MW01114098

The Family Voice

Book 5 in The Amish Singer Series

by Bob Nailor

Children are a heritage from the Lord,
Offspring a reward from Him.
Like arrows in the hands of a warrior
Are the children born in one's youth.
Blessed is the man whose quiver is full of them.

Psalm 127:3-5

ISBN: Book: **978-1-61877-179-7**
ISBN: Ebook: **978-1-61877-178-0**

This page left blank

The Family Voice

Discover other titles by Bob Nailor at
www.bobnailor.com

Dedication

This book is dedicated to my four sons:
Jeffory E. Nailor
David S. Nailor
Aaron D. Nailor
Robert L. Nailor

Cover collage by Bob Nailor

This page left blank.

Table of Contents

PRELUDE ~ The Dream 1

CHAPTER ONE ~ Day at School...2

CHAPTER TWO ~ School 6

CHAPTER THREE ~ Buying Land...13

CHAPTER FOUR ~ House Raising 19

CHAPTER FIVE ~ Hannah's Wedding 25

CHAPTER SIX ~ The Wedding 31

CHAPTER SEVEN ~ Jason 37

CHAPTER EIGHT ~ New Year, New Things.......................................46

CHAPTER NINE ~ Farming Issues 52

CHAPTER TEN ~ The Proposition...58

CHAPTER ELEVEN ~ Crop Planning..64

CHAPTER TWELVE ~ End of School 71

CHAPTER THIRTEEN ~ Gnomes 77

CHAPTER FOURTEEN ~ Jason's Wedding 84

CHAPTER FIFTEEN ~ Developments 96

CHAPTER SIXTEEN ~ Decisions 102

CHAPTER SEVENTEEN ~ Fighting Back 106

CHAPTER EIGHTEEN ~ Newborn 115

CHAPTER NINETEEN ~ Finality..118

CHAPTER TWENTY ~ Family Growth 123

CHAPTER TWENTY-ONE ~ End of and Beginning Year 129

CHAPTER TWENTY-TWO ~ The Development...................................138

CHAPTER TWENTY-THREE ~ Vacation Plans................................145

CHAPTER TWENTY-FOUR ~ Vacation 149

CHAPTER TWENTY-FIVE ~ New Year, New Changes 158

CHAPTER TWENTY-SIX ~ Baby Boom 165

CHAPTER TWENTY-SEVEN ~ Am-Lische....................................171

CHAPTER TWENTY-NINE ~ Mary's Wedding 182

CHAPTER THIRTY ~ Time Passes...187

CHAPTER THIRTY-ONE ~ Surprises 198

CHAPTER THIRTY-TWO ~ Fall Activities....................................209

CHAPTER THIRTY-THREE ~ Sarah and Bethany 220

CHAPTER THIRTY-FOUR ~ Grandpa Yoder................................226

CHAPTER THIRTY-FIVE ~ New Year; New Surprises...................230

CHAPTER THIRTY-SIX ~ Summer of 90 236

CHAPTER THIRTY-SEVEN ~ Bethany Wedding...........................244

CHAPTER THIRTY-EIGHT ~ Shipshewana 250

About the Author 259

Bibliography 261

BOOK SIX ~ The Englische Voice...263

PRELUDE ~ The Dream

Saturday, September 18, 1965 3:30 a.m.

Daniel bolted upright in the bed. Martha moaned at his action, but remained asleep.

He wiped the perspiration form his forehead.

"We are moving?" he asked the darkness of the room. His mind screamed. *The whole Amish community?* He shook his head. *That does not make sense. Why would the whole community move?* Then he remembered the water. Rushing flood waters everywhere. He watched his parent's home be swept away. He saw the Dawdi house crumble in the wake of the wave onslaught.

Daniel took a deep breath. *How do I interpret this?*

He lay back down and Martha snuggled closer.

CHAPTER ONE ~ Day at School

Saturday, September 18, 1965 4:40 a.m.

Daniel lay in bed, the dream still vivid in his memory. A small whimper from the nearby cradle caught his ear. He listened.

I am a father, he thought. *We are a family.*

He continued to listen to the rhythmic breathing of little Sarah.

Silence.

Daniel rolled over to lean closer to the edge of the bed, nearer the crib.

There was no sound. Sarah was not breathing.

He sat up in bed, alarmed.

Martha stirred. "Another dream?"

"No," Daniel replied. "Sarah has stopped breathing."

Martha sat up in the bed and listened, then smiled in the blue moonlight of the full moon shining through the bedroom window.

"It is all right, Daniel," Martha said "She did that earlier today and scared me. Your mother said it was quite normal." She paused. "Listen. Sarah is breathing, again."

Daniel held his breath and listened. He nodded; Sarah was breathing.

"Now, go to sleep," Martha chastised. "It will be morning soon."

She lifted her arm, pressing a hand against his chest, pushing him back down onto the mattress.

"I still cannot believe it. We are a family," he whispered.

"Yes," Martha replied, and dozed back to sleep.

#

Crying awoke them. Daniel wiped the sleep from his eyes and stared at the clock.

Ten more minutes, he thought.

"Sarah is hungry," Martha said. "I will take her to the main room and nurse her."

She picked up the baby and left the bedroom. Daniel, again, stared at the clock.

Nine more minutes. Can I sleep for nine minutes, or do I just get up?

Daniel sat on the edge of the bed, stretched across to the chair, grabbed and began to pull on his trousers.

I will help milk the cows with Papa, he thought.

Daniel paused in his thoughts.

I have a family. We need a home of our own. He gazed about the small bedroom of the *Dawdi* house and nodded in the moonlight shadows. *I will speak with Papa about the possibility.*

#

Saturday, September 18, 1965 6:00 a.m.

"Papa?" Daniel asked as they strolled to the barn. He watched Jacob race with the twins to the barn's door.

"Yes, Daniel." Noah placed an arm over Daniel's shoulder. "Your voice is serious."

"I have a family," Daniel started. "I think we should seek a home of our own." He hesitated. "The *Dawdi* house is fine, but..." He left the sentence unfinished.

"Your mother and I discussed the same thing the other night," Noah said. "There is no rush to leave the *Dawdi* house." He grinned. "Your mother is very happy to help take care of little Sarah."

Daniel laughed. "Between Mama and Sarah's young aunts, Martha has very little to do to take care of Sarah."

Noah gazed at Daniel. "Still, you feel you need your own place."

Daniel nodded. "Yes," he whispered.

"Tell you what," Noah said. "After breakfast, you and I will take the buggy and check out the area. We can stop at the grocery and call a realtor in DeMotte to see if any small farm is available." Noah opened the barn door. "Do you have an idea of the size or cost?"

"Martha and I thought maybe ten acres." Daniel shrugged as he stepped into the barn. "Cost? Depending on what is available, we have money in the bank."

"Let us milk the cows." Noah winked. "Are you ready to sing?"

Daniel nodded.

# # #

Saturday, September 18, 1965 9:30 a.m.

Daniel sat beside his father in the buggy. It seemed it had been a long time since he had sit in the buggy and his father handled the horse.

Beauty trotted as graceful as ever and he remembered Beauty's twin, Jezebel, owned by Jacob and Naomi Longenfelter in Pennsylvania.

Daniel jumped down from the buggy taking the reins, he tied Beauty to the hitching post on the side of Aaron and Jessica Shaw's grocery store. He quickly joined his father in the store.

"Good morning, Aaron," Noah said. "Have you heard of anyone wishing to sell farmland?" He put an arm over Daniel's shoulder. "My son is looking to establish a home."

Aaron scrunched up his face in thought. Jessica stepped up from behind him.

"Mrs. Jones, your neighbor, was in here the other day and mentioned that Richard wants to retire some day soon. He might want to sell a parcel of land."

Aaron leaned over and kissed Jessica on the cheek. "I was trying to remember who had said what a few days ago. Thank you, dear."

4

"I will check with him later today," Noah said. "Do you have a realtor you would suggest?"

Aaron stepped around to the front of the counter and snapped up a small business card.

"This is Linda Singer, a realtor in DeMotte. She comes by here at least monthly to see if anyone is wanting to buy or sell."

He handed the card to Noah. "Give her a call." He nodded toward the pay phone in the corner.

Noah took the card and walked to the phone, depositing a dime into the pay phone's coin slot. He dialed Linda Singer's phone.

"DeMotte Realty," a voice said. "May I help you?"

"I would like to speak with Linda Singer," Noah said.

"This is she," Linda said. "Who am I speaking with?"

"This is Noah Yoder of Centertown. I am looking for property in the area; a small farm."

"I don't currently have anything in the Centertown vicinity. But, Mr. Yoder, I do have a lovely small ranch farm just north of DeMotte. It is a three bedroom, two bath, on a well-landscaped five acres."

"Miss Singer," Noah started. "I am Amish. I am looking for a small crop of land for my son to farm and raise a family. We would prefer in Centertown. You say you have nothing?"

"I'm afraid not, Mr. Yoder."

"Thank you, Miss Singer. Good bye."

Noah hung up the phone and shook his head. "The woman did not understand what we want."

Daniel snickered. "I don't know if anyone ever told you. Martha's parents took her to DeMotte and they showed her a house in town. I think it was Miss Singer who showed the home that day. She was shocked we would want a horse in town, and a buggy, too. Martha had to explain we were Amish."

Noah handed the business card back to Aaron. "Thank you, but she was of no help. I will talk with Richard Jones in the next couple of days."

CHAPTER TWO ~ School

Monday, September 20, 1965 8 a.m.

Daniel pulled the buckboard into the school yard. Jacob jumped down to help his younger siblings.

"You are being very helpful, Jacob," Daniel said, a slight frown crossing his face.

"Simple, Daniel... uh, Mr. Yoder," Jacob started. "This is my last year of school. I graduate in the spring."

Daniel grinned. "If you pass."

Jacob stumbled. "Uh... what do you mean?"

Daniel shrugged. "Not everyone gets to pass. Some students flunk."

"But..." Jacob paused. "You have passed us for the last two years," he whined.

Daniel smiled. "Study and you will pass, Jacob. Now go play ball."

Little Anna stood near the steps to the school. "Will I pass, Mr. Yoder?"

Daniel gazed at his younger sister. "Like I told Jacob, study. Now, go play."

Daniel walked into the school house and immediately shook his head.

It is too tight, he thought. *We need more space. I will talk with the Bishop and see if another room can be added.*

"Good morning, Mr. Yoder," Elizabeth Troyer said. She moved from desk to desk, placing a bright, ripe apple on each desk.

"What are you doing>" Daniel asked.

"We had several apples this year and I thought it would be a nice treat for the students."

"Thank you, Elizabeth. Very thoughtful."

Daniel continued on his way to his desk and sat. He placed the stack of paper from his bag on the desk. Graded tests.

"Some of the students will not be happy with these grades," Daniel said to make conversation.

Elizabeth smiled. "I remember worrying about the test results."

"You were an excellent student," Daniel said. "Why would you worry?"

She shrugged. "I always worried I would flunk a test." She paused. "I never did, but that did not stop me from fretting."

"My brother, Jacob, had best start to study. He thinks it is his last year and can slide." Daniel made a face. "I will flunk him if necessary."

Elizabeth Wyse closed the school door behind her as she entered.

"Who are you flunking?" she asked.

"We are talking about my brother, Jacob," Daniel said. "He thinks he can slide this year because he is an eighth grader."

Elizabeth Wyse nodded. "He does have a certain air about him." She frowned. "Almost proud."

"I will discuss it with the bishop." Daniel stood. "Do either of you know of anyone who wishes to sell a small plot of land? Martha is wanting to have a home of her own."

"I can ask my uncle," Elizabeth Troyer offered.

Elizabeth Wyse shook her head. "Jeremiah works all the land we have left. He is also looking for extra land."

"Thank you. Another question. Do you think we need an addition? Another classroom?"

The two women assessed the open area of the classroom.

"It is very tight," Elizabeth Troyer said. "I think an additional room would be helpful."

"I agree," Elizabeth Wyse said. "And a larger storage area would be nice."

"That is another item I will discuss with the bishop," Daniel said. He looked at Elizabeth Troyer. "Let us begin class. Call in the students." He motioned for Elizabeth Wyse to come closer. "I will be headed out very shortly to work at the mill. Do you have any questions?"

7

She gazed at the stack of paper. "Last week's tests?"

Daniel nodded. "We may need to go back over some of the items learned. The scores were not good."

Elizabeth nodded, placing a hand on the stack of papers. "I will hand them out and go back over all of the covered material."

The students filed in and took their chairs. Quiet filled the room.

Daniel glanced at the smiling face. "Let us pray."

Heavenly Father, For the beautiful day you have given us, we thank you. Guide our feet and minds as we learn, listening to the teachers so we may pass into the next grade next spring. In Jesus name, Amen.

"Now we will all sing 'This Little Light of Mine.' If you do not know it, do not worry. You will learn." Daniel started to sing 'This little light...'" The students joined him. When they finished, the room was silent.

"We will now recite 'The Lord's Prayer' together. All the students joined Daniel in the prayer.

"Now we're going to sing 'The Ant Song' to help the new and younger students learn their numbers."

Daniel glanced at the clock; almost eight forty.

I must hurry, Daniel thought.

"Before I leave, did you listen to the first prayer? Mrs. Wyse will be passing back the tests from last Friday." Daniel took in a deep breath and slowly let it out. "I am not happy with the grades." He scowled at the older students. "Especially the seventh and eighth graders. I know you can do better. If not..." He left the sentence unfinished. "I will be back later."

Daniel strode to the back of the room and out the door to the buckboard. It was about a ten-to-fifteen-minute ride to the mill.

Plenty of time to think, Daniel thought. *Maybe my being at the mill and not at the school is bad for the older students.* He frowned, and his mind raced to another subject. *Where will I find a place for Martha, Sarah and I to live?*

# # #

8

Monday, September 20, 1965 10:20 a.m.

"Good morning, Daniel," Bob Sullivan said as he strolled into the wood carving office. "How are things working out? Is everything going well at school?"

"I am not sure, Mr. Sullivan," Daniel replied. "It seems the older students are failing. I am not sure my assistants are able to teach them or not." He paused. "My brother, Jacob, is in the eighth grade and I think he feels he can slide through the last year of school. Out of twenty questions on the math test, he only got four correct. His was the lowest grade in the class, but the others were not that much better."

"Tell you what, Daniel. Come into my office after lunch, after you've had time to evaluate this, and we'll discuss things." He smiled. "I'm not a tyrant. I like your work. We can make something happen to make it correct."

"Thank you, Mr. Sullivan." Daniel picked up his notebook and followed Bob out of the office so he could speak with his staff.

He approached Martin Smith who worked on the racing mustang replica. The young man was polishing the body.

"Looks very good," Daniel said, running his hand across the horse's wooden back. "Very smooth." He nodded approval. "What is your next project?"

"I plan to work on the parrot, Mr. Yoder," Martin said.

Daniel nodded approval. "When do you expect to start?"

"Right after lunch and I should have it finished before the end of the week."

"Very good," Daniel said and ambled to his other employee, Benjamin Heffel.

"Good morning, Benjamin," Daniel said and admired the rocking horse lawn chair Benjamin was working on.

"Good morning, Mr. Yoder," Benjamin replied. "How is Hannah doing?"

Daniel grinned. "I believe she is getting nervous. The wedding is next month."

"I and my wife have been asked to be *newehockers* (groomsman/bridesmaid)."

9

"Do you think John will be out of the hospital in time for his wedding?" Daniel asked.

"Aye, he is struggling, but I am told he will be allowed home next week and only need go back and forth to see the doctor three times a week."

Benjamin moved around the chair and tapped a corner.

"We have been blessed with John returning to us. My father… I mean the Bishop has been to visit him in the hospital and given him a baptism. John is now a member of the church, as is Hannah."

Benjamin nodded and tapped another peg onto the seat.

Daniel frowned. "Pegged, eh?"

"Not a nail in this one, Mr. Yoder," Benjamin said. "We altered the original plan to eliminate the nails." He frowned. "Did you know?"

Daniel nodded absently.

It seems I am failing in this job, too, Daniel thought.

"Good work," Daniel said and strolled back to his office.

I must decide what I need to do. Am I a teacher? Am I a mill worker? Is it wise to be both if I am failing in both jobs?

Daniel stumbled into his office and sat his desk. He pulled out the sketches of new projects.

My students are failing. My employees are making changes I do not know.

"A nickel for your thoughts," Ben said as he stepped into the office.

"Ben, do you think I am doing a proper job here?"

Ben sat down. "Whoa! Where did that question come from?"

Daniel shook his head. "My students are failing. Jacob only got four questions correct out of twenty questions. He failed." Daniel inhaled deeply. "Am I failing my students?"

"Danny boy," Ben started.

Daniel cringed but let it pass.

"You have two assistants. Are they failing in their teaching ability? Last year seemed to be satisfactory… yes?"

Daniel nodded.

"I don't think the problem is you. What else is bothering you?"

"They changed my plan for the rocking horse lawn chair," Daniel said, the dam breaking. "I... Martha thinks we should find a home of our own now that we have Sarah." Daniel shrugged. "Martha wishes to have a large family and the *Dawdi* house is very small. My sister, Hannah, is getting married..." He glanced at Ben. "Please do not say anything, it has not been properly announced yet." He grinned. "You know how we Amish wish to keep secrets."

Ben leaned back in the chair. "Hannah is getting married? To?"

Daniel took a deep breath. *The cat is out of the bag now,* he thought. "John Heffel. So far, only the families know."

"Are his burns healed?" Ben asked.

"He gets out of the hospital next week, at least, possibly." Daniel nodded toward Benjamin Heffel. "His uncle told me that this morning."

"John is a good man," Ben said. "I have wondered if Vietnam changed him."

Daniel rolled a shoulder. "It does not seem so. Martha and I have visited him a few times and he seems more confident, mature, and..."

"Daniel," Ben cut in. "You boys are growing up. Look at you. We all thought sure when you went to New York on *Rumschpringe*... well, most of didn't expect you to come back." He grinned. "Now you're married and have a lovely daughter." He paused. "How is Sarah doing?"

"With all the aunts, Martha says it is easy taking care of her."

Ben nodded and re-situated himself on the chair.

"I need advice, Ben," Daniel whispered. "Do I work here and remain a teacher? Or do I give up teaching? Or do I quit the mill?"

Ben leaned back against the chair. "I really don't know what to tell you, Danny boy. You do great work here. Plus, I know you love being a teacher." Ben rolled a shoulder. "Perhaps you and Bob Sullivan can work out a new schedule; perhaps spend more time at the school?"

Daniel leaned back in his chair. "Originally I was to come into the mill for an hour in the morning, but now I work at the mill almost all day." Daniel nodded. "I am to discuss this matter with Mr. Sullivan after lunch."

"Well, I see Leo wandering around. He's probably looking for me since I have a delivery. Catch you later."

Ben got up and left the office.

"Thank you, Ben," Daniel mumbled softly.

CHAPTER THREE ~ Buying Land

Wednesday, September 22, 1965 7:35 p.m.

A knock on the door startled Daniel. He looked to his father who placed the Bible to the side and nodded at him.

Daniel walked across the room to the front door as the person knocked, yet again. Daniel opened the door.

"Mr. Jones," Daniel said and pushed the front door screen open. "Come in. Father will glad to see you."

Richard Jones stepped inside, removing his baseball cap.

"Actually, I'm here to see you, young man."

Daniel led him into the main room where Noah stood, waiting. He offered a hand to shake. Richard smiled and grabbed his hand in a strong shake, placing his other hand on the grip, too.

"Have a seat," Noah said and offered the chair beside him. "To what do we owe the honor of your visit?"

Richard turned to face Daniel. "I heard this young man is wanting to strike out on his own. He's looking for a small piece of land to farm." He paused. "Is that true?"

Daniel nodded.

Rachel stood. "Martha, come help me get something to snack on." She nodded toward the kitchen. Martha tried not frown, and reluctantly followed Rachel to the kitchen.

"It is true, Richard," Noah said. "He is looking to get about ten to fifteen acres to farm." Noah grinned. "He is a teacher and works at the mill so he does not have a lot of farming time available."

This is the reason I wish to have my own land, Daniel thought. *I think Mr. Jones came to see me, but my father is taking control.*

Daniel smiled and nodded.

"So, Mister Daniel Yoder," Richard said. "How would you like about..." Richard hm-hawed. "Say about fifteen hundred feet across

13

the road, starting at the top of the south side of the ravine, going to the north. If we go back about four hundred fifty feet." He shrugged. "I'm guessing that would be close to fifteen acres." He held up his hand. "Yes, I know, that ravine. I couldn't farm it to save my life, but a good farmer, using equipment such as I've seen the Amish use; that would be viable land." He smiled. "Call the ravine area gravy. I won't charge you for it and see no reason you can't use it."

Daniel hesitated and took a deep breath. "How much are you asking?"

Rachel and Martha stepped back into the room with filled glasses of lemonade and a pile of cookies.

Richard reached up and rubbed his chin. "Do you think two hundred per acre is a fair price?"

"More than fair, Richard," Noah said. "Why so low?"

"I want my farm to be farmland. I'm thinking of retiring soon and there are those realtors... like buzzards over well-decayed meat, just waiting to get hold of my land."

"Lemonade, Mr. Jones?" Martha asked and handed him a glass.

"Thank you, Mrs. Yoder." He took the glass and sipped. "Delicious."

Martha glanced at Daniel and nodded her head ever so slightly.

Daniel gazed at his father and nodded.

Noah smiled. "I believe my son agrees to the deal."

Richard Jones stood and walked across the room to Daniel with his hand out to shake.

"We have a deal, son," Richard said and shook hands with Daniel. "I will have a surveyor out to mark the land. With luck we should be able to finalize and bank by Saturday morning."

Daniel nodded. "Thank you." He turned to his father. "I think I will ask Mr. Sullivan for some time off." He smiled. "I will have a home to build soon."

"There's nothing like a good barn-raising," Richard said and slapped Daniel on the back. "I look forward to it." He grinned. "It's been a while..." He gazed off to the corner of the room. "We raised the school, but I can't remember a barn raising in the last five to ten years. Noah?"

Noah shook his head. "It has many years."

"These are real good cookies," Richard said, biting another chunk out his cookie. "Did you make them?"

Rachel shook her head. "No, our daughter, Hannah, made them."

"You'll have to have Hannah share her recipe with Judy, my wife."

Rachel giggled. "Have Mrs. Jones come over any time. We are all willing to share our secret recipes."

# # #

Thursday, September 29, 1965 7:30 a.m.

"We, Sarah and I, are going with your mother to see Miriam," Martha said. "She should have delivered by now. I am sure your brother, Luke, is beside himself."

"I am off to school," Daniel said. "Like every other day, start school, go to the mill, go back to the school, finish school, go back to the mill, come home."

"Are you not happy, Daniel?"

Daniel shrugged. "I am… not happy, but I am not unhappy. I just feel my students are suffering with my absence." He leaned in and gave Martha a kiss. "See you this afternoon."

Daniel walked to the barn, hooked Bronk to the buckboard, and trotted him to the end of the kitchen walkway. His siblings came out and got in.

They headed for school.

# # #

"It's a girl," Rachel said. "You have a little baker."

Miriam attempted to smile although she was exhausted from the labor.

"Oh, Sarah," Martha said, holding her young daughter. "You have a new cousin to play with as you grow."

"Her name," Miriam whispered, while trying to sit up. "Her name is Naomi. Luke and I had decided on a girl's name." She slumped back onto the bed.

"You did not choose a boy's name?" Rachel asked.

Miriam shook her head.

"Luke!" Rachel yelled. "Come meet your new daughter."

Luke opened the bedroom door and entered. He held their son, Hiram. "A daughter? Naomi?"

Miriam smiled and nodded her head.

Rachel pulled the wraps closer around Naomi and handed the baby to Luke.

"Your new baby sister, Hiram," Luke said, a child in each arm. "This is Naomi. And Naomi, this is your older brother, Hiram."

# # #

Monday, October 4, 1965 9 a.m.

The two couples, Daniel and Martha Yoder and Richard and Jean Jones walked into the First National Bank in DeMotte.

"Are we ready to do this?" Richard asked.

Daniel nodded. "Yes, sir."

Richard went to a teller and told them they were there to see Alex Walker. Alex Walker, a bank associate, stepped from his office and waved for them to join him. He greeted each couple and offered them seats. He scurried behind his desk.

"Now, I can see all the paperwork has been done and the land is being transferred from Mr. and Mrs. Jones to Mr. and Mrs. Yoder. Is that correct?" He paused. "And the amount is a total of three thousand two hundred eighty-three dollars which includes the price, taxes, and processing."

"Sounds about right to me," Richard Jones said. "Daniel?"

"I agree," Daniel replied.

"So, we've drawn a check on Mr. Yoder's account in that amount, made out to Richard and Jean Jones."

Alex Walker pushed the bank withdrawal toward Daniel and Martha.

"If you both will sign to approve the check," he said.

Alex flourished a pen from seemingly nowhere for the signatures.

He took the withdrawal paperwork back and attached it to the file folder he had.

"Now," he looked at Richard and Jean Jones. "Do you wish to have this money deposited to your account…" Again, he hesitated. "Or do you wish to have it cashed?"

"Deposit it to our savings account," Richard said.

"Oh my, yes," Jean whispered. "Into the savings account by all means."

"If the two of you would endorse the back of the check…"

Alex pushed the check toward them. Again, he flourished a pen from the air.

Richard signed and slid it to his wife who signed. She pushed the check back to Alex.

Alex stood, pushing his hand out to shake.

"Gentlemen, it has been great doing business with you. If there are any questions, please don't hesitate to call…" He glanced at Daniel. "Or come visit me."

Jean turned to Martha. "It will be nice to have new neighbors. I insist you come over to visit once you get things settled." She frowned. "I mean, you do plan to build a home? Yes?"

Martha grabbed Jean's hands. "We most certainly do plan to build a home. I am already trying to think about what I will plant in the garden next year." She giggled. "Yes, I will come to visit and you… both of you are always welcome at our home."

Daniel turned and shook hands with Richard. "I remember you asking about a barn raising. First, we will have a home raising."

"Shouldn't be too difficult to find water, Daniel," Richard said. "I mean, with the ravine and the creek, water should be readily available."

Daniel frowned.

"Is there a problem?" Alex asked.

"No, sir," Daniel replied. "I was wondering if we will be able to have the house built before the weather turns cold."

"The bank is here to help in any way it can," Alex said.

"Don't fret, Daniel," Richard said. "I know the Amish community. I figure you will have a house within the next two weeks."

"Thank you," Daniel said. "Now I must get to the mill."

Daniel and Martha headed out of the bank with Richard and Jean following.

"We can drop you off at the mill, Daniel," Richard said.

"How will you get back to the school," Martha asked, her face full of worry.

"I can have Jason or Ben take me back to the school when I am ready to go." He leaned in close to Martha. "No need to worry. The buckboard is there to take us home when school is finished. Remember, you picked me up at the school.

Martha leaned over and gave Daniel a kiss and whispered in his ear. "Now I can start to go through all our wedding gifts and see what I need to set up our new home."

Daniel grinned at her. "First, make sure Sarah is taken care of."

Martha laughed. "With your mother and all those aunts, I am sure Sarah has been just fine in our absence." She gazed into the distance. "Still, it will be good to hold our daughter when I get home."

CHAPTER FOUR ~ House Raising

Friday, October 15, 1965 4:30 p.m.

"I've been meaning to ask you," Bob Sullivan said as he leaned against the doorway to Daniel's office. He ambled on in and sat.

"We talked a couple of weeks ago and agreed on an hour of work in the morning." He made a grimace. "Have the students' grades improved?"

Daniel nodded. "The tests I gave back this morning were much better grades than a month ago." Daniel sighed. "I think my being there is helping to encourage the students to work and study harder."

Bob Sullivan frowned.

"I think my aides are doing a good job, but I fear they may not know the correct answer themselves."

Bob Sullivan nodded.

"So, are you ready, Daniel?" Bob Sullivan asked as he stood.

"Ready?" Daniel asked.

Bob Sullivan grinned. "I take it Ben never said a word."

Daniel shook his head, still unsure of the conversation.

"Okay, let me explain. Tomorrow is Saturday. Ben has it all planned. Right now I have two trucks loaded with equipment like generators to run the air compressors and all the necessary tools. There is also a lot of wood to build a house."

"A house?" Daniel questioned.

"He spoke with your father and they talked with Martha. The three of them planned your new home."

"But..." Daniel stood, still in shock.

"Follow me, young man."

Bob Sullivan headed out. Daniel followed, still unsure of what was happening. As he left the building, he spied the two trucks and they were loaded with material to build a house. Bob Sullivan stood next to Daniel and pointed.

"There are two by fours, four by fours, siding, sheet rock, insulation, windows, doors, nails, screws, and everything else you could think of. It's all there, Daniel. Your new house." He paused. "And new barn."

"I see it," Daniel said. "I... When... Who? Who paid for all this?"

Bob Sullivan laughed.

"You will, Daniel." Bob Sullivan slapped Daniel on the back. "I have donated a certain amount, but the rest I will bill you. I know you will pay; besides, I know where you work."

Daniel stood there, gawking at the two trucks.

"How can we build?" Daniel asked. "There is no foundation."

"Yes, there is," Bob Sullivan countered. "Your father and Luke, your brother put it in and it was set this morning." Bob grinned. "It's a go."

"But who decided where the house would be?" Daniel shook his head, still unable to believe what he was hearing and seeing.

"Martha. She walked your father, brother, and Ben over to the property and picked out where she wanted the house."

Daniel gazed up at Bob Sullivan. "Martha did that?" he asked.

"She also showed where the barn, chicken coop, and garden would go." Bob Sullivan slapped Daniel on the back. "You, my young worker, have a wife who knows what she wants."

Daniel nodded and a sly grin crossed his face. He remembered the blue-haired girl at the theater who knew what she wanted and got what she wanted.

She is my Amish wife, he thought. *But, she is still Englische.*

"We're going to drop this off at the property. Do you want to go along and help unload?"

"Of course," Daniel replied and headed for a truck.

Ben waved. "Come, ride with me."

Daniel got up in the truck on the passenger side. Ben leaped into the driver's seat.

"Tomorrow is going to be one busy day," Ben said and put the truck in gear. "You have no idea how excited your father is, Daniel."

# # #

Ben stopped on the road in front of Daniel's parent's home at Daniel's request.

"I must check this out," Daniel said, opening the door.

He walked toward his new property. Ever so slightly, the mound of dirt that had been somewhat concealed from the road, appeared. He approached the hole in the ground. Amazed, he gazed at the basement floor, and the foundation walls.

How did I not see this? he thought.

Martha came running across the road.

"Is this not exciting?" she asked.

Daniel gazed across the road to his parent's house.

"This is where you wanted the house? We buy fifteen acres and you want a house across the road from my parents?"

Martha stepped back. "Yes, Daniel. This is where I wanted *MY* house."

"Oh, so I do not live here? This is *YOUR* house?"

Martha placed her hands on her hips. "I want my house here, near your mother and sisters. Now, you have the other fifteen acres to decide where you want your barn. The chicken coop…" She pointed. "Will be there. And the garden…" She pointed in another direction. "Will be there." She sighed deeply. "If you want your barn over there…" Again, she pointed at a distant point. "So be it, but you will be the one to go get the horse and buggy and the one to milk the cows."

Daniel grabbed her up, twirling her in a circle. "Your *Englische* is showing, my dear. It is said in Ephesians 5:22; *Wives, submit yourselves to your own husbands as you do to the Lord.*

Martha pushed at Daniel to release her. He held her tight.

"But, my love, it continues with Ephesian 5:25; *Husbands, love your wives, just as Christ loved the church and gave Himself up for her.*"

Daniel released his hold and let her slip to her feet. "If this is where you wish to have the home, so be it." He turned and stared at the property. "Now… as to the barn, I fear where you pointed might be too far. I think…" He placed a hand to his chin and rubbed. "I think… yes, I think the barn should go right there." He pointed at a location near where Martha had pointed the chicken coop."

"That is what I told your father and Ben," Martha said. "You are my husband and I know you, Daniel. Where else would you have placed the barn."

Daniel grinned. "Actually, over there." He pointed where Martha had pointed earlier. "Would have been nice, but the house would have too far away." He gazed at the basement foundation. "I don't think we can move this, so we will bring the barn closer."

Martha slapped him on his arm. "You are… are…"

Daniel turned, grabbed and kissed her. "You are the love of my life."

# # #

Saturday, October 16, 1965 8 a.m.

Daniel checked the foundation that had been poured. It was solid and ready to have a house built. He gazed back across the road to his parent's home. Buggies were arriving and Jacob and the twins were making sure the horses were properly tied, and there was food and water. They arranged the buggies off to the side of the barn. Even this far away, he could smell the food being prepped to feed everyone.

Martha stood momentarily on the back porch then scampered down the steps. She carried Sarah in her arms.

I think she is coming this way, Daniel thought.

Martha crossed the road and made her way to Daniel.

"Your father is about to make the assignments," Martha said and gazed about the property. "Tonight, we will sleep for the last time in the *Dawdi* house." She smiled. "Tomorrow, after church, we will move into our new home. You. Me. Sarah."

Daniel placed a loving arm around her and kissed her on the forehead.

"We are a family and we will have our own home."

A car pulled into the driveway of Daniel's parent's home.

"Is that your parents?" he asked.

"It is!" Martha exclaimed. "I told them about the raising, but I was not sure if they would come."

Dan Noble got out of the car and lifted a hammer into the air, waving it at them.

"Your father has come prepared," Daniel said. "We should go greet them."

They tramped across the ground and made their way to the house across the road where Dan and Emma Noble waited for them.

Emma had her arms outstretched. "Let me have little Sarah," Emma said as they approached. "My granddaughter." She cradled the baby in her arms and leaned down to give it a kiss.

"We're here to help," Dan Noble said.

"My father is about to assign jobs," Daniel replied. "Follow me."

The Amish community had showed up, as well as almost all the staff of the mill. Even Richard and Judy Jones had showed. Jason had spun into the driveway with his shiny yellow Mustang. He had Patty with him.

Aaron and Jessica Shaw wanted to help but had to keep the store open, so they donated food to help feed those who came to the raising.

#

Noah Yoder stood on a small wooden box. "I was going to say the first priority was the house, but we have such a wonderful turnout, we will break into two groups. A small group for the house, the rest for the barn." He paused. "Daniel will oversee the group building the house. I will oversee those working on the barn. Any questions?"

A hand went up. "When do we start?"

"We start now," Noah said. "I will assign thirty to the house." He stepped down and began picking. "The rest are on the barn. Follow me."

Noah headed across the yard and to the road and stopped. "I need six men to create a driveway from the road onto the property."

23

Again, he selected six men. "There are shovels and other equipment in my barn. Get what you need."

Noah motioned for the large group to follow him and they headed onto the property to begin assembling the barn.

Daniel led the smaller group of men to the foundation. Martha had marked where she wanted the inside walls of the first floor. She and Daniel had drawn pictures of the outside walls with the desired windows. Daniel held the picture of the second story and where the staircase would be.

First things first, Daniel thought. *Get the main floor done, then the second floor, then the roof.*

"Four men on the end walls. Six men on the side walls. The rest split and start on the foundation and roof trusses. Questions?"

The men broke into groups and began assembling the structures to raise.

# # #

Saturday, October 16, 1965 10:25 a.m.

Daniel stood back and watched as the walls were lifted into place.

This is my home, he thought.

Flooring was laid and overhead, joists were being installed for the second story.

Daniel joined the group and stuffed insulation between the studs before nailing up drywall. Windows went in quickly and were made airtight.

Tomorrow, after church, Martha and I will move from the Dawdi house to our new home. He smiled at the thought.

He gazed out a window and saw a wall being raised by the group working on the barn.

I will ask father if I may have Bronk, he thought. *At least, until I can buy a horse at the Shipshewana auction. I will need to get a buggy for Martha and I to use.*

24

CHAPTER FIVE ~ Hannah's Wedding

Sunday, October 17, 1965 9 a.m.

Noah stood before the congregation. He was about to start his sermon, but first, he had announcements.

"Brothers and sisters," Noah said. "I wish to thank each of you for your involvement yesterday. My son and his wife thank you dearly."

He paused.

"There are two announcements this morning. Anna Stutzman has chosen Samuel Beiler. They will be wed on Tuesday, November 2. Amos Stutzman wishes all the community to attend."

Again, he paused.

"My daughter, Hannah Yoder has chosen John Heffel. They will be wed on Thursday, October 28. I invite all the community to attend."

Noah opened his Bible. "Today, I will discuss on Hebrews 13:18 and having a clear conscience."

# # #

Jeremiah Wyse strode up to Noah. "Very interesting sermon today, Bishop."

Noah nodded.

"May I ask how an unbaptized boy, namely John Heffel, is allowed to wed your daughter?"

Noah took a deep breath before speaking.

"John Heffel is baptized, Brother Jeremiah. Due to his extreme burns, I went to him at the hospital and baptized him."

Jeremiah nodded. "So, he was baptized without the community to attend. Are we to believe this?"

"Did you not listen to my sermon?" Noah asked. "When I baptized John, there were in attendance, his parents and siblings, my family, his doctor and nurses." Noah turned to face Jeremiah. "John told me he would do another baptism when he was allowed to enter the water." Noah paused. "Would you denounce his baptism because you did not witness it?"

"Where did this baptism take place?" Jeremiah pushed.

"At the hospital. There is a marvelous garden space in the middle. People could watch the baptism from the windowed three floors above." Again, Noah paused. "It was quite moving."

Joshua Heffel approached. "Is there a problem, Bishop?"

Noah shook his head. "Nay." He gazed at Jeremiah. "Are all your questions answered?"

Jeremiah nodded and stepped away.

Joshua Heffel smiled. "You have had a lot of activity at your home. A raising. Now, a wedding."

Noah nodded. "The Lord has blessed us, Brother Joshua. I gain another son; you gain another daughter."

"Bishop?" Joshua started. "Do you think the community will accept my son? I mean, he went to war. He joined the Army." Joshua hung his head.

"There is no need for shame, Joshua." Noah put a comforting arm around Joshua. "Your son was on *Rumschpringe*. We judge not the actions of that time. He has confessed his sins, been baptized, and is one with the church. You should be proud of such a strong, young man."

"I feared with all his burns, the community might ignore him. I thought to hide him on our farm." He sighed. "But now he will be married."

"They will be a perfect couple," Noah said. "Hm? Can you smell that fried chicken. Shall we go, eat, and plan our grandchildren?" He grinned.

# # #

"Can I help?" Hannah asked.

"If you wish," Martha replied. "Your mother is caring for Sarah, so I do not have to fret about her."

Hannah gazed at the boxes. "You had all this hidden in here?"

Martha grinned. "My mother taught me how to pack. Some of it was under the bed, behind tables, or in closets."

Hannah shook her head. "Is this what I must do in a few weeks?"

Martha put an index finger to her lips. "The biggest secret? My parents are bringing over what I could not store here."

Hannah's eyes widened. "There is more?"

Martha smiled. "Everything to start a life together and set up a home."

Hannah picked up two smaller boxes and headed for the buckboard just outside the door.

Bronk waited patiently as they loaded the buckboard.

Daniel walked across the road toward them.

"The well is working," Daniel said. "You have a pump inside the house." He placed a loving arm around Martha. "Now, you need not go outside for water. In fact, Father is looking at the setup." He winked. "I think he may do something so Mama no longer will need to go outside to get the water from the hand pump, especially in the cold of winter."

Daniel went in the house, grabbed a large box, and headed out the door.

"Is this everything?" he asked and gazed up at the sky. "Cloudy. We may get some rain."

Martha nodded. "That is everything until my parents arrive." She joined Daniel to gaze at the sky then put her hand out where droplets collected in her palm. "It is starting to sprinkle."

Daniel helped Martha and Hannah up onto the buckboard then joined them.

"Okay, Bronk," he said. "Across the road to our new home. Let us hope we can get everything in the house before it really starts to rain."

Martha leaned over to Hannah. "Do you have everything ready for the wedding?"

Hannah sighed. "I have my dress. Mama has made sure there will be enough food. John has requested our *newehockers* (groomsman/bridesmaid) so..." Her voice trailed off.

Martha grabbed Hannah's hand. "My dear sister in marriage, Hannah, if you need anything, you know I am here for you." She took a deep breath. "You helped me with my wedding; allow me to help with your wedding."

Hannah whimpered. "I fear my wedding night," she whispered.

Martha frowned. "Fear?"

Hannah nodded as Bronk stopped in front of the new house. Daniel jumped down and helped the two down from the buckboard.

"I will move the boxes into the main room," Daniel said. "You can decide where each box goes later." He nodded at Hannah. "Go. Talk."

Martha nodded and led Hannah away toward the house and out of the light rain.

"Tell me, Hannah," Martha said. "Why are you fretful of your wedding night?" She watched Hannah. "It will be a natural thing. There is no need to be fearful."

"No, no," Hannah said, looking for a place to sit. "You misunderstand. I fear our wedding night will not be consummated." Hannah paused. "I mean, his burns. What will others say? I can only kiss him on the lips. His body is..."

Martha nodded. "Now, I understand. You love John. John loves you. Both of you can wait to consummate your marriage, if need be." She gazed about the room. "What others think and say will be gossip. Let them talk."

Hannah shook her head. "Never did I ever think I would marry John Heffel." She sighed. "He..." Hannah hesitated. "I love him."

Martha smiled. "I know you do. And, John loves you."

Hannah nodded and carefully sit on a sturdy box. Once more she gazed about the room. "You need furniture, Martha."

Martha giggled. "When my parents arrive, they will—"

A car horn cut her off.

"My parents are here," Martha said gleefully, looking out a window. "Now, we will have some furniture."

Dan Noble strolled in carrying two chairs. "Something to sit on."

Daniel followed with another two chairs.

"Come on, Danny-boy," Dan said. "Let's get that table in."

"My name is Daniel," Daniel mumbled, not wanting to offend his father-in-law, but at the same time, despising the term 'Danny-boy' from others.

"His name is Daniel, father," Martha said. "It is not Danny-boy."

"Yes, Marti," Dan said and strolled out the door.

"My name is Martha," Martha yelled to the receding figure.

"Your father is in rare form today," Emma said as she lugged in a box and placed it on the kitchen counter.

"Why is that?" Martha asked.

Hannah opened the box and noted all the kitchen items; she nodded.

"We received a letter yesterday from your sister, Bethan." Emma grabbed Martha's hands and danced in a circle about her. "She is moving back to Shipshewana."

"Bethan is coming home?" Martha gushed, letting go of her mother's hands. "When?"

Daniel and Dan carried the table into the kitchen. Martha and Hannah placed the chairs about it.

"Very soon," Emma said. "She didn't give a date, but said that she, her husband, Thomas, and their two children will move to Shipshewana soon."

"Two children?" Martha whispered. "Two?"

"Twins," Emma said. "Identical girls." Once more she grabbed Martha's hands and began to dance. "How exciting."

Martha let loose of her mother and slumped into a chair. "My sister is married. And twins."

"The name of the twins are Faith and Hope," Emma said. "How cute." She sighed. "If they'd had triplets, I bet the last one would have been named Charity."

"Twins," Martha whispered.

Dan stomped into the kitchen. "Whew! It is starting to come down." He placed a box on the table.

29

Daniel followed and placed his box on the counter. "I will take Bronk to the barn and settle him for the day."

"Do you need some help?" Dan asked.

"Nay," Daniel replied. "You visit with Martha."

Daniel stepped back out into the rain and quickly got on the buckboard and had Bronk trotting toward the barn.

The light rain fell stronger.

"This is your new life," Daniel said as he opened the doors of the barn and led Bronk to his stall. He grinned. "This is our new life," he whispered, listening to the rain on the barn roof.

CHAPTER SIX ~ The Wedding

Thursday, October 28, 1965 8:30 a.m.

Joshua and Jonah gathered the horses and buggies, taking them to Jacob who arranged them in the field. He made sure there was plenty of food and water for the horses and that the buggies were aligned nicely.

Jacob stood back to admire his work.

I should not be proud, Jacob thought. *Still, I have done a good job.*

Daniel and Martha helped greet people as they entered to wish the happy couple the best.

Ben Hopkins pulled his car into the driveway, ever careful of the horses and buggies. He inched closer and closer to Aaron Shaw's silver, 1963 Oldsmobile 88.

He turned to his wife. "At least we're not the only *Englische* at this wedding," Ben said. "We should be able to find Aaron and Jessica Shaw without too much difficulty." He smiled at his wife.

Linda Hopkins frowned. "I still don't see why we're here." She made a grimace. "They're all Amish."

Ben inhaled deeply and slowly. "I was the bus driver when Hannah was attending the *Englische* school." He shrugged. "She invited us. It would have been rude to refuse."

Linda got out of the car. "I guess I can spend the day with Jessica Shaw."

"My dear," Ben began. "You'll find the Amish to be quite friendly and..." He pointed to the back door of the house. "See that young man up there? That is Daniel Yoder, older brother to Hannah who is getting married. We work together at the mill, plus he is the school teacher for the Amish school."

Linda shook her head. "I don't understand your infatuation with the Amish." She locked her arms in Ben's and they headed toward the major group. "Oh, look! There's Jessica." She let go of Ben and waved to Jessica.

"I'll go talk with Daniel," Ben said and headed toward the back door of the house.

# # #

"Hannah," Noah called. "John is here and we are ready to discuss this marriage. As Bishop of the church, there are certain things we need to make sure you understand." He smiled. "It is more than just baptism."

"I understand, Papa," Hannah replied and stepped from her bedroom.

John Heffel stared at her. "You are beautiful."

Hannah bowed her head, hoping he wouldn't see the flush in her cheeks.

"Let us go to Daniel's old bedroom," Noah said. "We will have our talk there." He smiled at the couple. "It will be quiet and no one should bother us."

Noah led the way, Hannah followed and John held Hannah's hand and kept up with her. Noah sat on the bed with Hannah and John sitting on a bench.

"You have both joined the church," Noah began, noticing them holding hands. He frowned.

Hannah saw her father's frown and pulled her hand away. John gazed at her and ever so slightly nodded.

# # #

Noah led the way down the steps. At the bottom, he raised his hands.

"We are ready," Noah said and ushered those in the house to the outside.

The groups of people outside saw Noah, Hannah, and John. They immediately took seats; women to one side, men to the other. In front, two seats awaited the wedding couple.

The attending *Englische* were unsure of what to do and took seats in the back.

Noah opened with a prayer.

Daniel, as *Vorsänger* (song leader) for the occasion, stood and started to sing. It was hymn number 131 — *O Gott, Vater.* The rest of the church joined in the slow, monotone song.

There was a short break, then Daniel started *Das Loblied.* Again, the church joined in the song.

Linda frowned, unsure and unknowing of the song. She sat patiently waiting.

Ben leaned over. "Doesn't Daniel have a beautiful voice?" he whispered.

Linda shrugged.

The service continued with the *Englische* unsure of what was happening.

Finally, after three hours, John and Hannah were wed and led into the house to sit at the *Eck* (corner) table for the meal and festivities.

# # #

Rachel Yoder and her daughter, Ruth Mueller, walked toward the table where Ben and Linda Hopkins sat with Jessica and Aaron Shaw. They each carried two plates heaping with food.

"If this is not enough," Rachel said. "There is plenty more."

"Do I look like I'm starving," Linda asked Ben as the two women walked away. "Why so much food?"

"Enjoy the meal," Ben said and shoved a heaping forkful of mashed potatoes with a rich chicken gravy into his open mouth.

"The wedding service," Linda continued. "It was over three hours long." She heaved a heavy sigh. "Those benches. Hard. No back." Linda lowered her voice. "My butt is still numb."

"Eat," Ben said, hoping her tirade would end.

# # #

Ben led Linda to the *Eck* (corner) table and introduced his wife to the couple. Linda attempted to smile and quickly pulled Ben away.

Alone, at a table with the other *Englische*, Linda leaned over to whisper in Ben's ear.

"How can she love him? His scars are terrible." She made a face and shook her head. "They say love is blind, I don't think this one has ever seen the light of day."

Ben reared away. "How can you say such things?" he asked. "John Heffel served in the Army. He was injured in a bombing incident in Vietnam."

"Pshaw," Linda said. "He is Amish. They would never have sent him to Vietnam."

Ben inhaled deeply. "He never told the Army he was Amish. He joined the service with Jonathan Bell. Remember him and the mix-up about his death?" Ben nodded at Jessica. "By the way, Jessica was Jonathan's aunt." Ben wiggled his finger in the air. "Let me see, Jessica's husband, Aaron, is Jonathan's mother's sister. They're related through marriage."

Linda frowned. "This is the John that everyone thought was dead?"

"Yes, dear," Ben said. "I never realized you were so against the Amish."

"It's not that I'm against them, Ben," Linda said. "It's just that they are so... well, different."

Ben shook his head. "They are a soft-spoken, easy-going people, Linda. They don't wish to be better than anyone else, that's one of the reasons they all look alike." He paused. "How many times have you gotten upset because Nancy got a new dress and was putting on airs, as you called it." He nodded toward the Amish sitting around them. "They wear similar clothes hence none are better than the next." He shrugged. "Maybe something we could consider."

Linda paled. "I... I don't think I could do that," she whispered.

Ben looked up to see Daniel and Martha walking toward them.

"I am glad you could make it," Daniel said, sitting opposite them. "And, you must be Ben's lovely wife... ah, it is Linda, yes?"

Linda nodded.

34

"This is my wife, Martha," Daniel continued, introducing Martha who joined Daniel. "And, this is my daughter, Sarah." He reached out to let Sarah grab his index finger.

"What a lovely daughter," Ben said. "I was hoping to meet her today."

"You seem so young," Linda said. "I..."

Daniel smiled. "I will be nineteen this coming December." Daniel leaned over the table to get closer to Linda. "We Amish marry early."

Linda patted her chest and took in a light breath. "I guess you do."

"Daniel has been working at the mill for several years now. I think I told you; he is also the school teacher."

"You have two jobs?" Linda asked.

"I work at the mill, and I teach grades first through eight at the school." He grinned. "In addition, I also have a family and..." He gazed across the road. "A homestead that I will begin to farm next spring."

"How do you find the time?" Linda asked.

Daniel shrugged. "I do not spend a lot of frivolous time on television and shopping."

"Proverbs 16:27 says idle hands are the devil's workshop," Martha said. "We keep busy."

Linda nodded.

Hannah and John strolled nearby.

"Hannah! John!" Daniel called. "Come meet my coworker Ben Hopkins and his wife,"

John shook hands with Ben, giving him a strong grip. Hannah eased onto the bench by Martha.

"John, this is my old school bus driver, Ben Hopkins." Hannah pointed to Ben.

"I wish you both all the luck in the world," Ben said.

"Yes," Linda added feebly. "Such a pretty, simple dress, Mrs. Heffel. Where did you buy it? If I may ask."

"I made it," Hannah said. "Most Amish women make their wedding dresses." She paused. "We also make our *newehocker's* (bridesmaid) dresses."

Linda frowned.

"Bridesmaid," Martha said.

"Hannah," John said. "We had best visit other guests."

They departed.

"Actually, we should be about our job as *newehockers* (bridesmaid / groomsman)," Daniel said and got up from the table. Martha joined him.

"It was nice to meet you," Martha said and shook hands with Linda.

"And you," Linda mumbled and watched them walk away.

"I guess they're not so bad once you get to know them," Linda whispered.

CHAPTER SEVEN ~ Jason

Thursday, December 16, 1965 6 p.m.

"You had best bring in extra firewood," Martha said. "The supper meal is almost ready."

"More firewood?" Daniel asked.

Martha nodded. "Please? I did not feel well today. I was going to ask your mother to care for Sarah, but she needed to be over to your sister's house." She smiled. "Rachel gave birth to another young farmer. They named him Jeremiah."

"Rachel had her baby today?" Daniel questioned.

Again, Martha nodded, then placed a hand to her stomach. She gazed at the food on the stove, and covered her mouth, running into the bedroom.

Daniel frowned, considered following her, but decided to get the wood. He gazed out the window as the snow began to fall. He came back into the house with a load of firewood.

Martha stood at the doorway of the bedroom. She wiped her lips.

"I am sure," Martha said. "I remember this. I am pregnant, again."

"Pregnant?"

"I thought I would visit Dr. Braeburn, but will hold off another month to be sure."

"Pregnant?" Daniel questioned again.

Martha nodded. "I think this one will come during the summer — maybe June and July."

Daniel rushed to her and lifted her into the air. "Maybe this time I will get my Ezra."

"Or Elizabeth," Martha said. "Now, put me down.

#

Monday, December 20, 1965 7:30 p.m.

Daniel sat in his chair reading *The Budget*. He would gaze at the table, and frown. The papers stacked there caused him concern. They were tests he needed to grade, but kept avoiding the job.

Headlights flashed through the windows into the room.

"I wonder who that is?" Martha asked.

Daniel folded the paper and got up from his chair. "Probably just somebody turning around in our driveway."

He peeked out the window to see a man and woman walking toward their door.

"Somebody visiting or lost," Daniel said and headed for the door.

He opened the door and watched the man walk up to the front porch in the wintry weather. Snow had fallen earlier in the day and there was at least three inches on the ground the strangers sloughed through.

The people kept their heads down against the wind and stomped their feet at the base of the steps leading to the porch.

"Good evening, Daniel," the male stranger said.

"Jason?" Daniel questioned.

"We came to visit my favorite niece," Jason said. "Patty came along."

"Come in," Daniel said and opened the door to allow Jason and Patty into the house.

"Good evening, Jason," Martha said. "Oh, Patty! How good to see you."

"And to you," Jason replied. "Now, where is my niece? Where is Sarah?"

Martha giggled. "You insist on calling her that but you're not related." She shook her head.

"Daniel and I have been friends since second grade," Jason said. "If that doesn't make us almost brothers, I don't know what would."

Again, Martha giggled. "Having the same mother could help."

"Short of the ceremony," Jason jibed. "Daniel and I could be blood-brothers."

"Please, have a seat," Daniel said. "Martha will get Sarah."

"Oh, is she asleep?" Patty asked. "I was afraid she might be."

"Why do you wish to see Sarah?" Martha asked as she slipped into the bedroom where Sarah slept in her cradle.

Jason sat by Patty on the bench and took the glass of water offered.

"It's Christmas," Jason said. "I brought Sarah a gift for the holidays."

Martha stepped into the room.

"A gift?" Daniel questioned as he sat back in his chair.

"A gift?" Martha echoed as she carried Sarah in her arms.

"Yes," Jason said. "I..." Patty jabbed Jason with her elbow. "We, I mean, we got her a gift."

He reached into his coat pocket and brought out a small, holiday themed wrapped package. There was a bright red bow on it.

"This is for Sarah." Jason handed the package to Martha.

"Would you like to hold Sarah?" Martha asked Patty and handed the baby to her.

"Whatever is it?" Martha asked, taking the present and pulling the bow off.

Jason grinned. "Patty and I were in Shipshewana the other day and we spotted this and knew we had to get it for Sarah."

Martha pulled the paper away from the small box.

"I'm sure it might too big for her," Patty said, bouncing Sarah on her lap. "But she can grow into it."

Martha frowned and opened the box. She lifted the folded petite white apron from the box.

"Oh, how darling," Martha said and held the small apron in the air. "I know Sarah will enjoy wearing this." She held it against Sarah. "How perfect."

"Why did you not tell me you would be here tonight when we were at work this afternoon?" Daniel asked.

"I wasn't sure," Jason said. "Patty is going to school at night for her nursing degree." He shrugged. "She skipped class, but has to attend the next two nights for exams. So, here we are." Jason grinned and gazed about the room. "Other than helping on the barn,

I never really got a chance to see the house." He nodded. "Nice place."

"Would you like to see?" Martha asked, putting the apron back in the box.

"That isn't necessary," Patty mumbled.

"Sure," Jason replied and stood.

Patty stood. "I guess we'll see your home." She smiled feebly at Martha. "Where is the bathroom?"

Martha grimaced. "Outside."

Patty stared at Martha, horror on her face. "I forgot." She shrugged. "I guess I can hold it a bit longer."

Martha wrinkled her nose and smiled. "We do use a chamber pot, if you would want to use it." She reached for Sarah. "Let me take her and I will show where the chamber pot is. Trust me, Patty. It is so much better than going outside, especially at night."

Patty followed Martha to a bedroom. "There it is." She pointed at the item. "I will close the door and leave you alone."

Martha left, closing the door behind her.

"You have seen the barn, Jason," Daniel said. "This is the kitchen." He reached over to the water hand pump and gave it a few pumps. Water gushed out. Daniel grinned. "Indoor plumbing."

"I bet your mother is envious," Jason said. "How well I remember pumping water for a meal."

"Actually, Papa put one of these in the house. Mama is very happy."

Daniel led the way back into the main room. He pointed at the doorway with the steps leading up.

"There are four bedrooms upstairs, plus we have two on this floor." A tinge of flush came to Daniel's face. "Martha wants a large family."

"Nothing wrong with a large family," Jason said. "Patty and I are talking and..."

Martha walked into the room holding Sarah. "When?" she asked.

"Let the man finish the sentence," Daniel said.

"We're thinking of getting married next summer, maybe June."

Patty entered the room.

"Oh, you told them?" She lifted her hand with the engagement ring. "I was thinking perhaps the last weekend in June." She did a little twirl. "I've always wanted to be a June bride."

"Congratulations, Jason," Daniel said, offering his hand to shake.

"I am so happy for you," Martha said. She placed Sarah in the cradle and hugged Patty.

"One thing I can assure you," Jason said. "It will not be a three-hour ceremony sitting on hard no-back benches." He looked at Patty. "One hour, tops." He grinned. "Then we party."

"Party?" Daniel asked.

"Unlike the Amish," Jason said. "We will have music and dancing. Yes, there will be a meal; most likely catered, but nothing, I'm sure, to match the Amish for eating."

Daniel grinned, remembering the long agonizing time spent during his Amish wedding and the others he'd attended, including his sister's wedding.

"I am guessing we will be included in the guests?" Martha asked.

Patty froze for a moment.

"If you don't show up," Jason said. "I'll consider it an affront. Too many... uh, we'll call them incidences between Daniel and I for him not to be at my wedding."

"It is my wedding, too," Patty added. "Of course, you're invited." She glanced at her watch. "Oh, Jason, we should be going. It's getting late and I'm sure they would like to go to bed."

Jason grabbed Patty's coat. "I guess we really should be on our way."

# # #

Monday, January 3, 1966 8:30 a.m.

Daniel stood by the stove, letting the heat warm his hands. The chill had been taken off the room and shortly, he knew it would be comfortable for the students who were still outside playing in the snow.

Elizabeth Wyse stood at the door watching the students.

"Call them in, Elizabeth," Daniel said and moved toward his desk.

The students filed in and took their seats.

"Good morning, students," Daniel said.

"Good morning, Mr. Yoder," they replied.

Daniel moved to the front of the classroom.

"Bow our heads for prayer." He paused.

Heavenly Father, bless us this day as we begin a new year. Open our hearts to Your ways. Allow us to learn and guide our feet in the proper direction. Amen.

Daniel raised his head and studied the students. A sly smile crossed his face.

"A new year; a new song. Do you want to learn a new song?" he asked.

"Yes!" the students said loudly.

"Fine. It is called *This Little Light of Mine*." He paused and looked at the eager faces. "Does anyone know it?"

Two of the eighth graders raised their hands.

"How do you know it, Philip?" Daniel asked.

"I learned it in the *Englische* school when I went to first grade."

"Me, too," Mark Troyer said.

"Fine. You will be able to help me teach it then." Daniel moved to the middle of the class room where he was in the middle of all the students. "Here are the verses. We will take them one at a time. Ready?"

The students nodded.

Daniel cleared his throat. "Listen carefully. The lyrics repeat." He began to sing:

> This little light of mine,
> I'm gonna let it shine.
> This little light of mine,
> I'm gonna let it shine.
> This little light of mine,
> I'm gonna let it shine,

Let it shine, let it shine, oh, let it shine.

"Shall we try?" he asked and began again. The students joined in.

The class room filled with the joyous sound of the students singing.

"Now," Daniel started. "The next two verses are just as easy. Listen."

Ev'rywhere I go,
I'm gonna let it shine.
Ev'rywhere I go,
I'm gonna let it shine.
Ev'rywhere I go
I'm gonna let it shine,
Let it shine, let it shine, let it shine.

"Third verse."

Jesus gave it to me,
I'm gonna let it shine.
Jesus gave it to me,
I'm gonna let it shine.
Jesus gave it to me,
I'm gonna let it shine,
Let it shine, let it shine, let it shine.

"Ready? Starting with verse one again and going through all three."

Daniel began to sing. Mark and Philip joined in and the students followed suit. The song ended.

"We shall now all recite The Lord's Prayer together."

All the students bowed their heads and recited the prayer with Daniel.

"Now, I have graded the tests from last year. Mrs. Wyse will pass them back to you after I leave." Daniel sighed. "You may want to review the tests in my absence. I will be back in a little over an hour. If you have any questions, please see me." Daniel smiled. "I want to see you all graduate in May." He shrugged. "Some of you may not."

He handed the test papers to Elizabeth Wyse. "I will be back as soon as possible."

Daniel headed out of the school house. Jason, sitting in the heated yellow Mustang, blasted the radio while waiting for him. He turned the radio off as Daniel opened the door.

#

"Patty was so excited," Jason said as Daniel got in the car. "The wedding invitations came in the Monday after Christmas." He put the car in gear. He sighed. "So, we have been addressing invitations for the last few days." Jason shook his head. "I told Patty I could give you your invitation, but she was adamant it had to be mailed." He shrugged. "Expect it in the next couple of days." He held up an envelope. "This one is for the guys at work if they want to come."

"How many do you expect?" Daniel asked.

"I'm figuring between two hundred and..." Jason shrugged. "Maybe three hundred?"

"That is a lot of people," Daniel said.

"Her father is paying for all of it," Jason said. "Me? I wanted a small wedding, maybe fifty people." He shook his head. "Patty wants a big, BIG wedding. Her day. It's okay with me."

"You love her," Daniel said. "That is what counts. Not the ceremony. Not how many people. Not the food. Well... maybe the food."

They laughed.

"I am glad you were there when I got married the first time in Shipshewana," Daniel said and shook his head. "I had no idea what was happening."

"That's what best friends are for, Daniel. To be there. I was wondering.... Would you... can you... be one of my groomsmen? I need five. My brother will be my best man. I want you to be my number one after him."

44

"To be part of your *Englische* wedding? Me? An Amish man?" Daniel shrugged. "I will ask my father… I mean, the Bishop and see if it is allowed."

"Check with Martha, too. I don't want her mad at me," Jason said.

"I will," Daniel replied.

Jason pulled the Mustang into the parking lot. "I work full-time the rest of the week and then I start back to college."

"An hour and I need to get back to school," Daniel said. "My students need me. I still think my absence is the cause in the learning failure."

Jason parked the car. "Well, then, best get inside, get your men working, and Ben will take you back to school. Sooner in, sooner out." He laughed. "So, beat feet, Danny boy."

Daniel frowned. *Danny boy*, Daniel thought. *Will they ever stop calling me that?*

CHAPTER EIGHT ~ New Year, New Things

Monday, January 3, 1966 9:35 a.m.

Daniel stepped into his office and gazed at the paperwork on his desk. What caught his attention was a plastic man sitting on a pile of papers.

What is this? Daniel thought and picked up the item.

It was lightweight, cute, and about twenty inches tall. He gazed at the red hat, the white beard, and colorful clothing.

"Sort of cute, isn't he?" Martin Smith, Daniel's youngest employee stood in the doorway. "My mom bought it this weekend to put in the flower bed."

"What is it?" Daniel asked.

"They call it a garden gnome."

"What does it do?" Daniel rotated the item, gazing at it.

"It sits in the flower bed and looks pretty," Martin replied. "That one is plastic, but when I saw it, I immediately thought - We could make these."

Daniel nodded. "How long do you think it would take to carve one?"

Martin shrugged. "Not sure, a day? Maybe two?"

Holding the gnome toward Martin to take, he nodded. "Try it. I think this might be an interesting item for the team to try." Daniel frowned. "Do you think you could make different positions? Faces?"

"Sure," Martin quipped without hesitating. "Right now, the store only has this one type of gnome." He grabbed the gnome and held it. "We could make gnomes working, bending over, stretching." His eyes alight with excitement. "Big gnomes. Little gnomes."

Daniel nodded. "I like it."

Martin turned and disappeared into the workshop.

I will check on the others and then head back to school, Daniel thought and strolled into the workshop.

"*gut'n mariye*, (good morning)" Benjamin Heffel greeted Daniel.

Daniel nodded and gazed at the horse Benjamin was working on, unsure if he liked what he saw. "You changed it?"

"I thought rather than standing, I would make it rearing up."

"Did you ask Mr. Sullivan before changing?"

Benjamin shrugged. "No. I decided to do it and see what everyone thought."

Daniel took a deep breath. "It looks nice, but we needed a standing horse for an order. I need you to stop on this and start immediately on a new horse." He paused. "Standing, not rearing up. Am I understood?"

"Whatever you want," Benjamin said.

"No, it is not what I want, it is what the mill needs. It is what Mr. Sullivan expects."

Benjamin nodded, put his tools down and headed to get new wood.

Daniel checked the inventory and then walked toward the main office.

# # #

"Is Mr. Sullivan available?" Daniel asked when he walked into the office and interrupted Cynthia's typing.

She glanced at the telephone. "He's on a call right now."

"I can wait," Daniel said. "If that is okay."

"Fine. Have a seat."

Daniel sat, watching Bob Sullivan on the other side of the big window between the offices. He seemed upset.

Maybe I should come back at a different time, Daniel thought.

"How are things at the school, Daniel?" Cynthia asked. "I bet your little one is really growing."

"School is getting better, I think," Daniel said. "Little Sarah is trying to crawl." He shook his head. "Soon she will be walking. That should keep Martha busy." He smiled.

Daniel noticed Bob stand and motion him into his office.

"I think he wants to see me, now."

The intercom crackled. "Send young Daniel in."

"You're right," Cynthia said. "Go on in."

Daniel walked into Bob's office.

"Is there a problem?" Bob asked and motioned Daniel to a chair.

"I am not sure," Daniel said. "It seems Benjamin Heffel decides on his own what he wants to carve."

"Uh-huh," Bob said absently, moving paperwork around on his desk.

"We have an order for a standing horse," Daniel continued. "He decided to make the horse to be rearing up on its back legs."

Bob cocked an eye. "That could be attractive."

"Yes," Daniel said. "It does appear to be, but it is not what the customer ordered and hopes to pick up this coming Friday."

"Do you want me to talk with him?"

"This is the second time he has decided to make something different." Daniel shrugged. "I think the last time he talked with you."

Bob frowned. "I don't recall having that conversation."

Daniel nodded. "He said you had approved his new method."

"Oh, that." Bob shrugged. "He did show me, but I told him to pass it by you before pursuing it much further."

"He is my brother-in-law's uncle." Daniel gazed at the floor, wringing his hands. "Still, you are the boss and tell me what you need. I relay that to my staff, and they have always done what I tell them. When there are no orders, I allow them the luxury of creating new things." Daniel sighed. "Today, Martin brought in a... a... yes, I gnome. It was different and I told him make one and we would see what you thought."

"A what?" Bob asked. "A gnome." He thought. "Oh, yes, I saw that at the store the other day. Cute little guys." Bob leaned back in his chair. "Good call on that one, Daniel. They might be big sellers come spring."

"I will go out and oversee your department. I'll check on Benjamin and see what he is doing." Bob leaned over his desk to Daniel. "I may need to keep a closer watch on your department in your absence." He folded his hands together. "Are the students getting better in their studies?"

Daniel shrugged. "A little, I think." He glanced about. "I should get back to them."

"Haven Ben Hopkins take you." He paused. "You didn't come into town in your buggy, did you?"

"No, Mr. Sullivan. Jason brought me."

Bob nodded. "Yes. During the winter I think that is the best." He smiled. "When it warms, you can start using your buggy, plus school will almost be out." He picked up a pencil. "Any other issues?"

"No, sir," Daniel replied and stood. "I'll make one last check of my department and be back later today. Thank you." He stuck out his hand and shook hands with Bob.

# # #

Monday, January 3 5:30 p.m.

Jason drove the yellow Mustang into the driveway.

"See you tomorrow morning," Jason said as Daniel got out of the car.

"*denki*, (thank you) Jason."

Jason leaned down to look out the passenger door. "You know, I think that is the first time you've spoken Amish to me." He smiled. "It means something special, like we're brothers or something. By the way, I know Patty is going to ask, did you find out if you can be in my wedding?"

Daniel frowned, having forgotten to ask his father.

"I will ask tonight," Daniel said. "I am sorry."

"No big deal," Jason replied. "Don't sweat it." He laughed. "Okay, when the temperatures get warm, then sweat. Now, close the door; you're letting all the heat out."

Daniel closed the door and waved as he stomped up the stairs, trying to get as much snow off his feet. He opened the door. The scent of a meal cooking assaulted him.

"That smells delicious, Martha," Daniel said. "You have the meal ready early? I have chores."

49

"No, I have done most of your chores, today," Martha said. "If you wish to go check and make sure I did everything..." She paused then nodded at the door. "Go. Check. When you get back, we will eat." She smiled. "Then we will go to your parents. The neighbor, Richard Jones, wishes to talk with us this evening."

"Us?" Daniel echoed.

Martha shrugged. "He stopped by and said he would be talking to your father tonight and we should be there. He said it was important."

Daniel frowned. *What could be so important for both my father and I?* he thought.

"If you said you did the chores, I see no reason to check," Daniel said.

"Sarah and I collected eggs and fed the chickens. She watched as I prepared the meal. Then we milked Clara and I made sure she had feed." She hesitated. "Have you thought we should breed her again? Oh, and I made sure Bronk had feed and hay."

He grinned. *Maybe I should have her plow the fields in spring,* he thought, but knew wiser not to say it aloud.

"What are you grinning about?" Martha asked. "Go get Sarah and I will have the table set when you get back."

Throwing caution to the wind, Daniel explained. "I was grinning because maybe you would like to plow the fields this spring."

With wooden spoon in hand, and hand placed on her hip, she glared at him. "The garden, maybe. The fields? That is your job, my husband. Now fetch Sarah." She smiled and turned to the stove and the food cooking.

# # #

Daniel said grace and they began to eat.

"I know it is the Amish way not to talk during meals, but I thought I would tell you. I had morning sickness today."

Daniel stopped in mid-chew. "Morning sickness?" he echoed. "Do you mean?"

Martha nodded. "Yes. I am definitely pregnant, again." She pulled at her dress. "I think about three months. I was not sure last month, but this month, a woman knows. I was pretty sure, but being sick again earlier today confirmed it." She shrugged. "Guess I will visit Dr. Braeburn to make sure."

"Perhaps Ezra, this time?" Daniel asked.

Martha shrugged. "Perhaps Sarah wants a baby sister named Elizabeth."

"It is the Lord's choice," Daniel said.

He leaned over and gave Martha a peck on the cheek.

"I am going to be a father, again." He smiled and continued chewing the roast beef with a smear of beef gravy. Daniel scrutinized the mash potatoes and the beef gravy flowing to the top of the wooden bowl he'd made.

You are the next on the fork, he thought, eyeing the potatoes. He sighed. *My family grows.*

CHAPTER NINE ~ Farming Issues

Monday, January 3, 1966 about 7:45 p.m.

The knock at the front door startled Noah, even though he knew Richard Jones was coming.

"That must be Richard Jones," Rebecca said.

"I will get the door," Noah said as he placed *The Budget* on the table beside his rocker before standing and walking to the door.

"Good evening, Noah," Richard Jones said in the darkness of the porch. "I hope I'm not too late for visiting."

"Come in, Richard," Noah replied. "It is still early. Have a seat."

Richard entered and noticed Rebecca, Daniel, and Martha immediately. "Good evening, Mrs. Yoder, Daniel, Mrs. Yoder." He grinned. "I hope you are all doing well."

Rebecca stood. "I am fine, Mr. Jones." She motioned to a seat on the settee. "Would you like some fresh lemonade?" She nodded to Martha. "Come, help me?"

"That would be nice," he replied before turning to Noah. "I came to discuss an issue." He sat. "I have my fields scheduled to plant for the year, so I will wait until I harvest them, at least."

Rebecca and Martha left the room for the kitchen.

Noah frowned as he sat in his rocker. "What do you mean?"

Richard smiled. "I'm getting old, Noah. I just don't have it in me anymore." He sighed. "I had a long talk with Judy and we've decided to give up farming."

Noah's eyes widened.

Richard continued. "I asked each of my sons and my daughter if they were interested in the farm." Richard's full body heaved a sigh and he shook his head disgustedly. "They're not. R.J. - Richard Junior, that is... well, he's content being the plant manager at the factory in

Auburn. Alan, I don't think has any idea what he wants, but I'm pretty sure he has no desire to be a farmer since he is studying to be an accountant." Richard smiled weakly and shrugged. "Or, a teacher… or some type of fancy chef." He made a grimace and raised his eyebrows. "Like I said, I don't know, and neither does he. And, well, Ruth Ann is adamant about becoming a full partner at the law firm where she works in Fort Wayne." He shrugged. "If she marries, more likely it will be to a city slicker."

Noah nodded. Rebecca and Martha entered with lemonade and cookies. Richard took a tall glass and a cookie to munch. He cleared his mouth and throat.

"I considered selling a plot of land to your daughter, Hannah, and her husband. I discovered his father had already procured a place for them. So, as soon as the crops are in this fall, I think I will offer the farm for sale."

Rebecca stared at Noah then continued back to the kitchen. Noah frowned, wondering why Richard was telling him of his plans.

Richard cocked an eye. "I see you evaluating my words and wondering why I'm telling you this. The answer is simple. I know you, Noah. You're a farmer. And a good one, at that. If you bought the farm, I know it would remain a farm, being properly tended by a real farmer, not those 'play' farmers who have those big tractors and all the equipment that only take three passes to do a field." Richard watched Noah. "I also don't want my farm going to one of those new-fangled cooperative farms."

"I feel blessed you would think of me first, Richard," Noah replied.

"I will sell it to you at a very reasonable price, Noah. You and your children could divide it up into individual plots."

"You will not sell until this fall? Is that correct?" Noah asked.

"Not until the crops are in," Richard confirmed, then offered a sheepish grin. "That will allow me all summer to make sure I and Judy have decided on the right course of action." He sighed. "We've considered traveling, yet I hear Florida and Texas are wonderful for old people during the winter."

Richard popped the last chunk of cookie into his mouth, chewed and then guzzled the last of his lemonade to wash it all down.

"Maybe you could have Rebecca come over and share her cookie recipe with Judy so she can make me cookies that taste this good." Richard rubbed his stomach area. "Your wife really knows how to cook and bake."

"Perhaps I should make you wait until next summer for Rebecca to teach Judy." Noah laughed and winked at Richard. "That way you will stay another year."

Richard waggled an index finger at Noah. "No cheating, Noah. I will await your answer." He stood. "At least, until the end of September at which time I will consider other options."

"I will let you know of my answer, Richard. The offer is most generous."

"I will leave you to your thoughts," Richard said and headed to the front door.

Noah followed and saw him out the door then turned to Rebecca who stood at the kitchen doorway.

"Make sure Luke is here tomorrow night after the supper meal." Noah paused then nodded his head approvingly. "Be sure to invite Ruth's husband, Joshua, Rachel's husband, Jacob, and Hannah's husband, John."

"What do I tell them?" Rebecca asked.

Noah grinned. "Tell them we need to discuss farming and the family."

# # #

"Papa," Daniel started. "Before I return home, I have a question for the bishop. Can I be allowed to participate in an Englische wedding?" He paused, watching his father. "It is Jason. He is getting married and wishes me to be a groomsman in the ceremony."

"What is a groomsman?" Noah asked.

Martha slipped up and placed her arm around Daniel's arm.

"A groomsman," Martha started. "It is a person who will stand up in front during the wedding, like a witness; like *newehockers* (groomsman/bridesmaid).

"Englische weddings are different," Noah said.

Daniel nodded. "I know."

Noah snickered. "I know you know. I see no reason you cannot participate in such a manner." He leaned in close to Daniel. "Please use discretion, Daniel. I am sure there will be pictures. We do not want any Amish to see you misbehaving." He shook his head. "Your *Englische* wedding had the community whispering for weeks."

Daniel hung head. "I have been shunned so many times growing up. I will respect my elders and refrain from anything that would cast a shadow on my actions."

"Then attend with my blessing, Daniel."

Noah stood and strode to the kitchen.

"I will tell Jason tomorrow. We will attend the wedding in June."

Martha sighed. "And I will be a full seven or eight months pregnant."

Daniel took Sarah and helped Martha to the door.

"Good night, Mama, Papa," he said.

Martha echoed his words.

He helped Martha down the steps as he carried Sarah.

"I will go see Doctor Braeburn in the next day or two," Martha said. "You know, just to make sure everything is fine."

Daniel nodded, grabbed her hand and they walked to their home across the road. Sarah was asleep.

# # #

Tuesday, January 4 5:30 p.m.

Daniel got out of Ben's car and gazed at the collection of buggies at his parent's house.

Joshua Mueller, Luke Yoder, Jacob Metz, and John Heffel, Daniel thought. *I am the last.* He looked at his house, Martha did not appear. *I am sure Martha has been over to help Mama with the meal.*

He walked the driveway and slipped into the kitchen.

"Daniel," Noah called from the main room. "Join us. We have been waiting."

The scent of fried chicken made Daniel's head swirl. *My favorite*, he thought. He smelled again. *Potatoes, corn, cornbread, and... and apple pie. I hope this meeting is short.*

"Daniel," Noah said and pointed to a chair beside his younger brother, Jacob. "Have a seat. We need to discuss Mr. Jones' proposition.

Noah gazed at his sons and sighed.

"Mr. Jones visited last night." He nodded at Daniel. "Daniel was here. Mr. Jones wishes to sell his farm and has offered it to me. It is a little over five hundred acres."

"That is a lot of land," Luke said.

"Mr. Jones said he had five hundred and fifty acres. He sold a little over fifteen acres to Daniel. I am guessing we are talking somewhere around five hundred and thirty-five acres." He lifted his hand and wobbled it. "More or less."

"Jacob is thirteen," Noah started. "He will graduate this year..." His voice trailed off as he gazed at Daniel who shrugged. "We hope, and he should be available to help farm." He smiled. "Even the twins could help, but I think Mama wants them to help with the garden."

From the other room came the sound of "Darn!"

"Joshua! Jonah! You should not be listening to your father's meeting," Rebecca said. "Now, scoot upstairs and play with the others."

The sound of two boys making their way upstairs filled the house.

Noah laughed, as did the rest in the meeting.

"They might be able to help," Luke whispered. "But we will not tell them that."

"Do you think I should bring the information to the community?" Noah asked. "As Bishop, I can announce the offering at church on Sunday, or I can have the Elders meet."

"I do not think this is something we can decide," John Heffel said. "I think you should consult with the Elders."

"How much is he asking?" Joshua Mueller asked.

"I do not know," Noah replied. "He sold the property to Daniel at two hundred dollars per acre. Five hundred acres would be over one hundred thousand dollars."

Daniel's eyes widened.

"That is a lot of money," Luke said, shaking his head. "Is he willing to negotiate?"

Noah frowned. "I could ask. Or, I could go to the bank."

Daniel frowned, he knew how much his father didn't like dealing with the bank, but knew it to be a necessary evil.

"There is an option," John Heffel said. "I heard a buddy in the Army…" He allowed his voice to fade.

"Go on, John," Noah said.

"He said he was buying his house on something called a land contract. He paid so much down and makes monthly payment to the owner until it is paid off." He shrugged. "We could do something like that with a yearly payment." He paused. "Of course, there is interest on the unpaid amount." John stared down at his shoes. "I may have spoken out of place."

"No," Noah replied. "It could be an option Mr. Jones is willing to accept. We could pay fifty percent now and the rest in yearly payments for five or up to ten years."

Jacob Mueller sighed. "Fifty thousand is a lot of money." He gazed at his in-laws. "I maybe have three or four thousand." He paused. "Nowhere near the fifty thousand we are discussing."

"Allow me to discuss this with the Elders," Noah said and lifted his head and smelled the air. "I believe the evening meal is about ready."

"The table is set and the meal is ready," Rebecca said, appearing at the doorway between the rooms.

CHAPTER TEN ~ The Proposition

Wednesday, May 11, 1966 10 a.m.

Rebecca was tidying the kitchen with Hannah and Martha; both young women were showing their pregnancies. They heard the car pull into the driveway. The urgency of the knock on the kitchen door startled all of them. Rebecca answered the door with hesitancy and caution.

"May I help you," she asked, opening the door and staring at the stranger standing on the other side of the screen door.

"My name is Timothy Hagen. I would like to speak with Mr. Yoder," the gentleman said. "Is he available."

Rebecca shook her head. "Nay. He is out in the field and will not return until near sunset. I will be taking his lunch to him later. Would you like to leave a message?"

"Which field is he working... uh, Mrs. Yoder?" Hagen glanced about the surrounding area, scanning the horizon for any activity.

"Yes, I am Mrs. Yoder. He is working the north field this morning with our son, Luke."

"Point me in the direction of the field, Mrs. Yoder. It is imperative I speak with your husband today... immediately. I need his answer."

Rebecca frowned and continued to dry her hands in the apron even though they were no longer wet. She was nervous.

"As I said, my husband will be back this evening. What is the message I can give him?"

Hagen inhaled deeply.

"I'm the purchaser for the local grocery chain - Meadow Markets - and just had a vendor back out of a deal for this summer and fall's produce. I need a new avenue of supply." He grimaced, tightening his lips in the process. "I was told Mr. Yoder might be interested in producing the needed items." Hagen shrugged. "I need a response today." He paused. "Perhaps I should check with another." Hagen turned to leave.

Rebecca's brows knitted in thought. "If you wish to speak with my husband, I can show you the field." She glanced down at the wing-tip shoes and then appraised the suit Hagen wore. "The field is dirty. Are you sure you…"

"I'm fine with dirt, Mrs. Yoder. Lead the way." He reached to open the screen door for her.

Rebecca leaned back into the kitchen. "Hannah. Martha. I will be back shortly."

She led Hagen across the open area toward the barn, veering to the right to trudge around the barn. She pointed.

"See this field? The next field over is where my husband is working. Stay close to the fence row and you should not get too muddy or dirty. When you have reached the other side of this field, you should be able to see where Noah and our son, Luke, are working." Once more she gazed at Hagen. "Are you sure you…"

"Thank you, Mrs. Yoder," Hagen said and tromped across the field, his shoes sinking into the freshly turned soil. He finagled himself toward the fence row, pushing the new growing weeds aside.

# # #

Wednesday, May 11 10:25 a.m.

"Papa," Luke called to his dad.

Noah looked up to see Luke nod toward the field closest to the house.

"We have a visitor," Luke said.

"Mr. Yoder!" Hagen yelled and hailed with a flailing arm in the air. "I need speak with Noah Yoder."

"Aye, I am Noah Yoder," Noah replied, bringing the team of horses to a stop. "What do you need?"

"My name is Timothy Hagen. I have come to ask if you would be interested in supplying watermelons, cantaloupes, pumpkins, squash, and some gourds for our chain?"

Noah's eyes narrowed. "What chain?"

"Meadow Market," Hagen replied. "We have three stores."

Noah trudged through the rough plowed ground. "Exactly how many of these do you need, Mr. Hagen?"

"We can discuss the logistics and numbers when we sign contracts," Hagen replied between huffs, catching his breath.

"Nay," Noah replied. "I need know the number to see if I have the space to grow your needs."

Hagen leaned against a fence post, slightly bent over, his paunchy build huffing. "I have the paperwork in my briefcase…" He pointed back at the house. "In my car." He inhaled deep, expanding as he did so. "Could we talk about this in your home?"

Noah glanced at the field.

"I will tend the field, Papa," Luke said, speaking Amish. "Go, see what the *Englische* desires." He leaned in close to Noah. "This could be a profitable opportunity."

Noah scrutinized Hagen. "Since my son helps me with the farm, we shall both return with you to the house to discuss this matter." Noah turned to Luke. "Unhitch the teams and put them in the paddock until we return."

Noah began the trod across the field. "Shall we return to the house, Mr. Hagen?"

They trudged along the field, keeping to the fence row and out of the newly turned dirt. Noah examined it, more to assure himself the field was ready for planting. As he walked, he shrugged, unsure of what to plant.

"If you will allow me a few minutes, Mr. Yoder," Hagen said. "I need to get my briefcase from the car."

"That is fine," Noah replied. "I will await you at the kitchen door." Noah ambled toward the back kitchen door and contemplated each step up to the porch and the waiting screen door. *Is this a blessing for our family?* He thought. *Is this the answer to buying the Jones' property?*

Timothy Hagen slammed the door of the car and rushed across the small yard. He took the steps two at a time. Winded, he paused to take a deep breath.

"You need not rush, Mr. Hagen," Noah said while opening the screen door. "We have plenty of time to talk."

Hagen stepped inside the kitchen and Noah followed, placing his hat on the nearby hook.

"This way to the front room," Noah offered and led the way across the kitchen. "You met my wife." He turned to Rebecca. "Some lemonade, please."

"I will get some cookies," Hannah offered.

"I will get the glasses," Martha added.

"Please, Mr. Hagen." Noah directed the man toward the front room and chair. Noah took his favorite rocker. "Now, what is it that is so important you would fancy yourself traipsing across my plowed fields in your Sunday clothes?"

Hagen cleared his throat. "Mr. Yoder. I had a contract with…" He shook his head. "No, that doesn't matter. They are unable to fulfill the contract and your name was given to me as a possible replacement."

Noah nodded his head. "Go on."

"As I stated earlier, I need somebody to supply our small chain of groceries with watermelons, cantaloupes, and other garden vegetables." He drew a breath. "We pride ourselves on offering fresh farm items whenever possible."

Again, Noah nodded as Luke entered the room.

"What I'm asking, Mr. Yoder. Would you consider providing the items? I was told you have the best-tasting cantaloupes in the county."

Noah smiled.

"We do," Luke said. "I have no problems selling them in the towns from my wagon when I go."

"Ah, there is a catch, Mr. Yoder. This contract requires exclusivity."

Noah frowned.

Hagen attempted a smile, his face reflecting the possibility of losing the deal. "We can't have you selling your veggies in competition with us. We require an all-inclusive sale. You can't sell except to Meadow Market. Do you understand?"

Noah inhaled, leaning back in his rocker. "If I agree to this contract, it is with me, and me alone. My children also farm with me and it is part of their income. They need to be able to sell at the farm markets and from the wagon."

"I'm afraid that can't work for us, Mr. Yoder. Again, we seek exclusive sales."

Noah shook his head. "Then we have no deal, Mr. Hagen."

"Perhaps if you spoke with the bishop, he could help you to see your way clear to sign with us."

"Mr. Hagen, I am the bishop," Noah replied.

"But you farm and..."

"The bishop oversees the religious welfare of the community. It is not an occupation. I see no way we can do business, Mr. Hagen." Noah stood.

"Do you know of another who might be interested in such a contract?" Hagen gazed up at Noah, sweat breaking out on his forehead.

Noah considered Hagen's words, all the while tugging on his beard. "Nay, Mr. Hagen. We Amish all deal the same." He grinned. "We all have families to provide for."

Hagen grabbed his briefcase and stood to follow Noah from the main room.

"I have a thought," Hagen mumbled. "A possible solution." He grinned. "A loophole, so to speak."

"Here is the lemonade and cookies," Rebecca said, gently pushing the men back into the main room. "Sit, and discuss."

Hagen sat on the settee across from Noah who eased into his rocker.

"What is this possible loophole?" Noah asked.

Hagen opened his briefcase and removed papers from it.

"I will make the contract between you and the chain. It will not entail your family." He nodded toward Luke. "This will allow your married children to continue to sell as they have done."

Noah nodded approval.

"But, Mr. Yoder, your unmarried children, those who live with you, will not be able to sell any goods." He gazed hopefully at the Amish man. "Do you think you could agree to such terms?"

"I see no problem," Noah said and lifted his lemonade to his lips and sipped. "Daniel, my married son who lives across the road, this would allow his wife to sell our goods as usual from our greenhouse."

Hagen frowned. "It would appear that for you it will business as usual."

Noah smiled. "Yes, it would appear like that. Now, exactly how many of each item are you desiring?"

Hagen nibbled on his cookie. "Could we go the kitchen table to discuss the terms?" Hagen stood. "This way I can place all the papers out for you to see."

Noah nodded and led Hagen to the kitchen. Luke followed.

CHAPTER ELEVEN ~ Crop Planning

Saturday, May 14, 1966 Early Morning

"Martha!" Daniel hollered. "I am going to milk Clara, and then go over and help Papa with his cows."

"I can hear quite well, Daniel. You need not wake Sarah. Go."

Daniel strolled to the barn and quickly fed Clara and then milked her. He fed Bronk and thew some feed out for the chickens to scratch and forage. Daniel carried the milk into the house and set it on the counter.

"Fresh milk," he whispered.

"Why are you whispering?" Martha asked.

"I do not want to wake Sarah," he continued to whisper.

"Honestly!" Martha slapped his arm. "You are... are..."

"Your loving husband," he finished and gave her a quick kiss. "Off to help Papa."

# # #

"Papa," Daniel yawned. "Have you decided how to plant for the contract?"

Noah gazed at his son as they joined together to go to the barn. "Are you sleepy? Not enough sleep last night?" He reached for the barn door and opened it. He motioned inside. "See? Jacob has already started to feed the herd."

Daniel yawned once more then stepped through the open door to appraise the cows he would be milking. *Hm? Papa never answered*, he thought.

"When we finish, we shall eat breakfast." Noah moved to the back of the barn. "By then, Luke should be here and we will discuss the contract and decide what to plant, how much, and where."

Daniel nodded, grabbed a bucket and stool. He gazed at the line of waiting cattle, and smiled. Soon they would be milked and ready to spend the day in the field. The thought of breakfast brought juices to his mouth, he swallowed. He envisioned the eggs, the ham, the warm biscuits, fresh homemade butter and jam, and… Daniel grinned. *Maybe Martha will make her delicious fried potatoes*, he thought.

"You are dreaming, my son," Noah chastised. "You will be back with Martha, shortly. Get on with the milking."

# # #

Luke scratched his head and gazed once more at the crude map of the farm. "Do you think we can grow enough to supply the demand of the stores?"

Noah tugged on his beard. "It will be possible, Luke. The Lord will see us through this. Daniel has offered his land to help grow what is needed."

A knock on the kitchen screen door caught their attention. Then it opened.

"Excuse me." Richard Jones opened the screen door slightly. "May I come in?"

Noah stood while motioning the man in. "Enter, neighbor."

Luke and Daniel stood to greet the man.

"Rumors spread fast, Bishop Yoder," Richard said. "I have heard you made a contract to supply a small chain with your produce."

"Aye," Noah said and motioned for Richard to have a seat at the kitchen table.

"You remember our discussion earlier this year?" Richard asked.

Noah nodded.

"To show you the fertility of my farmland, I'm going to make you an offer." Richard gazed at the crude map of the Amish man's farm. "Here." He pointed at the valley just to the south of Daniel's house across the road. "It isn't many acres, but I am sure it would suffice for you to grow some of your vine crops on."

Noah gazed at where Richard pointed, nodding.

"I've not been able to really plant in this area because of it being a ravine and washing out the seed from time to time." Richard shrugged. "Once a plant is growing and has roots to hold it in place, the minor occasional flood is of no consequence. Of course, I've been letting it go to weeds and carefully, very carefully, plowing it under each fall. I'm sure that action has enriched the soil over the years."

Again, Noah nodded. "I can have Rebecca grow some seedlings and we can plant them in that area." Noah cocked his head and gazed at his neighbor. "Are you sure of this plan?"

Richard spread his hands across the table. "I want you be sure the land is adequate and worth a good price."

"What are we talking?" Luke asked. "An acre, more or less?"

Richard smiled. "I was thinking if you use most of the ravine that I don't plant..." The old man rubbed his chin in thought. "Maybe a couple acres. Say, five?"

Noah eased back from the table. "Five acres?" His eyes wide. "Do you realize how much we can plant in that land?"

Richard snickered. "Maybe you'll consider giving me a pumpkin or two for my wife to can."

Noah nodded. "Aye, that will be no problem." He gazed about the table. "With what we have already planted, to have some of the items for the contract I thought we were going to have to double crop some of the land... like pumpkins with the corn. Daniel offered his land to help with the crops." Noah leaned in and placed folded hands on the table. "The Lord has seen fit to oversee our endeavor and bless it. I see a blessing here." He stood and offered a hand to Richard. "It is a deal, my friend." They shook.

Noah leaned in and whispered to Richard. "I wish to discuss the purchase at some point in the future; such as your price, etc."

Richard patted Noah on the shoulder. "There is no rush, my friend. We have all summer. Now, I'd best get back to my farm. The corn is waiting to be planted." He snickered. "Now, don't you get any idea of sneaking into my corn field at harvest."

Noah laughed. "Field corn. Sweet corn. I think the shoppers of Meadow Markets would know the difference. I will be sure to keep my sweet corn from your corn fields. No need to cross-pollinate."

66

# # #

Noah saw Richard to the door and returned quickly to the table. He turned once more to the crude map and added another awkward square across the sketched road and home. "This is Mr. Jones property he has given us." Noah smiled. "We will keep the squash on this property and away from the watermelon and cantaloupes. No reason to allow them to cross pollinate. The creek should not dry too early in the year and we should be able to water the plants without too much difficulty."

Luke scratched some numbers on a sheet of paper. "If we average the hills about six feet apart, and I think the ravine is about twenty feet; so..." Luke continued to scribble numbers on the sheet. "That would be three rows of about one hundred eighty feet. Plants five feet apart would give us..." Again, he calculated. We should be able to have over one hundred hills of pumpkins." He shrugged. "That could easily be four to five hundred or more pumpkins." He roughed some more numbers, all the while nodding his head. "Yes, this will work. We will have more than enough land to plant all the needed items for the contract." Luke leaned back slightly from the table, a satisfied grin on his face. "Five acres from Mr. Jones and the almost fifteen acres from Daniel..." He nodded. "We have the extra acres needed to plant."

Noah turned to Daniel. "Tell your mother to begin filling pots to plant some of the seeds into so we can transplant them in about week or so." He grinned. "Pumpkins, watermelon, squashes, and cantaloupe germinate in just a few days. With luck, Luke and I can have the fields ready by next weekend and the family can help plant."

Noah stood. "I will take the buckboard and Beauty to town to get the seeds necessary for the fields."

"I will join you, if you allow," Luke said and gazed at Daniel.

Daniel nodded. "I will tell Martha..."

"You will tell Martha what?" she said, coming into the kitchen.

"I am going with Papa and Luke into town to buy seeds," Daniel said.

67

"We will have lunch ready when you return," Rebecca said as she joined Martha. Behind her followed Miriam, Luke's wife.

"Have the children start to fill pots with good soil to plant the seeds." Noah pushed the kitchen screen door open. Daniel, Luke, Jacob, Joshua, John and little Jacob headed out the door.

"Jacob," Noah said to his young son. "Stay and help oversee getting the pots filled, please."

Jacob scuffed his shoe. "Yes, Papa."

Luke put a hand on Jacob's head. "If you need more cans or pots, take Miriam to our house and check beside the barn." He grinned. "We have many there." He leaned down to whisper. "See? You are needed here."

Jacob smiled.

# # #

"I've been expecting you," Aaron Shaw said as Noah and the others walked into the store.

"Expecting me?" Noah asked.

"I heard about the offer and contract," Aaron said. "I know I don't have what you will need, but..." He placed both hands on the counter. "I will give you what I have and go to DeMotte and get what you still need and bring it to your home today."

Daniel nodded. "Sounds fair to me," he said.

Noah cast a glance at Daniel and he immediately was quiet.

"I will need about three pounds each of pumpkin and cucumber seeds, about four pounds each of cantaloupe and watermelon seeds." Noah pulled out his crude map. "Plus, about a pound of cabbage seeds, two pounds of carrots and...." He paused. "About forty pounds of sweet corn. If you can, I would like the bi-color, but if not, I wish to have Golden Cross Bantam or Iochief."

Aaron paled. "I have a few bulk seeds, maybe a up to a half-pound of some items right now." He paused. "Jessica!" he yelled.

"What do you want?" Jessica answered from behind the next row of shelves. "I'm right here. I heard."

"I'll be leaving for DeMotte in ten minutes... as soon as I give Mr. Yoder all the seeds I have available."

"How much will I owe?" Noah asked.

"We can settle the account when I get what you need," Aaron said. "Now, if you'll follow me, I will get you started with a starter amount of seeds for your project."

Aaron started for the garden supply section.

"Do you think you'll have any extra to offer me to sell?"

"Nay," Noah said. "I can only sell to Meadow Market." He grinned. "But my married children might be able to supply you with some.'

The five men behind Noah all nodded in agreement.

Aaron smiled. *I will be selling some of the best grown vegetables*, he thought.

# # #

Saturday, May 14, about 1 p.m.

Daniel smiled at Martha as she swiped a dirty hand across her forehead creating a trail of smeared dirt. He glanced at the back of his hand before wiping his brow. Martha frowned at him.

He reached up and gently attempted to remove the smudge, but only made it worse. He grinned.

"Quit!" Martha said and pushed his hand away. "I know there is dirt there and you are only making it all the worse." She pushed the three pumpkin seeds into the pot. "I will clean my face when we finish. Soon, I will need to help Mama with the supper meal." She shrugged. "These seeds need..."

"Supper?" Daniel asked. "Chicken?"

"If you want fried chicken, Daniel Yoder," Martha said, placing a dirtied hand to hip. "You will need to..."

"More work, less talk," Noah said with a smile as he entered the greenhouse. "We have just finished our lunch. Allow it to settle before fretting about the next meal."

Rebecca stood, placing hands to her back, she stretched, all the while quietly appraising everyone working.

Ruth and Joshua were working with the cantaloupe seeds; Luke and Miriam pushed watermelon seeds into pots; Rachel and Jacob quietly stuffed different squash seeds. Hannah and John repotted tomato plants. The other siblings filled various pots with the rich, dark, loamy soil.

Noah eased beside Rebecca and nodded approval. "I believe you have this all under control, even the Lord would be impressed." He gave her waist a slight, almost invisible squeeze. She smiled. "I will take the older ones," Noah said. "We will finish up the fields." He turned to the door of the greenhouse and called back over his shoulder. "Luke, Daniel, Joshua, Jacob, John and yes, even you my son, Jacob. Do you wish to play here with the women and children or..." He grinned. "Return to the fields and do a man's job?"

Daniel leaned in toward Martha. "I will see you at supper. Chicken, right?" He turned to join his father at the greenhouse door, hoping to escape any possible repercussions from Martha. She slapped his shoulder before he could get away.

"You will eat what the good Lord provides and what we cook. Do you hear me, Mr. Daniel Yoder?"

Rebecca lowered her head so most couldn't see her grin. Without even hearing the full conversation, she knew Daniel was asking for chicken. She shook her head. *That boy loves his chicken meals*, she thought. *I will teach Martha my secret chicken recipe.*

CHAPTER TWELVE ~ End of School

Thursday, May 25, 1966 7:20 p.m.

Daniel sat at the kitchen table going over the final exams given that day. He was being careful and somewhat gracious on some answers.

He smiled. "Hm,' he said. "I should dismiss this as an error, but I will allow it since it is not critical to our Amish life." Again, he stared at the answer and then the question.

What town is England is where the time meridian begins?

Bethany Sutter wrote 'Sandwich.'

Daniel printed "Greenwich" beside her answer, but didn't mark it wrong.

A knock on the door startled Daniel.

"Who could that be?" Martha asked while nursing Sarah. She brought a blanket to cover the baby.

Daniel went to the door and was surprised to see Jacob standing there.

"I thought I could over and help you grade papers, if you wanted," Jacob said.

Daniel opened the door. "Come in." He appraised his younger brother. "So, you thought you would help grade."

Jacob shrugged. "It is my last year."

"I have already graded the tests for the eighth graders." Daniel smiled. "I think you might be a little late to help with that."

"Oh," Jacob said, scuffing his foot on the floor. "Guess I might go home."

"As you wish, Jacob," Daniel replied.

Jacob turned and headed back out the door.

Daniel leaned out the door at the figure sloughing his way to the road. "You will find out your score tomorrow, Jacob. Okay?"

"Sure," Jacob mumbled and stomped down the driveway.

"See you in the morning," Daniel said.

"Uh-huh," Jacob grunted and continued on his way across the road.

Daniel closed the door, turned to Martha and began to laugh. "My young brother hoped to see how he did on his test." He shook his head. "He is worried he might flunk and need to do eighth grade all over."

"He did pass," Martha said.

"Of course," Daniel said. "But I am not going to tell him that until tomorrow."

"You are an evil man, Daniel Yoder," Martha said. "He is your brother."

"No, Martha," Daniel replied. "He is my student."

"It's a fine line." Martha pulled the blanket from over Sarah. "I say you are being mean. Period."

"I still have papers to grade." Daniel walked back into the kitchen. "By the way, did I mention that Clara is pregnant? She will calve next January." He frowned and gave a shrug. "Not the best month, but Clara was uncooperative these last few months."

# # #

Friday, May 27, 1966 7:45 a.m.

Daniel guided Bronk down the road toward the school.

"Can you tell me if I passed?" Jacob asked.

"Are you asking me, your brother, or are you asking Mr. Yoder?"

"Uh, Mr. Yoder?" Jacob replied.

"Mr. Yoder will notify you along with the rest of the class."

Jacob slumped on his seat and was silent. *I guess I should have said brother*, Jacob thought.

Bronk trotted into the schoolyard to his hitching post.

Jacob jumped down and tied him up, making sure there was food and water.

Daniel smiled, knowing Jacob was upset and hoping to pass.

Elizabeth Troyer opened the school door.

"Mr. Yoder! Please! We have a situation inside that needs your immediate attention."

Daniel frowned, grabbed his papers, and rushed up the steps to the school.

What could possibly be that important to need my immediate attention? he thought.

Elizabeth held the door open and Daniel rushed into the school house.

A woman stood at the far end of the classroom. She turned.

"Ruby Mueller!" Daniel said. "I mean, Ruby Hockstetler. How good to see you."

He rushed to her and gave her a hug. She giggled.

"What brings back to Centertown?" Daniel asked.

"I came to visit my brother and decided to make sure I came to the school." She gazed about. "There are so many great memories here." She nodded. "I enjoyed my days helping to teach the children."

"Do you wish to come back?" Daniel asked.

Elizabeth Troyer and Elizabeth Wyse both frowned.

Ruby tittered. "Oh, I could not do that. I live in Shipshewana."

Both Elizabeths sighed relief.

Ruby grabbed Daniel's hand, patting it as she held it.

"You made my day, Daniel Yoder," Ruby said. "To ask me back shows you care and my assistance was not in vain."

Daniel smiled. "We had our days, Mrs. Hockstetler, but we honored each other and the students were the most important to each of us."

"True," Ruby replied. "May I call the students in?"

In unison, Daniel, Elizabeth Wyse and Elizabeth Troyer spoke. "Yes!"

"Well, I guess that makes it unanimous." Ruby giggled and practically skipped her way to the front door of the school house.

She rang the bell and watched the students line up; the older students surprised to see her. Each student walked into the classroom, the younger ones casting a questioning glance at Ruby.

The older students smiled, seeing a friend once again. When the students were seated, Daniel began.

"We will open with prayer." He bowed his head, as did everyone else.

Thank you, Heavenly Father, for another finished year of learning. With your grace, each student will pass. We thank you for this beautiful day, and also for allowing Mrs. Ruby Hockstetler to join us for this day. In Jesus name, we pray. Amen.

"I do not believe Mrs. Hockstetler knows the Indian song. We will sing that one now in her honor."

The younger students enjoyed it because they could hold up their fingers as an Indian, going from one to ten and back to one.

They sang another song and finished with the Lord's Prayer.

Daniel stood at the front of the classroom holding the test papers.

"Today is the last day of school," he said. "I will return your final tests." He paused, watching the eighth graders who nervously watched. "First, second and third grade students all passed and will move to the next grade." Daniel gave a heavy sigh. "The remainder of the tests I will place face down on your desk. Do not peek. When I return to my desk, I will have you turn over your tests. You will see the grade for the test...." Again, he paused. "Also, you will have in the upper right corner your placement for next year. In other words, if you are in fourth grade and see a five, you will move to the fifth grade. The only exception will be those in the eighth grade. You will see either an eight, meaning you must return, or it will be blank."

He placed the last test on the desk.

"Only a few more seconds," Daniel said as he walked to his desk.

He turned to face the students.

"You may turn your test papers over."

The sound of rustling paper filled the room. Sighs of relief were next.

Jacob cautiously turned over his test paper. He immediately saw the 82% on his test score. He glanced at the upper right corner. It was not blank. He read:

You passed, Jacob. Do you wish a job at the mill?

Jacob slumped back in his chair, relieved, and glanced at Daniel who watched. Jacob nodded. Daniel smiled; he had already discussed the possibility of Jacob getting a job at the mill helping Jason as a janitor.

Jason had told Daniel he was hoping to get a new position as a pallet maker. It was full-time, and Jason decided he would go to college part-time in the evenings, now that he would be a married man.

"Does anyone have a suggestion of what to do next?"

"Can we sing the Ant song next?" Ester Yoder, Daniel's youngest sister asked.

"Yes, we will," Daniel replied. "We shall march about, everyone follow me."

Daniel began and the students quickly joined. Daniel began to march about the classroom with each grade, starting with first, following him. He made a grand circle of the classroom, noting both Elizabeths and Ruby had joined in the fun. He glanced at the door and made a decision. He marched out of the classroom to the yard. The students followed. When they finished, everyone was outside.

"We are outside now," Daniel said. "What shall we do? It is the last day of school."

"Can we play?" James Schmucker asked. "Maybe baseball?"

Joshua and Jonah stood beside him, vigorously nodding their heads in agreement.

"What do you think, Mrs. Hockstetler? Do we let them play? Or, do we go back inside to learn?"

Ruby grinned. She gazed at the door of the school. Then she gazed up at the sky.

"It is a beautiful day," she said. "It would seem wrong to waste a beautiful day like today inside." She shrugged and looked at the two Elizabeths. "I think the three of us would like to be outside today." Both Elizabeths smiled and nodded.

"So it shall be," Daniel said. "I will go to the mill and get things done there and be back shortly." He grinned at the boys. "I do not want to miss a rousing game of baseball."

Ruby frowned.

"I go to the mill and make sure my department knows what to do during the day in my absence. Then, after school, I go back to the mill to complete the day. Next Tuesday, after the *Englische* holiday, I will work full-time until school this fall."

Ruby nodded.

Jason pulled up in his yellow Mustang. He stepped out of the car.

"There's a party? Am I late?" He laughed.

Daniel approached. "Last day of school. Unlike you *Englische*, we can have fun on the last day."

Jason smiled. "Ah, you forget our early school years, Danny boy. Remember? We had picnics during the last week of school when we were in first and second grade."

Daniel cringed at the 'Danny boy' but nodded. "I do not remember such when we were in eighth grade."

Jason shrugged. "True. Get in. Work awaits. Some of us are adults and don't go to school all the time."

Daniel sighed. "I am not going to school, Jason. I am the teacher. Now, being an adult..." He left the sentence unspoken as he got in the Mustang.

CHAPTER THIRTEEN ~ Gnomes

Friday, May 27, 1966 9:15 a.m.

Jason pulled the Mustang into the parking lot. The place was alive with people milling everywhere.

Daniel frowned. *Why are there so many people here?* he thought.

Bob Sullivan strolled to the car.

"I can't believe it, Daniel," Bob said. "I put them out less than an hour ago and it has been jam-packed ever since."

"Put out what?" Daniel asked.

"Your gnomes," Bob replied. "I found about twenty of them in the back. I didn't realize you were making them and had so many."

Daniel stared into the mob. *Twenty?* he thought. He remembered telling Martin to make a few, perhaps two or three.

"These are hotcakes, Daniel," Bob said. "Your horses have always been good sellers, but these? I think we're down to maybe ten remaining." He gazed at Daniel. "Do you have any more in the back?"

"I will ask Martin," Daniel mumbled, still in shock. He strode to his office and saw Martin working on a small horse.

"Martin," Daniel said. "Do you have any more gnomes? Mr. Sullivan put the ones you made out for sale."

Martin, with a guilty look, gazed over at the open stockroom. The gnomes were gone.

"How many do you need?" Martin asked.

"Mr. Sullivan said there were about twenty to start and he thinks there might be only ten lefts."

"Ten?" Martin exclaimed. He shrugged. "I have some I made for my mother, I think maybe another six or seven." Martin winced.

"I think she might be willing to give them up until I can make her some more."

"Go explain it to Mr. Sullivan. If he agrees, go home and get them. Mr. Sullivan is very excited the gnomes are selling so fast." Daniel smiled. "We will need to make more and very quickly." He paused. "But, still maintain our craftsmanship. No shoddy work from this mill."

He strolled over to see what Benjamin Heffel was working on.

"When finished, this will be a porch swing," Benjamin said. "Amish built." He slid his hand along the arm rest.

Daniel nodded. *Again, he has decided what to make without asking,* Daniel thought. *I do not wish to terminate him, but he needs to discuss things.*

"Did Mr. Sullivan know of this?" Daniel asked.

"I mentioned it to Mr. Sullivan and he said he thought it a good idea."

Daniel nodded. "Did he say to make it or talk to me?"

Benjamin gave a small shrug. "I thought I would make one and see what you thought." He gazed at Daniel, hoping.

Daniel appraised the swing, noting the angles and size. He was impressed.

"I think this would make a good item for the collection," Daniel said.

Once again Benjamin had saved his job.

Daniel walked into his office and barely had time to sit in his chair when Martin was at the door.

"Mr. Sullivan wants me to get the gnomes, Mr. Yoder. I will be back shortly." He shrugged. "We may need to clean them a bit, but they should be saleable."

Daniel nodded and watched the young man disappear from the doorway. He noted the orders and gazed at the inventory sheet.

We have everything, Daniel thought. *Now, I will have Benjamin finish his swing then he can complete Martin's horse. No, the horse can wait. I will have both Martin and Benjamin work on gnomes. I will be back later and help make gnomes, too. I think tomorrow will be a very busy day selling gnomes.*

Daniel sat back in his chair. *Did Martha have anything planned for tomorrow?* He let his mind wander in thought. *Would Martin and Benjamin be agreeable to overtime on Saturday?* He grimaced, hoping. *Next week, everyone will be making gnomes.*

Daniel filled out the forms for the orders and put them in his out box. Cynthia would pick it up within the hour.

He walked to the door and hailed Benjamin.

"Are you willing to work some overtime tomorrow? Making gnomes? In fact, when you finish with the swing, I want you to assist Martin with gnomes. Is there a problem?"

"No, Mr. Yoder," Benjamin said. "Overtime is nice. Gnomes?" He shrugged. "I will learn." He grinned. "I should be finished with the swing by the time Martin gets back."

Daniel nodded. "I will be back after school and I, too, will learn to make gnomes."

# # #

Saturday, May 28, 1966 Early morning

Daniel strode to the barn. He fed and gave Bronk fresh water. He moved to Clara, making sure she had food and then he milked her. He stepped out of the barn and gazed at the chicken coop. Carrying the bucket of milk, he went to the coop and opened it, allowing the chickens free. He cast grain into the air and watched as the chickens ran and scratched to get the food.

Picking up the bucket of milk, he continued to the house.

"I will go and help Papa milk his cows," Daniel said.

"Let me get Sarah around and I will come over and help your mother with breakfast."

Daniel nodded and headed out the door, noting his father going into the barn.

I will not be too late, Daniel thought and quickened his steps across the road.

He opened the door and saw Jacob with a pail headed for a cow. Up in the loft, the twins were pushing fresh hay and straw for the cattle.

"Ah, Daniel," Noah said. "Just in time. Sing us a song and calm these cows so we can milk them."

Daniel grabbed a pail and headed for the middle of the line of cows. He sat and began to milk. His voice filled the barn with *"Where Could I Go But to the Lord"* with his father and three siblings joining.

The song finished and Daniel began *"Take My Hand and Lead Me Father"* which let the others join.

That song finished and Noah called from the other end of the cows. "Daniel, sing the song about walking."

Daniel frowned and then quickly remembered the song he requested was *"Where're You Walk."* He cleared his throat and began, letting his voice fill the barn as he had been taught by his chorus teacher back in high school, Miss Bronson. *No,* he thought. *Her name is now Mrs. Jones.*

The cow Daniel milked offered a deep, but soft bellow. Others followed.

"They like this song," Noah said. "They are content. Can you hear them?"

Daniel nodded. *I must remember to sing to Clara,* Daniel thought.

"When we finish here," Noah said. "We will eat breakfast and then all the family should be here to plant the last of the fields for Meadow Markets."

Eyes wide, Daniel realized he had forgotten he was to help in the fields today.

"Papa?" Daniel called. "I need to work at the mill today. Yesterday, Mr. Sullivan put out the gnomes and they were a hit."

"He put out what?" Noah asked.

"Gnomes," Daniel repeated. "My youngest employee, Martin, showed me one and I had him carve a few. He made twenty. Mr. Sullivan found them and put them outside to sell. When I arrived from school yesterday morning, the parking lot was filled with cars and customers wanting to buy them."

"So, you need to work at the mill today?" Noah asked.

"Yes, Papa," Daniel mumbled. "I am sorry."

"It is only a half day," Noah said. "You will back shortly and can help at that time."

Daniel grabbed the bucket of milk to pour into the big canister. He was relieved his father had not pushed the problem.

# # #

Daniel searched the sky. It was clear with only a few clouds.

It is a beautiful day, Daniel thought. *I will ride my bike into work.*

He strolled across the road to his place and got his bicycle and rode it back to his parent's home.

Martha carried Sarah and came outside.

"I will be back for lunch... late," Daniel said as he sat astride the bike. "Some of the leftover meatloaf in a sandwich would be nice."

"You will get what the good Lord provides," Martha said with a grin. "I think I might be able to save you a slice for a sandwich." She shrugged. "Of course, your siblings might eat it all, and you will need to eat peanut butter and jelly, instead."

Daniel pushed down on the pedal to start riding. "You know you should maybe go back into the house and hide me a slice of meatloaf." He blew her a kiss and began to pedal away.

"I will do no such thing, Daniel Yoder," Martha yelled as she turned and went back into the house.

# # #

Daniel rode his bike into the parking lot of Sullivan's mill. The number of cars surprised him. People milled about the open area where many of the carvings were on display.

"I saw it first," a woman yelled. "It's mine!"

Daniel saw her tugging a gnome from a man's grip.

"Do you hear me?" she continued. "Let go of it."

Daniel shook his head, surprised the gnomes were such a big hit.

Mr. Sullivan and Cynthia approached the quarreling duo.

Daniel decided to hide and hustled into the building to see what his staff was doing.

Martin looked up as Daniel came into the department area.

"Did you see the mob of people?" Martin asked. "They're fighting over the gnomes."

Daniel laughed. "They still are. Do we have more to offer?"

Martin glanced at the inventory locker. "We have maybe another five." He looked over at Benjamin. "He should be finishing up that one within the hour and I have this one I will be done before lunch."

Daniel strolled to an empty workspace. "I will start on one." He grabbed a chunk of wood and picked up the chisel. He had only started when Bob Sullivan raced through the door."

"We have five more over there," Daniel said and motioned toward the inventory locker.

Bob Sullivan heaved a big sigh. "Only five?" he asked.

"We should have at least two more this morning," Martin said, offering a shy glance at Daniel. He shrugged. "Maybe three?"

"Who knew these things would be a hot item?" Bob Sullivan asked and turned to Daniel. "Do you think we can handle the demand?" He stared at Daniel. "The woman who was fighting out there, she is from DeMotte." Bob shrugged. "Word is traveling."

Daniel attempted to remain calm, but he knew he would be sweating shortly. He gazed at his two staff and thought.

With the three of us carving, we could produce maybe seven or eight gnomes per week. He shook his head. He didn't like the answer, but it had to be said.

"No," Daniel blurted. "We..." He motioned to include the three of them. "We can maybe do eight per week."

Bob Sullivan leaned against a table. "So few."

"Maybe..." Daniel started. "My brother, Jacob, was hoping to get a job here as a janitor helping Jason. He can carve. That would give us four making these gnomes. We might be able to produce..." Daniel calculated. "Say maybe a dozen per week, maybe more if we lessen some of the details."

Bob Sullivan cupped his chin with his hand. He stood there stroking his chin as he thought. He watched the two men chisel away at the wood continuing to create gnomes.

"Are you sure Jacob wants to work here? Remember, your father has a contract with Meadow Markets in DeMotte. Will your father allow Jacob to be away from the farm?"

82

Daniel's eyes widened.

"I did not think of that," Daniel mumbled. "I will check with my father. It is summer and stays light out quite late."

"Check with your father," Bob Sullivan said. "If he is agreeable, Jacob can start on Monday as another person in your department until further notice."

Bob Sullivan ambled to the inventory locker. "I'll take these and as you finish those, bring them out."

Daniel analyzed the chunk of wood he was working on, visualizing the gnome. He worked on a gnome.

CHAPTER FOURTEEN ~ Jason's Wedding

Friday, June 24, 1966 4:30 p.m.

Jason appeared at the door of Daniel's office.

"I see the gnome rush has eased up," Jason said and sauntered into the office and sat in the chair opposite Daniel.

Daniel leaned back in his chair. "I think so," he said. "Benjamin is back working on horses and Martin says we now have about eighteen gnomes in the inventory locker."

"Will I be getting my assistant?" Jason asked, a smirk crossing his face.

Daniel frowned. "Oh! You mean Jacob," Daniel said.

"Yes, Jacob," Jason repeated. "I got the job in the pallet department, but I've had to wait to train Jacob who was assigned to you as an emergency to help cover the gnome bonanza."

"I will talk with Mr. Sullivan before I leave work," Daniel said. He leaned forward, and wrote on a sheet of paper. He nodded. "Jacob will start Monday working for you unless Mr. Sullivan disagrees."

Jason nodded. "Great. So, do you want me to pick you up about five-thirty for the rehearsal dinner?"

"Rehearsal dinner?" Daniel echoed and frowned. He shook his head, confused. "What?"

"My bad," Jason said. "I forgot. The Amish don't do rehearsal dinners." He sighed. "Tonight, we will rehearse for tomorrow's wedding." Jason shook his head. "I can't believe I will be a married man tomorrow night. Anyway, we rehearse then we have a dinner where everyone gets to know everyone else in the wedding party."

"I…" Daniel was unsure what to say.

"Bring Martha and Sarah. They can sit in the church and watch then enjoy the meal when we finish. My mom and dad weren't sure what to serve, so mom ordered fried chicken from Kentucky Fried Chicken."

Daniel's mouth began to salivate. *Fried chicken,* he thought.

"Plus, she was going to make mashed potatoes and that green-bean casserole everyone likes. I know she baked up three apple pies yesterday and I'm guessing that will be dessert with ice cream."

"I think Martha will have our evening meal almost finished when I get home," Daniel said. "I will let her know." He shrugged. "We... I do not know, Jason. I wish you had mentioned this earlier."

"Don't sweat it, Danny-boy," Jason said. "I'll stop by and, if nothing else, pick you up for rehearsal and bring you back home."

Daniel inhaled deeply, hoping Jason didn't see him cringe at the name.

Jason glanced at the clock. "Almost time to shut down. You go talk with Mr. Sullivan." He stood and left the room, hesitating at the door. "See you a little before six. That will give you time to talk with Martha before I pick you up." He shrugged. "It's my wedding, so if we're late, I guess I'll be late... at least, tonight; not tomorrow, though." He laughed and disappeared.

Daniel gazed at the clock and realized if he wanted to talk with Mr. Sullivan, he'd best be headed to the office.

# # #

Cynthia was arranging things on her desk when Daniel walked into the office.

"Is Mr. Sullivan available?" he asked.

"Send Daniel in," Bob Sullivan's voice sounded through the intercom.

Cynthia nodded. "Go on in. Have a nice weekend." She grabbed her purse and headed out.

"What brings to you my office this late on a Friday afternoon?"

Daniel decided not to sit since it was late and Friday.

"I just spoke with Jason..."

"And he was wondering when Jacob would become his assistant?" Bob asked.

85

"I think we have enough gnomes now," Daniel said. He placed his hands on the back of the chair. "I see no reason why Jacob cannot start his janitor duties."

"I think a week of training would be sufficient," Bob Sullivan said. "I know Jason is itching to start work in the pallet department." He grinned. "It comes with a salary increase which he will need since he will be a married man this weekend. Are you going?"

"I am a *newehocker*, I mean, a groomsman," Daniel replied. "Tonight is a... a... rehearsal dinner?"

Bob Sullivan smiled and nodded. "Yes, it is the *Englische* way. You're part of the wedding party?"

Daniel nodded.

"Jason must hold you in very high regard." Bob Sullivan leaned back in his chair, putting his hands behind his head.

Daniel grinned. "We have been best friends since second grade."

"I will let Jacob know when I get home tonight. Thank you, Mr. Sullivan."

"Have a good evening, Daniel." Bob Sullivan shook Daniel's hand and walked with him to the door. "I'll see you tomorrow night."

Daniel headed back to his office where Ben Hopkins waited to take him home.

# # #

Friday, June 24, about 5:30 p.m.

Daniel strolled up the steps to the house and went in. He sniffed the air. It lacked the scent of a meal cooking.

"I see you sniffing," Martha said. "Tonight, you get leftovers. There is some cold fried chicken."

"Dress up," Daniel said. "Jason will be here shortly to take us to the wedding rehearsal and dinner."

"What?" Martha stood from the rocker where she held Sarah who was sleeping.

Daniel shrugged, glanced at his feet which he scuffed against the floor.

"Daniel Yoder!" Martha exclaimed. "I spent several hours cleaning that floor and making it shine. Do NOT scuff your feet."

"I did not know," Daniel started. "Jason came in and told me he would pick us up for the rehearsal and dinner tonight."

Martha's eyes widened. "I totally forgot. I have been Amish for so long now; the *Englische* do that." She handed Sarah to Daniel. "You hold her while I freshen." She patted her skirt. "No, I cannot wear this." She scurried from the room to the bedroom.

Daniel followed, placing Sarah on the bed.

"I need to clean up, also," he said. "I just got off work."

They hustled about, washing and putting on clean clothes.

Daniel began to laugh.

"What is so funny?" Martha asked.

"You offered me cold fried chicken. Jason says his mother ordered fried chicken from Kentucky Fried Chicken." He paused. "I wonder if it will be as good as you make?"

"It is fried chicken, Daniel," Martha said. "You will like it."

Daniel nodded then picked up Sarah.

"I will get items for the evening so Sarah is not a problem," Martha said and left the room.

Daniel followed and headed for the door.

He saw Jason pull up into the driveway.

"Jason is here," Daniel said, and walked out the door to greet him.

Martha joined him and the two walked down the steps to the yellow Mustang convertible. Jason had the top down.

"I will sit in the front seat," Martha said, a sly grin on her face.

"You will take Sarah with you," Daniel said. "There will be too much air in the back with me."

Martha grabbed Sarah and moved back to allow Daniel to get in the back of the vehicle.

"I should hand Sarah to Jason and drive this myself," Martha mumbled. "But I know it is not the Amish way."

"I can let you drive it while we are in rehearsal," Jason said.

Martha glanced back at Daniel to see him shake his head. "Papa said for us not to bring attention." He shrugged. "I think driving the car... especially this bright yellow Mustang convertible, somebody from the community will see you."

"I will be content to ride in the front seat," Martha said with a pouty smile.

Jason engaged the gears and the car turned around and headed out.

# # #

Daniel did as he was told and stood in the line behind the best man. He listened and watched as the minister spoke with Jason and Patty repeating words. He was reminded of his *Englische* wedding, yet this one was different.

Perhaps tomorrow will be different, he thought.

"Now," the minister said. "Jason Muirs and Patty Zimmer will walk out..." He motioned them forward. "Tomorrow they will have the same name. Now, the best man will offer his arm to the maid of honor..." He motioned them forward. "Now, each groomsman will offer his arm to a bridesmaid and follow the others out."

Daniel moved forward and repeated the motion the best man had done, offering an arm for the bridesmaid to hold.

As he walked past Martha, she grinned and winked. Daniel stumbled but caught himself and continued to the back of the church.

Jason came up and slapped him on the back.

"Now, we eat, Danny-boy," Jason said.

Daniel grimaced at the term of 'Danny-boy' but kept a smile as Martha and Sarah joined them.

"Where do we eat?" Daniel asked.

"Follow me to the Fellowship Hall," Jason said and put his arm around Patty. He lifted his head and sniffed. "Can't you smell the chicken?"

Daniel gently sniffed. "Yes," he said, nodding.

Patty gazed at Martha. "You are quite pregnant," she blurted.

Martha nodded with a grin. "Next month," she said. She rubbed her extended stomach. "With this heat, I will be glad when this baby is born." She smiled. "I am enjoying the air-conditioning."

Patty shook her head. "It will only be hotter when we leave this place." Once more she gazed at Martha's stomach. "I don't envy you."

Martha nodded. "Air conditioning. A convenience I had forgotten." She inhaled. "I will enjoy this luxury as much as I can."

They stepped into the Fellowship Hall. Tables, placed in a U-shape, had lavender and pink table cloths decorated with an off-center row of lavender lilacs and pink gladiolas. A white streamer twirled within the row of flowers which held them together. Plates and silverware were on the wider side. Two goblets with the names Jason and Patty were in the very center of the middle table. Other settings had goblets with names.

Daniel saw his name on a goblet, beside it was a small placard with Martha's name on it.

"We thought we'd make this a buffet style dinner," Mrs. Muirs said. "If you need help, my husband, I and Patty's parents are willing able to assist."

Jason and Patty took their place in the center.

"Very similar, sort of," Martha said. "But not quite the *Eck* table."

Daniel nodded as he led Martha to their seats.

Jason stood, tapped on his goblet to get attention.

"Ladies and gentlemen," he said. "Tonight, we celebrate tomorrow's marriage. Enjoy the meal. My bride-to-be and I will begin; the rest follow as you wish."

Mrs. Muirs came up to Martha.

"Martha. Right? My name is Violet Muirs, Jason's mother. If you will allow it, I can hold the baby while you get your food." She held out her hands for Sarah. "Honest. I will sit right here until you return."

Martha laughed and handed Sarah to Mrs. Muirs.

"Her name is Sarah," Martha said, struggling to stand. "I will be right back."

"Oh, my," Mrs. Muirs said. "Perhaps I should go get the food for you."

Martha eased herself from the chair. "I will be fine."

She followed Daniel and was amazed at the amount of food available. She was reminded of all the Amish food at their wedding.

Daniel gazed at the food, eyeing the fried chicken.

A leg and a thigh, Daniel thought. *Some mashed potatoes with… oh, good, chicken gravy.* He began to salivate. *And some green beans.*

Jason slipped by Daniel. "Don't be polite. Eat hearty," he whispered. "Get two legs."

Daniel turned to talk, but Jason was gone, already back to the table and sitting beside his bride-to-be.

# # #

Saturday, June 25, 1966 6:00 p.m.

Daniel walked into the room where Jason told him to come. The other groomsmen were there, changing, putting on their tuxes.

"Thank the Lord," Jason said. "I thought you weren't coming." He reached over and grabbed a tux from the rack. "Here's your tux."

"My tux?" Daniel said and frowned. He gazed down at his new, clean clothes. "Can I not wear my clothes?"

Jason put an arm about Daniel. "Danny-boy, we're all wearing tuxes today. I thought you knew that. Remember your *Englische* wedding. You and I wore tuxes."

Daniel nodded. *I did not discuss this with my father*, Daniel thought. He hesitated. "Will there be other Amish at your wedding?"

Jason shrugged. "I don't know. I invited the factory, but I don't remember any of the Amish saying they would be here."

"The bishop allowed me to participate in your wedding," Daniel said. "I did not ask about wearing *Englische* clothes."

"Tell you what," Jason said. "Put these on, and, as soon as the wedding is over, you can come back and change out of them." He smiled. "Plus, if you don't wear the tux, I'm pretty sure Patty will be upset. Even if you decided now to drop out of the wedding party…" He nodded. "Yup. She'll be totally ticked."

"I will wear the tux," Daniel said and began to remove his shirt, noting the others in the room weren't watching.

Modesty, Daniel thought and kept an eye on the others.

As Daniel removed his Amish trousers, Jason moved so none in the room could see Daniel.

"Thank you," Daniel whispered.

"No problem, Danny-boy."

Daniel found he wasn't upset with the name this time and was quickly changed.

"Okay, gentlemen," Jason said. "We'd best boogie up to the church and wait for Patty to make her grand entrance."

Daniel frowned.

"Sorry, Daniel. What I mean is when Patty walks down the aisle to marry the best guy in the world - me!"

Daniel nodded, remembering his *Englische* wedding and seeing Martha walk with her father toward them.

# # #

Daniel stood in the line with the other groomsmen. He remembered the rehearsal and it had not taken this long. His legs were getting weak; he hoped he could continue to stand for the whole service.

"I now pronounce you man and wife. You may kiss your bride," the minister said.

Daniel watched as Jason swept Patty into his arms, leaned her back, and kissed her.

Those sitting in the pews began to clap.

Daniel waited.

"I now present to you, Mr. And Mrs. Jason Muirs," the minister said.

Jason and Patty walked down the aisle to back of the church.

Daniel remembered this part and knew he would soon be out of these *Englische* clothes and back in his Amish clothes.

Daniel walked down the aisle with the bridesmaid, all the while searching for Martha in the hundreds of people in attendance. The person he didn't expect to see was Molly Pearce.

Do not stumble, he thought.

When he arrived at the back with Jason and Patty, Jason motioned for Daniel to come over.

"Here's the key to the room. Go change and hurry back," Jason said.

"I will wait until I see Martha," Daniel said. "Then I will go."

91

"Whatever you wish, Daniel. Thanks for being a part of my special day."

Daniel waited and Martha appeared, carrying Sarah.

"My *Englische* Amish boy," Martha said. She ruffled his hair. "If not for this haircut and beard, you'd look almost fully *Englische*."

"Now I will go change," Daniel said. "I will return shortly. There is a reception and..."

Molly Pearce popped up behind Martha.

"Daniel! Daniel Yoder! What a surprise to see you." She glanced at Martha. "At this wedding, no less." She pressed his lapel. "And wearing *Englische* clothes, no less."

"Hello, Molly Pearce," Daniel mumbled. "This is my wife, Martha, and my daughter, Sarah."

Molly's eyes widened. "I heard you married. A baby already?" She glanced at Martha's pregnancy. "And another?"

Martha leaned into Daniel somewhat protectively. "This is the Molly I heard about from high school?"

Daniel nodded.

Martha straightened the lapel on Daniel's tux that Molly had played with. "I know how *Englische* weddings are done, Daniel," Martha said. "Jason's parents are taking us over to the hall." She winked at him. "You go and change."

"That's correct," Jason said, appearing behind Daniel. "Go change and when you get back, my best man, my brother, Jack will bring you to the hall. Okay?" He turned to Molly. "Oh, hi, Molly. I figured you'd show." He grabbed her arm. "Come with me. I'm sure Patty will be happy to see you." He led her away, turning back to wink at Daniel.

Daniel nodded, turned, and left.

\# \# \#

Daniel sat at the table with Martha and Sarah. He watched the activity around them. Suddenly, people wearing white jackets and gloves appeared carrying plates of food which was placed in front of the guests. Jason, Patty, and those sitting at the wedding table were served first. Daniel had decided to not sit with them.

A plate was placed before Daniel and he stared at the contents.

A small piece of meat with bacon wrapped around it, a half dozen large grilled shrimp on a skewer, a baked potato and a half ear of corn on the cob. There was a parsley sprig garnish beside the corn.

Daniel frowned, unsure.

Martha leaned over. "Somebody is paying a lot for this meal," she whispered. "Imagine it. Fillet mignon. Jumbo shrimp. Surf and turf that could only be topped if it was lobster instead of shrimp. Still, fillet mignon? You are in for a treat, Daniel."

"I have heard of this," Daniel said. "I will enjoy this meal, even if it is not fried chicken."

Martha giggled.

# # #

Daniel watched as Jason and Patty danced alone on the floor for the first time as Mr. And Mrs. Jason Muirs. The other wedding party soon joined them. Daniel continued to sit with Martha. The bridesmaid he had walked down the aisle stared at him.

"You should at least dance with her," Martha said.

"I do not know how to dance," Daniel whispered and shrugged.

A man walked up behind the bridesmaid, whispered, and the two joined the others on the dance floor.

A few minutes later, a minor flurry, and the wedding party dancers broke up, rushed to tables, and grabbed their chosen partners.

The party continued with a father/daughter dance. A custom Daniel was not familiar with, which then followed with the dollar dance. He found that interesting. Attendees paid to dance with the groom and/or the bride.

Daniel watched Jason's grandmother dance with Patty. They talked and talked as they slowly danced until finally, the person collecting the money suggested a new partner for the bride.

The DJ lowered the lights, the atmosphere changed, and Daniel knew things were about to change.

Paint It Black by The Rolling Stones vibrated the hall.

Daniel leaned back in his chair, listening to the music, knowing if he was to do anything, he was sure the church would find out and he would be shunned. He didn't want that. He watched and waited.

Finally, out of breath, Jason sat down in the empty chair by Daniel.

"Are you having fun?" he asked.

"This has been a very nice evening," Daniel replied.

Patty came up behind Jason and place her hands on his shoulders.

"I fear the evening is about to end for us," Daniel said. He glanced at Sarah. "My daughter is trying to sleep and this music is…"

"A bit too much for a child her age," Patty finished. "It was great of you to come and be a part of our special day."

Martha struggled to stand. "It was our pleasure, Patty."

"I thought we'd be going on our honeymoon tonight," Patty said. "But it seems Jason must teach another his job next week. So, we will leave next weekend for a week in Acapulco, Mexico." She grinned. "Then he will start his new job." She shrugged. "Things change, we change with them."

The strains of *When A Man Loves A Women* caught Jason's attention.

"See you Monday." He turned to Patty. "This is our dance, my love," he said, stood, and took Patty's hand and led her to the dance floor.

Bob Sullivan approached as Daniel and Martha were about to leave.

"Hold up, young Yoder," Bob Sullivan said. "I want to talk with you. I think we were a tad hasty on moving Jacob to janitor. Jason had scheduled vacation for his honeymoon and I totally forgot. I see two options. I want Jason and Patty to go on their honeymoon as planned."

Daniel nodded.

"I think the best option is for you to oversee your brother as a janitor. You know the routine. When Jason gets back, he can make sure Jacob has things under control yet start work in the pallet department." He paused. "The other would be to keep Jacob in your department and the men…" He laughed. "Sure. The men clean their own stations until Jason returns."

"I can oversee Jacob until Jason's return," Daniel said. "I think Jason will be happy to go on his honeymoon tonight instead of next week."

"I know Patty will be happy," Martha said.

Jason and Patty returned from the dance floor.

"I thought you were leaving," Jason said.

Daniel nodded. "We were, but Mr. Sullivan has something to say."

Bob Sullivan nodded, "You said you'd delay your honeymoon so you could train Jacob. How about you two leave tonight and Daniel will train his younger brother. Remember, Daniel was a janitor before you."

Jason's eyes widened in surprise.

Patty clutched Jason's arm. "That would be wonderful." She leaned up to give Bob Sullivan a kiss on the cheek. "Thank you, Mr. Sullivan."

"When you return, you will start in the pallet department, but the first day you will oversee Jacob Yoder…" He grinned and gave a sly look at Daniel. "Just to make sure he knows his janitorial duties." He shrugged. "After all, Daniel has been away from being a janitor for some time."

They all laughed.

"We must go," Daniel said and helped Martha toward the door.

"Not sure how you got here," Bob Sullivan said. "But I and my wife can give you a lift home, if you'd like that."

Martha leaned back, placing her hands on her hips to stretch. "That would be nice."

CHAPTER FIFTEEN ~ Developments

Thursday, July 7, 1966 10:15 a.m.

Ben Hopkins strolled into Daniel's office.

"Have you heard the latest?" he asked.

Daniel gazed up from his orders and frowned.

"Latest what?" Daniel asked.

"I was getting a cup of coffee at the newsstand in DeMotte. There were a couple of gentlemen talking with a realtor. Seems they are looking for land."

"Why is that different?" Daniel asked.

"They are looking for a large farm with a creek." Ben plopped into the chair.

Daniel shrugged. "So?"

Ben smiled. "The interesting aspect is they are wanting to buy in the Centertown area."

Daniel nodded.

"Seems they want to develop a lake resort type thing. They're calling it Amish Acres."

"Amish Acres?" Daniel questioned.

Ben nodded. "I heard the guy say they wanted at least five hundred acres." He shrugged. "Know anyone with that size farm near the Amish?"

Daniel's eyes widened and inhaled deeply. "Richard Jones?"

Ben nodded. "That was the name I heard being bandied about. The realtor lady was sure Richard would be willing to negotiate and that he had one of the larger farms in the area."

"There is no lake on Mr. Jones' property," Daniel said and leaned back in his chair, realizing this conversation was going to take a while.

"That's the catch with the creek," Ben said. "Richard's property has a creek which can be dammed and the area flooded."

Flooded! Daniel paled at the thought. The dream rushed to the forefront of his mind. He inhaled, gasping for air.

"Are you okay?" Ben asked.

Daniel leaned forward and wiped the perspiration from his forehead.

"Just a memory," Daniel said. *I will need to talk with Papa tonight,* he thought, realizing the dam would be near his property. *The contract!*

"I can see something has you bothered, Daniel. Spit it out."

"The creek on Mr. Jones' property runs along my property. My father has many crops growing on the banks since Mr. Jones cannot farm it." Daniel inhaled. "To flood that would mean my father's crops would be destroyed."

"And…" Ben added. "He wouldn't be able to fulfill the contract with Meadow Markets. Right?"

Daniel nodded.

Ben leaned back in his chair, placing an arm over the back of the chair. "Let's not jump to conclusions. I only told you what I heard this morning. They may choose another location." He frowned in thought. "Of course, ol' man Barrington… he has about six hundred acres." He paused. "Hm? Not sure if there's a creek on his property. I see two problems using his property. One; he's tight and will want double the worth of the property, and two; it's to the north of the Amish community."

Daniel shrugged. "Another property. Maybe yes. Maybe no."

"I'd best get to my next delivery. They should have the truck filled."

Ben got up and headed for the door, standing in the opening, he gazed back at Daniel.

"Again, Daniel, don't fret too much; at least, not yet."

# # #

Friday, July 8, about 7:30 p.m.

The knocking on Daniel's front door startled him. He'd not heard anyone come into the driveway.

"Who can that be?" Martha asked, and rubbed her belly.

"I shall answer the door and find out," Daniel said with a smile.

"Good evening, young Yoder," Richard Jones said. "I hope I'm not disturbing you and your family, but I thought you might want to join me at your parent's home for the discussion."

Daniel's heart sank. He knew the discussion. He'd already spoken with his father the day before and they decided to wait and see what happened.

"Yes," Daniel replied. "I will join you." He turned to Martha. "I am going with Mr. Jones to my parents."

"I will join you," Martha said and struggled from the rocker. She grabbed Sarah from the cradle and handed her to Daniel. She stretched, pushing with hands on her back. "I think I can walk to across the road."

"Do you want me to hook up Bronk?" Daniel asked.

"No," Martha replied. "If we take it slow, I will make it."

"I didn't mean to cause a problem," Richard Jones said.

"No problem, Mr. Jones," Martha said and started down the steps. "I am only pregnant, not incapacitated."

Daniel held Sarah with one hand, the other arm he offered to Martha to hold and use as support.

"You walked?" Daniel asked as he gazed at Richard.

"I needed time to think," Richard said. "Fresh air always helps me think." He snickered. "I think that's why I'm a farmer." He also offered an arm to Martha. "Here, use my arm for more support."

Martha stepped carefully as they made their way along the driveway, across the road, and into Daniel's parent's driveway.

She labored up the steps. Rebecca stood in the kitchen doorway.

"I saw you coming across the road," she said, walking to the edge of the steps. "Martha, do you want to deliver today? My goodness, you only have a couple of weeks."

"I am fine, Mama,' Martha replied, but reached for Rebecca's offered hand.

"I hope Noah is home," Richard said.

Rebecca nodded. "He is in the main room, waiting for you."

Richard raised an eyebrow, questioning. "He is expecting me?"

Rebecca smiled. "At some point. Go on in."

Daniel led the way; Richard followed.

"Please, have a seat," Noah said, leaning forward in his rocker. We have much to discuss."

Richard sat on the settee. "It seems you know more of why I am here than I guessed."

"Please," Noah said. "I will allow you to discuss that which we will talk about."

"As you seem to already know," Richard started. "I was approached early this morning by a DeMotte realtor and two men wishing to purchase my property." He paused. "Judy thinks we should take the offer..." Again, he hesitated. "Which was quite lucrative. But they want to turn my farm into a lakeside development." He gazed at Daniel. "First, they will build a dam very near the edge of your property and begin to flood the creek. Then they will bulldoze the land to create the lake they intend to have. About half of my farmland will be under water. They rest they will divide into small lots to sell for homes to be built."

Noah nodded.

"They plan to call it Amish Acres." He grinned. "They'll destroy the Amish community." Richard gazed at Daniel. "They will probably approach you to buy your property young Yoder, and..." He gazed at Noah. "And, your property, too, since it will be dangerously close to the dam and could be washed out." He eased back in the settee. "They will approach the others whose land the creek flows through and could possibly be in danger of the dam."

"Why would I sell my property?" Noah asked.

"Or I?" Daniel added, but frowned, remembering the dream.

"Refreshments," Rebecca said, entering the room carrying a tray of glasses filled with lemonade."

Mary, Daniel's younger sister followed with a tray of cookies.

Daniel gazed out to the kitchen where Martha sat at the table, fussing with Sarah.

Richard shrugged. "If you do not sell, Daniel, just remember, I figure the dam will be near the road by your property."

"What of my crops?" Noah asked.

"I tried to tell the men of the situation, they said they would compensate you for your loss." Richard shrugged. "They assured me they would pay for all my crops I'd lose."

"Meadow Market will not take compensation for my loss," Noah said. He leaned back in his rocker. "What are you planning to do?"

"Again, Noah, I will ask. Do you wish to buy my property? I still want it to be kept as a farm."

"I spoke with my sons about our discussion. Five hundred acres is a lot of land. How much are you asking per acre?"

"Again, like young Daniel, I don't ask much. Maybe two hundred per acre?"

Noah grabbed his beard at his chin. "Over one hundred thousand," he whispered. "Even if the whole community contributed, I am not sure we could raise that much money."

"We can negotiate," Richard said, sipped his lemonade and then nibbled on the cookie.

Noah held up a hand. "My newest son, John Heffel, made a suggestion. I will mention it and allow you to think it over."

"Sounds fair, Noah," Richard said.

"We do not have the funds to pay in full. Would you consider a partial payment with yearly payments until the full debt is paid." He paused. "With interest, of course."

"What amounts are you thinking?" Richard asked.

"We think forty thousand now, and ten thousand for the next six or so years."

"With interest on the unpaid amount?" Richard asked.

Noah nodded. "Yes."

"I will discuss this with Judy," Richard said and popped the last of his cookie into his mouth. He leaned toward the kitchen. "I know you can hear me, Mrs. Yoder. I still hold you to your promise to share your baking secrets with Judy."

Rebecca walked to the doorway.

"I will teach her," she said. "I will visit her this next week, unless she would prefer to come here."

"I think she would prefer to use her kitchen," Richard said. "No offense."

"I understand," Rebecca replied. "*Englische* conveniences."

Richard stood. "I will return to my house and think over your offer, Noah. Judy and I will discuss it well into the night."

"My prayers go with you, neighbor," Noah said.

"Yes," Daniel added. "We shall lift you up in prayer to find the right answer."

Richard shook his head. "Flood out the Amish, build a lot of homes and the irony, call it Amish Acres."

Daniel paled as the memory of the flooding dream once more raced to fill his mind. He slumped in the chair.

"Are you okay, young Yoder?" Richard asked, noting Daniel's look.

Daniel nodded. "I am fine," he mumbled. "Tell Mrs. Jones a hello from us upon your return."

"I will," Richard said and headed for the arch between the kitchen and main room. He stopped in front of Martha and Sarah. He placed a finger out for Sarah to grab. "I will not allow them to destroy your home, my little one."

Sarah cooed and leaned forward to put her mouth on his finger. Martha pulled her back. "No need to bite the nice man," Martha whispered.

"I will pray on the matter," Richard said as he approached the kitchen door to the outside. "I will give you my answer next week. That is what the realtor gave me as a time line. She expects an answer no later than Wednesday. You will know by Tuesday evening."

Richard Jones opened the door and left. Ambling down the stairs, he continued on his walk to the end of the drive, and turning left, he disappeared down the dusty, dirt road.

Noah placed an arm over Daniel's shoulder.

"Next Tuesday," he whispered. "I pray the answer favors our family." He gazed about the kitchen. "I do not wish to sell." He inhaled deeply. "But I do not wish to live with a dam across the road holding back a lake."

101

CHAPTER SIXTEEN ~ Decisions

Tuesday, July 12, 1966 7:40 p.m.

Daniel watched as Richard Jones drove into his father's driveway.

"I will be back," he hollered into the house for Martha to hear him.

He walked down the steps and headed across the road to his parent's house.

"Daniel," Richard yelled as he stepped from the vehicle. "You will be joining us?"

Daniel nodded and picked up speed to cross the road and joined the older man. They walked up the steps to the house and Daniel held the door open for Richard.

"Good evening, Mr. Jones," Rebecca said and showed Richard to the main room.

"Ah, Richard," Noah said. "Come. Sit."

As before, Richard sat on the settee across from Noah.

"I have come to a decision," Richard said. "I felt I should let you know first."

Noah eased back into his rocker, unsure of the meeting.

"The developers offered me three hundred an acre, one hundred more than what I was asking of you. Judy wanted us to take the offer and immediately move to Florida."

Noah sighed. Daniel felt the wind knocked out of him. His dream of the flooding homes seemed even more vivid.

"I asked Judy what she really wanted for our farm. I mean, did she care it was no longer farm land? Did she want to see the Amish neighbors land flooded?"

Both Noah and Daniel frowned, unsure of Richard's answer.

"After a lot of soul-searching and prayer, Judy and I came to a decision. The Lord has guided our feet to your door."

Daniel held his breath.

"We will take your offer. It will allow us a tidy sum to start a new life in Florida. Plus, the money coming in for the next several years will be nice." He smiled. "Judy said it need not be ten thousand dollars each year, but anywhere between five and eight thousand with the adjusted number of years for the amount of time."

"You are selling the farm to us?" Noah asked. "For the agreed upon amount?"

"If you could raise the fifty thousand, that would be good. Still, if you are short, say only forty thousand; I will accept that amount, too." He inhaled deeply. "I want my farm to remain a farm and who better than the Amish to do it?"

"When do you wish to sell?" Noah asked.

"I want to get my crops in first..." He gazed out the window. "They are coming in very well this year, so I should see a reasonable profit. It will be this fall, say October, no later than early November, if that is okay with you."

Noah nodded. "By then I should have the money saved up from the contract to help make the forty thousand, maybe even the fifty thousand." He stood and shook hands with Richard. "I will discuss this again with my sons and we can finalize this fall."

"Sounds good to me," Richard said. "I will tell Judy you have accepted the offer."

# # #

Wednesday, July 13, 9:30 a.m.

"Good morning, Mr. Jones. Remember me? My name is Linda Singer with DeMotte Realty." She stood at the front door.

"Come in," Richard said, noting the two developers with her.

"Again, this is Mr. Ronald Hudson and Mr. Bob Smyth from Wonder Lake Development."

"I made some fresh coffee," Judy said. "Would you like a cup?"

"That would be nice," Linda said. "Gentlemen?"

The two men nodded. Judy left the room.

Linda scanned the area. "Shall we talk at the dining table? That way we can lay out all the paperwork for signing."

Judy brought the coffee cups into the dining room. "Here we go." She placed a cup in front of each person and the cream and sugar in the middle of the table.

"So, Mr. Jones," Ronald Hudson started. "We are offering you three hundred dollars per acre for your farm of approximately five hundred and forty-three acres. That totals out to one hundred sixty-two thousand and nine hundred dollars." He grabbed the coffee cup and eased back in his chair to sip. "A very nice retirement sum."

Judy placed the plate of cookies on the table. "The neighbor lady made these for me," she said as she sat in the chair by Richard.

"All you need to do, Mr. Jones, is sign the paper here on this line," Linda said. "That done, you and your wife can be off to Florida as soon as you wish."

"The offer is very tempting," Richard said. "But this is a farm, not some development land. I wish to keep it that way."

Bob Smyth leaned in over the table, pushing his coffee cup before him. "Am I to understand you are rejecting our offer?"

Richard nodded. "I am rejecting your offer."

"Fine," Ronald said. "Let me sweeten the deal. "I will offer you four hundred an acre. That would be..." He calculated. "That is over two hundred thousand." He paused. "Pushing close to a quarter million dollars."

Judy glanced at Richard and grabbed his hand under the table. She squeezed it.

"I think the—" Richard started.

Ronald cut him off. "Also, you will be allowed to harvest your crops and not vacate until after Christmas." He shrugged. "That way you can have a nice family Christmas one last time."

Richard eased back in his chair, rubbing his chin in thought.

I made a promise to Noah Yoder, he thought. *I shook hands with him. We made a gentleman's agreement.*

"Gentlemen... and Miss Singer," Judy said. "We are farmers. This is our farm. It has been in the family for five generations." She shook her head. "To allow it to become some type of development, even if we are not here..." She shrugged. "It can't happen. I love this farm and I want it kept as a farm."

"Are you sure there is nothing we can offer to change your mind?" Ronald asked.

"Perhaps more money?" Bob offered. "Maybe even a prime lake front piece of property?"

"My wife has expressed our wishes," Richard said. "I had another offer and have accepted their conditions."

Ronald gulped the last of the coffee from the cup. "If there are no other options." He glanced around. "I guess we are finished here." He stood.

Bob Smyth and Linda Singer joined him.

"Thank you for your time, Mr. Jones," Linda said.

The three headed for the door and Richard followed to close the door after they'd left.

"Did we do the right thing?" Judy asked. "They were offering us almost a quarter million dollars."

Richard pulled Judy close and hugged her, giving her a long, lingering kiss.

"You, my dear, said exactly what I was feeling. His attempt to pull at my heart string with a last Christmas was empty since the kids usually send gifts and call. I was trying to think of the last time we all got together for that holiday. You and I spend Christmas, alone, together. They come the weekend before, one day, to celebrate." He shrugged. "Just not the same as what he thought he was offering."

"Well, we spoke with the kids and none of them wanted the farm. I think Noah Yoder will treat this land with love. It will remain a farm. Young Daniel Yoder has already created a farm from our land. I'm sure others of the family will build on this land, too. If not Noah's offspring, others of the Amish community will."

Judy snickered.

"What?" Richard asked.

"Amish Acres," she said. "They planned to call it that and what we've done is assure it will be."

Again, Richard hugged his wife and held her for a long time.

CHAPTER SEVENTEEN ~ Fighting Back

Wednesday, July 13 about 7 p.m.

Richard pulled into Daniel Yoder's driveway.

Daniel stepped onto the porch. "Good evening, Mr. Jones."

"Come," Richard said. "Is Martha up to travel? Bring her and Sarah. We need to go to your parent's home. I'll drive which will be easier for Martha."

Martha carried Sarah out onto the porch and lumbered toward the car. Daniel grabbed Sarah and got into the back of the vehicle.

"Thank you, Mr. Jones," Martha said getting into the front seat.

"I believe your father will be pleased with this morning's outcome," Richard said and pulled the car around and across the road to the other house.

"Everyone out," Richard said with a grin.

Again, Rebecca met them at the kitchen door, helping Martha up the steps and into the house.

Richard ambled into the main room.

"Good evening, Noah," Richard said and sat on the settee.

"Good evening to you, Richard," Noah replied, easing forward on his rocker. "May I ask what brings you to our home this evening?"

"The realtor and developers came to my house this morning." He took a deep breath. "I was offered twice what I was selling my land to you." He paused. "Satan was definitely playing aces to me. But... I had the Lord at my back and I stayed true to our agreement."

"The Lord truly was on your side, Richard," Noah said.

"Imagine. They offered me four hundred an acre for five hundred forty-three acres. That's over two hundred thousand dollars; almost a quarter million dollars."

Noah frowned.

"They wanted to buy me, then they would buy you and the others, flood all the land, move out the Amish, and then call the new development Amish Acres. How ironic."

"What will they do now?" Noah asked.

"I heard Miss Singer say something about another larger farm to the north. I think she means Arnold Barrington's place." He shook his head. "I don't think he'll sell, either."

"Perhaps we should call a Centertown hall meeting," Noah said. "We could promote having these developers look elsewhere than our area." He frowned. "Wait, does Barrington's property have a creek or some type of water accessibility?"

"A town meeting would be great," Richard said. "Do we need another five hundred homes near Centertown?" He paused. "As to Arnold's property; I don't remember any creek, river or low land that could be made into a lake."

Daniel shook his head. "So, they would need to do major construction... digging and moving huge amounts of dirt."

"How fast can we get a town meeting together?" Noah asked.

"I will talk with Aaron Shaw and stop at the fire station. School is out but I know I can talk with John Teegarden, the school's board president." He shrugged. "With them, the word could get out and we could maybe have something by this Friday."

"That sounds good," Noah said.

"I can mention it at the mill," Daniel said. "I know Ben will spread the word."

"We have a plan," Richard said. "We will protect our farms."

# # #

Friday, July 15, 1966 7 p.m.

Richard Jones sat at the front of the room. Beside him was John Teegarden on one side, Noah Yoder on the other. He gazed at the assembled people, surprised the turnout was this good, at least fifty people filled the gymnasium.

Richard stood.

"Good people of Centertown," Richard started. "For those who don't know, a development team has attempted to purchase my farm to create a man-made lake with approximately five hundred lots for homes. I declined the offer which, in its final offer, was quite lucrative." He paused. "I just confirmed with Arnold Barrington earlier today that he, too, was approached and offered a great sum of money for his property. He has not made his decision from what I have heard." Richard gazed about the room, but didn't see Arnold.

"Do we want this development in our midst?"

Richard sat, hoping someone would step forward.

Aaron Shaw stepped forward, adjusting the microphone.

"I, for one, have mixed emotions about this development. As a businessman, I see my store expanding, but, also, I see competition coming into town which might force me to close. DeMotte is not that far away, Meadow Market could open another store in our town and I would not be able to compete and be out of business. I, for one, do not see this development as a good thing."

Aaron sat down as another moved forward.

"My name is Roger Marshall. I am a farmer. My property abuts Mr. Barrington's farm. If it is developed as a lake, I might see destruction of my property." He paused. "Even possible flooding. Will this company compensate me? Buy me out?"

"I don't know," Richard replied.

"Let me address that issue," Ronald Hudson said and stepped forward. "First, we have, indeed, offered Mr. Barrington a fair price for his farm and he is currently mulling our offer. As to nearby farms, we will assure everyone the flooding will be controlled and should not have any effect on nearby properties." He started to step back and then leaned once more into the microphone. "I hope that answers any questions." He stepped back to sit by Bob Smyth.

"Next?" Richard asked.

Bob Sullivan stepped forward.

"The name is Bob Sullivan. I own the local mill. Would this development be good? I am sure the people living at this new man-made lake would become summer clients. I see many of DeMotte's citizens taking advantage of having a summer vacation home. I already have DeMotte customers, so I don't see this as creating that large of surge in customers. My vote would be to have these developers move to another area beyond Centertown. We don't need them." Bob stepped back to the bleachers and sat.

Noah stood, moving the table microphone closer to him.

"My name is Noah Yoder. I am Amish. The original plan was to flood Richard Jones' property, forcing me to sell my land and several of my neighbors, including my son who just built his home. They will force the Amish to move, but yet, they plan to call the new development Amish Acres. There will be no Amish in the area. We will move." Noah sat.

There was murmuring in the bleachers.

A woman approached.

"My name is Kathleen Bergo. I am new to Centertown having only moved here two months ago. Why did I choose Centertown? It was a small community filled with families with the right values. I enjoy the Amish and their easy lifestyle." She hesitated. "I didn't mean their life is easy, but the simplicity they live. I came from New York City where the hustle and bustle of city life was just too much for me. Another five hundred homes? I might as well live in New York City again. I say to the developers, find another place." She stepped away from the microphone.

Bob Smyth moved forward.

"I think the community has lost sight of what this development can do. Yes, another possible five hundred families will move in, but you will see Centertown burst with growth. More churches. Bigger and better schools. More business opportunities." He glanced at Aaron Shaw. "Maybe your store might close, but the options will enhance Centertown and make it better."

John Teegarden stood and moved the table's microphone to him.

"I have been doing a little calculation. If we get five hundred more families and only half of them live at the new lake on a full-time basis, that would mean possibly over three hundred new students. Our school system can't handle that influx." He stretched out his arms. "We just consolidated our schools. With this number of students, Centertown would need to have its own school again, building extensions to class all the students." He paused. "Can the other schools exist without Centertown in the consolidation?"

Daniel smiled, remembering the issues when the Amish school was built and the Amish students were removed from the consolidated schools. The high school was in Centertown, the other three towns handled the elementary students which meant being bussed away which the Amish didn't like or want.

Another gentleman approached the floor microphone.

"My name is Alex Walker with DeMotte Bank. I see this development as a chance for Centertown to grow. Yes, new businesses, more families, bigger schools, more churches, and... and... well, the list goes on and on."

"But, Mr. Walker," Noah said. "Do we, as residents of Centertown, want to see this expansion? Do we want to lose our somewhat sleepy, small-town ambiance?"

Daniel wanted to stand and applaud his father's words.

Applause broke out in pandemonium. Some attendees stood.

Alex Walker stepped back. He joined Ronald Hudson and Bob Smyth as they stomped from the gymnasium.

Ronald stopped, turned, and yelled into the gym. "We are not defeated. Not yet." The trio left.

"I think we have made a decision," Richard said. "I will talk with Mr. Barrington tonight when I leave here."

"I will join you," Noah whispered. He patted Daniel on the shoulder. "My son will tag along."

Richard nodded. "If you don't mind, I'd like to go along, too." Richard smiled. "As a trio, we may be able to convince Arnold to see our way."

Daniel frowned. *Am I not part of the process?* he thought.

# # #

Friday, July 15, 1966 8:115 p.m.

"Looking at my watch, I see it is still early enough to visit Arnold tonight," Richard said while getting into his car.

Noah, John, and Daniel crawled in; Noah and Daniel taking seats in the back.

110

"They've called Arnold Barrington the ol' tightwad for so many years, yet he's not that old." Richard laughed. "Just tight. I do believe he can squeeze a dime and get nine cents change out of it."

Daniel frowned, having never heard such a thing.

As they pulled into the driveway, the front porch light turned on. Arnold Barrington stepped onto the porch.

"Come on in," he said. "Been expecting you." He gazed at the four men exiting the car. "Didn't expect a party, though. Come in. Come in." He waved them up the steps, onto the porch, and into the house.

"Have a seat, gentlemen." He gestured toward the couch and chairs in the spacious living room. "Anywhere is fine, except for the recliner. That's mine." He turned to the kitchen. "Jacquelyn? You want to make some coffee for these gentlemen?"

"Not I," said Noah. "Just a glass of water is fine."

"Same here," Daniel echoed.

"With cream and two sugars," John said. "Please."

"I'll take mine black," Richard said.

"Hey, Jackie. Make that two waters, one coffee with cream, double sugar, and two black. Did you hear me?"

"Yes, I heard you," Mrs. Barrington said, entering the room. "You needn't bellow. You're not out in the field."

Arnold waved her back to the kitchen. "Just the drinks, dear."

She wiped her hands on the ruffled apron she wore. "Fine."

"Now, let me guess. The four of you are here to convince me to not sell my farm. Am I right?"

"The reason they came to you is because I wouldn't sell my farm to them. You weren't their first choice."

"I figured as much, having heard the rumors down at the AJ Store. Aaron is about as subtle as a corn sheller choking on a cob."

Daniel frowned. *Again, another phrase I have never heard*, he thought.

"Have you given their offer any thought?" Noah asked.

"With six hundred and eighty-five acres, at their offer of two hundred and twenty-five per acre…" He drew a deep breath. "Jackie and I have had some heated discussions over the measly one hundred fifty plus dollars."

John Teegarden frowned. "Heated?" he asked.

111

Arnold laughed. "We're both fighting on the same side." He shrugged. "She wants to keep the farm for the children to have when we are gone. AJ, Arnold Junior that is, will be a senior this fall in high school. He's a great farmer."

John Teegarden nodded. "How well I know."

"Becky and Hans I'm not sure about. Sure, they help me, but they don't seem to have the same love of farming as AJ."

"So, you want to leave the farm to AJ?" Richard asked.

"I'm a farmer, Richard. Like you, I want to keep this as a farm. The offer is quite a substantial amount. The kids could go to college and I could help them start life with a little ease."

"You are considering selling?" Daniel asked.

Arnold scowled at Daniel. "You're Amish. You have no idea about higher education costs."

"I am a teacher, Mr. Barrington," Daniel replied. "I attended two years of high school. I went to New York City and learned the trade of being a singer and actor on a Broadway stage. I have a very good understanding of the *Englische* ways and the costs of higher education. I had to work at a Chinese restaurant to pay for my singing lessons."

Arnold nodded. "Ah, so you're the one who made all the fuss a few years back."

"Let us not be distracted by my son's life," Noah said. "Are you considering the offer from the developers?"

"Not really, gentlemen," Arnold said. "Yes, one hundred fifty thousand dollars is a lot of money, but at my age, I am only forty-one, it won't last the rest of my lifetime." He smiled. "Especially if I decide to help my children."

"Do you think they will offer you more?" Richard asked. "They did me, but I wanted my land to continue as a farm, not a lake."

"Even if they were to offer me four hundred an acre which is over a quarter million dollars — no, I wouldn't sell." He smiled at the men and eased back into his recliner to sip his coffee. "Therefore gentlemen, you have made a trip to visit me tonight as a waste of time."

"Not really," Richard said. "We received the answer we were searching for. The community seems to back us and not want the development because it would ruin our lifestyle."

"I don't know why they even considered my property," Arnold said. "I have no viable water source to make a lake unless they were lucky enough to strike a strong artesian spring or two."

"That would be lucky for them, but where would the excess water go? Whose land would become a flooded marsh over time?"

"Most of the excess rain water drains to the southwest and that is Roger Marshall's farm. He has a low area in the one field that tends to flood quite often during the year. He plants it and hopes for the best. With a lake and excess overflow water, his land would be flooded, destroying any possibility of crops growing there."

"The developers argued that point. They even promised Mr. Marshall that such flooding would not occur."

Arnold laughed. "I can't control it now, exactly how are they going to stop it? Nature has its own rules and plans. A man-made lake is not natural. There will be issues. I want no part of it."

Noah finished his glass of water. "I think our work here is done, gentlemen. We will see what happens next." He turned to Arnold. "When are you to give them your answer?"

"Monday morning," Arnold said. "They won't like it."

"I will talk with Roger Marshall tomorrow," John said. "I think he should know the consequences if a lake were to be developed on this land and the possibility of an artesian well."

"Very well," Arnold said. "May I show you to the door? Not wanting to rush you."

"That is fine," Richard said and stood. He headed for the front door. "Are we finished here, gentlemen?"

John Teegarden, Noah and Daniel Yoder stood, nodding their heads.

"Good evening and thank you, Mrs. Barrington," Daniel said, leaning back so he could see her standing, like his mother always did, at the doorway from the kitchen.

"Good evening, gentlemen," Jacquelyn said.

Arnold saw them out, watching them go down the steps and across the yard to the car. As the car pulled out of the driveway and onto the road, he turned off the porch light.

"Do you think the developers will offer more?" she asked, coming into the room and sitting beside Arnold.

"Even if they did, could we exist on it?" Arnold asked. "I don't think so." He grabbed her hand and held it in his. "We are farmers, my dear. We will stay here." He shook his head. "I can't believe I'm about to say this — money isn't everything."

Jacquelyn blew him a kiss.

CHAPTER EIGHTEEN ~ Newborn

Sunday, July 17, 1966 11:30 a.m.

Martha squirmed on the bench. She couldn't get comfortable. Suddenly, it hit. A twinge. A few minutes later, another, with more force.

Her eyes widened.

I am in labor, she thought. She gazed at those around her. *In church, no less*.

Another contraction coursed through her. There was no hiding that one.

Rebecca stared at her, then realized what was happening. Noah, her husband, the Bishop, was about to finish his talk on the traps of lying. She leaned toward Martha.

"Labor pains?" she whispered.

Martha nodded and froze as another pain wracked her body.

"They are strong," Martha whispered. "And fast. I do not…"

Again, she began to take short breaths.

"Come," Rebecca said, grabbing Martha's hand. "If we do not leave now, you will deliver here during church."

Rebecca stood, and helped Martha stand.

"A problem?" Noah asked.

"No," Rebecca said. "A delivery."

Two more women stood. "We shall help."

Daniel began to stand when a strong arm pushed on his shoulder and he was held in place. He glanced at Luke.

"They have no need for you," Luke whispered.

The four ladies left the room and headed for a quiet spot where Martha could give birth and not be disturbed.

"This way," the older woman said. "The main bedroom is here." She led the way.

"I do not wish to be a burden," Martha said.

"You are delivering a baby," the older woman said. "You are not a burden. Another one of God's miracles is about to join us."

Martha listened, hearing the church sing.

If I can hear them, they can hear me, Martha thought, holding back a scream as another wave of pain hit. *This child is coming and coming fast.*

Martha felt the wetness. *My water broke!*

"I am sorry," Martha said. "My water—"

"Do not fret," the older woman said. "It is not the first time it has happened in this bed."

The baby shifted.

"The baby is coming," Martha said. "I want to push."

Rebecca checked, and nodded. "You are ready. Push."

Martha pushed, feeling the baby move.

"You have a little farmer," Rebecca said as the child gasped its first breath and cried. "Let me guess, Daniel wants to name him Ezra."

A woman dabbed a cloth on Martha's forehead.

"A son? Yes," Martha said. "Daniel says his name will be Ezra."

# # #

"You are a father, again," Luke whispered. He glanced at his father who was finishing the service. "You will meet your new one shortly."

Daniel sat on the bench, his leg bouncing up and down, impatient, hoping the service would end.

Noah began the Lord's Prayer and the congregation joined in.

Almost done, Daniel thought. *Is it a boy, or is it a girl? I hope a boy. Ezra.*

A wail of the child filled the rooms.

"Amen," Noah said. "Now, if I am not wrong, I believe we have a new member to the community." He gazed at Daniel and nodded. "Go see your newest family member."

Daniel stood and quickly maneuvered around the men and headed for the kitchen to see where he would go next.

Following the sounds of the crying baby, Daniel located the bedroom where Martha was. She held the baby in her arms.

"Come," Martha said. "Meet Ezra Matthias Yoder."

Daniel nodded. "I like the name." He walked over the bed and sat near Martha's shoulder. He leaned over and peeked at the baby. "He is handsome."

"He has your eyes, Daniel," Martha whispered. "He will be a little Daniel as he grows."

Daniel smiled. *My family grows*, he thought.

CHAPTER NINETEEN ~ Finality

Monday, July 18, 1966 11:30 a.m.

Ben Hopkins strolled into the office with his cup of coffee and sat in the chair opposite Daniel.

"Congratulations, Daniel," he said. "I heard you're a new father as of yesterday. A boy?"

Daniel nodded. "Ezra Matthias. Martha named him. She knew I wanted Ezra, she decided on the middle name."

Ben leaned back in the chair and sipped his coffee. "That is a nice strong name. I like it."

Daniel shuffled the papers on his desk. "I know you did not stop here to talk about my new son."

Ben grinned. "What? A friend can't stop in and talk?"

"Talk about what?" Daniel asked.

"Rumor control. When I stopped at the newsstand in DeMotte, I heard Arnold Barrington turned down the development offer."

Daniel sighed relief.

"I also heard he told the developers to consider a piece of ground up north of Madison."

Daniel frowned. "Madison?"

"He told them his cousin has a large farm there and much of the land is ravines and gullies. Plus, there is a river running through his property that they might be able to dam, depending on the state's laws and restrictions."

Daniel smiled. "Sounds like they may have found their property, but there aren't any Amish near there." He shrugged. "It does not matter. Amish Acres, it is only a name."

"I've delivered stuff up in that area. It really is a lot of rolling land. Flooding that area would make more sense than trying that around here." He paused. "Especially ol' man Barrington's place. Talk about flat land."

Daniel attempted not to laugh, but couldn't hide the fact.

# # #

Wednesday, August 9 8:30 a.m.

Noah used the back roads to get to DeMotte. Meadow Market was on the edge of DeMotte and he was able to pull the horse-drawn wagon laden with vegetables into the parking lot.

He walked into the store and found the manager.

"I have the first shipment of goods," Noah said. "There are tomatoes, carrots, corn, melons, and beets."

"What are you talking about?" Thomas Harwood asked then scrutinized the Amish man before him. "Your name is Noah Yoder?"

Noah nodded.

The two men walked outside to the horse and wagon.

"You are under contract for melons, pumpkins, and squash." He shrugged. "I don't think Tim Hagen wanted any more than that."

"Tim Hagen said he wanted vegetables, such as melons, pumpkins and things like that. I have grown vegetables and have brought them to your store."

"Let me get Tim Hagen on the phone. Come with me."

Noah followed into the store and office, and sat on a chair near the desk. He waited.

Thomas talked on the phone, waving his hand in the air.

"He wants to talk with you, Mr. Yoder." Thomas handed the phone to Noah.

"Hello?" Noah said.

"You have brought tomatoes and other vegetables?" Tim asked.

"Aye," Noah replied. "I have fresh tomatoes, corn, carrots, beets, watermelon and cantaloupes."

There was a heated discussion from the other end of the phone.

"I see," Noah said. "I will leave the melons. The rest my family can sell."

119

"Now wait a minute," Tim countered. "You signed a contract to not sell to anyone else but me. You can't take your vegetables elsewhere."

"But," Noah said. "You do not want my vegetables. So, they are mine to do with as I wish. My contract, as you have just told me, is for only melons, pumpkins and squash. I will supply those."

"But you signed an exclusivity clause with Meadow Market. You can't sell your vegetables but only to us."

Noah frowned and thought a moment. "You say it is an exclusivity clause. I cannot sell my vegetables to anyone else, but you do not want my vegetables except for melons, pumpkins and squash. The others you do not want. Am I to let them rot in the fields?"

"I... Well... You can't sell them, Mr. Yoder."

"I will not sell them, Mr. Hagen," Noah said. "My children will sell them, as per our agreement."

There was silence.

"Mr. Hagen?" Noah said into the phone. "Are you there? Mr. Hagen?"

"I'm here. I'm thinking."

"I have the contract," Noah said. "I misunderstood. I will bring you my pumpkins, squash and melons. The other vegetables, as per our agreement, my children are allowed to sell."

"I guess that is correct," Tim Hagen whispered.

"I may be Amish, Mr. Hagen, but I am not stupid. I, like you, are a business man. If you do not want my other vegetables, my children will sell them."

"Let me speak to Mr. Harwood," Tim said.

A few minutes of discussion ensued.

"Yes, the vegetables look really good. Fresh. In fact, they look better than what we're currently selling."

Thomas gazed at Noah.

"Mr. Hagen says he will be at your home tomorrow morning to renegotiate the contract."

Noah nodded.

"Also, I am to offer you funds for the other vegetables." He smiled. "I am not to allow you to leave with them."

Again, Noah nodded. "I look forward to seeing Mr. Hagen tomorrow morning."

#

Wednesday, August 10, 1966 8:30 a.m.

Tim Hagen knocked on the kitchen door of the Yoder residence.

Rebecca answered. "Come in, Mr. Hagen," she said, and led him into the front room where Noah waited.

"I understand there was a misunderstanding of the contract," Tim said. "I thought you understood we only wanted you to grow pumpkins, melons, and squash."

"Aye, that you did, but you also kept saying vegetables. So, I grew vegetables."

"Mr. Harwood was very impressed with your selection and quality of vegetables," Tim said. "We have a contract with another person for many of the other vegetables, but Tom was adamant he wanted your vegetables."

Noah smiled.

Tim held up a hand. "You may think you have the upper hand, Mr. Yoder, but rest assured, I am a businessman first."

"As am I," Noah said.

"Shall we go to the table?" Tim asked.

Noah stood and went to the kitchen. Tim followed.

"Here is some fresh lemonade and a few baked goods," Rebecca said. "Enjoy." She placed the glasses and plate of cinnamon rolls on the table.

"Okay," Tim started. "I am willing to pay ten cents per dozen ears of sweet corn."

"Make it a penny an ear," Noah said. "If so, we have a deal." He paused. "This is the sweet bi-color corn. It might be the sweetest sweet corn you have ever tasted."

Tim grimaced. *This might be tougher than I thought.*

"Fine, a penny an ear," he consented.

"Now, for tomatoes, I'll be generous and offer ten cents a pound."

Noah nodded. "For the carrots, make it five cents a pound."

"Done," Tim said. "Tom said your carrots were some of the finest he'd seen in a long time. Good color and straight." He snickered. "Even said they were sweet and super crunchy."

Tim scanned the sheet in front of him. "Oh, beets. I can offer you a penny a pound. Is that acceptable?"

Noah nodded. "Aye, a penny it be."

"Now, Mr. Yoder, beyond what we've discussed today and the original agreement for the pumpkins, melons, and squash; do you have any other vegetables you want to sell or are growing?"

Noah shook his head. "I have cantaloupes, watermelons, pumpkins, and three types of squash: acorn, butternut, and zucchini."

"Fine, Mr. Yoder." Tom skipped his pencil down the list. "I see no problem. I look forward to your future shipments, as does Thomas Harwood."

Noah stood and offered his hand to shake. "It is a deal."

Tim Hagen firmly grabbed Noah's hand and shook it.

"I enjoy doing business with you, Mr. Yoder and look forward to next year." He paused. "In fact, I will probably contact you right after the first of the year to see if you would want to do this again. Perhaps we can expand with peas, beans, potatoes, strawberries and maybe, even asparagus." He cocked an eyebrow. "Interested?"

"I will see you next year," Noah said. "I will think on what we have discussed."

CHAPTER TWENTY ~ Family Growth

Monday, August 29, 1966 9:10 a.m.

Hannah felt the first twinge of labor. She eased into the rocker and rubbed her belly hoping it would alleviate some of the pain.

She rocked. Another half hour later, pain again caught her attention.

I am in labor, Hannah thought. *John will be happy to have a son*. She smiled. *I would love to have a daughter*.

"Hannah," John said, coming into the main room of the house. "I was thinking of going to visit…" He paused and stared at her. "Are you okay?" he asked.

Hannah smiled. "I am in labor. Today, we will have a baby." Again, she rubbed her belly. "I think I have been pregnant for the last ten years. It will be nice when it is over."

"Stay in the rocker," John said. "I will go get my mother to help you."

Hannah nodded. "*denki* (thank you)."

# # #

Monday, August 29 9:35 a.m.

John Heffel walked back into the house. His mother, Sarah, followed behind him.

"First, young lady," Sarah said. "We are going to get you to bed." She helped Hannah from the rocker. "It will make it all that much easier."

"Hello?" Rebecca stood at the front door. "Is anyone home?"

"Come in, Mrs. Yoder," Sarah Heffel said. "Your daughter is in labor. You have come at a very good time."

"Mama," Hannah whispered, another pain wracking her; this one stronger than the last.

"How far apart?" Rebecca asked, gazing at Sarah Heffel.

"About ten minutes," Sarah replied.

"Soon," Rebecca whispered. "Martha wished to come, but Ezra was coughing and she thought it best to stay home."

Sarah nodded. "Wise. We are very excited." She shrugged. "My husband thought John would never marry. He is excited to know John will be a father soon."

Hannah yelped.

"The contractions are closer," Rebecca said.

"No, Mama," Hannah said. "My water just broke. Little Miriam or Tobias is near."

Rebecca nodded. "Soon."

The two older women waited as the contractions came closer and closer. Each time, Hannah writhed in pain.

Sarah brushed Hannah's forehead with a damp cloth.

"I want to push," Hannah said.

Rebecca looked. "Not yet, my daughter. Wait."

'I cannot wait," Hannah cried. "I... I..." A labor pain forced her to curl upward. "The pain!"

"Be still, Hannah," Rebecca scolded. "You will deliver soon, but not yet."

"Mama, the pain," Hannah whined. "I did not know it would..." Another labor pain hit.

Rebecca checked. "You are near, Hannah. Get ready to push."

Hannah began to take short breaths in and out.

"Push, Hannah," Rebecca demanded.

She did as her mother said.

"Again!" Rebecca ordered.

The sound of a new baby filled the room.

"You have a son, Hannah," Sarah said. "My son has a son."

"His name is Tobias," Hannah said. "John and I spoke often of this. It is his choice."

"Tobias," Sarah repeated and nodded.

"Tobias Jonathan Heffel," Hannah whispered.

Rebecca frowned. *Why that middle name? Who chose it?*

Sarah repeated the full name.

Hannah saw her mother's frown.

"The middle name..." Hannah started. "The middle name is to honor Jonathan Bell. It was John's decision. They were friends."

"So be it," Rebecca said.

# # #

Tuesday, October 15, 1966 5:30 p.m.

The front door slammed shut with the fall wind catching it.

"You are home," Martha said. "Good news! Your sister, Ruth, has given birth to a boy. His name is Joel David Mueller." She rushed over to give him a kiss. "The meal is about ready.

Daniel slumped onto the bench at the table, placed his arms folded on the table, and lay his head down.

"Are you not feeling well?" she asked, placing an arm over his shoulder.

"I have had a headache most of the day," Daniel mumbled from around his arms. "With the rain this morning, the students were stuck inside and had no chance to burn off the last of the fall anxiety. I tried to have them march around the classroom as we sang *The Ant Song*, but I think it made it worse."

"I thought we would go visit Ruth, but if you are not feeling well..."

Ezra wailed from the cradle in the other room.

Daniel sat up. "I will check on him. Maybe I will hold him in the rocker and perhaps a little sleep before I go to bed down the animals for the night."

Martha shrugged. "Most of the family will probably visit tonight. We can wait until tomorrow night, if you wish."

Daniel shuffled into the main room to get Ezra. He was almost asleep as he walked. Grabbing Ezra from the cradle, Daniel cooed with him then sat in the rocker.

Moving the rocker back and forth, Ezra smiled, cooed, and slowly closed his eyes. Daniel matched him, the rocker slowing as the two slept.

Carrying Sarah on her hip, Martha stepped to the arch between the kitchen and main room. She saw Daniel and Ezra asleep. Martha tapped Sarah's nose. "We will let them sleep a little then wake them for the evening meal." She turned and went to the stove, making sure things were simmering and keeping warm without burning.

"Shall we go feed Bronk and Clara?" Martha asked, gazing at Sarah. "Would that be fun?"

Sarah giggled as the two made their way out the kitchen door and toward the barn.

Daniel is trying to do too much, Martha thought. *I can feed Bronk and Clara. I know how to milk a cow.*

Coming back into the house, Martha saw Daniel and Ezra rocking in the chair.

"He woke me up," Daniel said. "He was wet. I changed him."

Martha nodded. "I will have the meal on the table in a few minutes." She put Sarah down. "Go play with Papa," Martha said and gave her a little pat on the butt to send her on her way.

Sarah giggled and toddled toward Daniel who swooped her up into his arms with Ezra.

"My little babies," he whispered.

# # #

Saturday, November 12, 1966 3:40 p.m.

Rebecca pulled the small buggy into Daniel's driveway.

"I have just returned from Luke and Miriam's home. You have a new nephew, Daniel. His name is James Matthew Yoder." She smiled. "He is a cute one; that he is."

Daniel ambled over to the buggy. "Another boy for Luke?"

Rebecca nodded. "This is his third child. Two boys, one girl."

Nodding, Daniel reached up to help his mother down from the buggy. "Do you wish to talk with Martha?"

Rebecca pushed Daniel's hand away. "Not now," she said. "You, Martha, and your two children join us for the evening meal. I do not think Martha has..." She sniffed at the air. "No, she has not

126

started the evening meal." She nodded at the house. "Go tell your wife you will be joining us. Now, get a haste about you."

She snapped the reins and turned Beauty around in the driveway.

Daniel ambled up the steps of the kitchen doorway and entered the house. Martha was coming from the main room into the kitchen.

"Did you mother not wish to come in?" she asked.

"You have Ezra," Daniel said. "I will get Sarah and we will go visit them. Mama invited us for supper."

"I was about to make your favorite, Daniel," Martha said. "I know you love your fried chicken."

Daniel hesitated, unsure of what his mother was planning for supper. *How can I pass up fried chicken?* he thought. He took a deep breath. "Mama will probably want to talk to you about Luke's newest child." He frowned. "I think they named the boy James... James... James Mark? No, that is not right. James Matthew. Yes, James Matthew Yoder."

Martha turned to look at Daniel. "Miriam had her baby. A boy?" She started to the front door. She gazed at Daniel. "Do not stand there, Mama is waiting for us. Grab Sarah." Martha opened the door and headed down the steps. "Are you coming, Daniel?"

Daniel pulled the door closed behind him. "Do you want me get..."

Martha was already headed down the drive, almost to the road. He shook his head. *No, I do not think she wants me harness up Bronk*, he thought.

# # #

Daniel walked with his father, Jacob, and the twins, Joshua and Jonah. They headed to the barn to milk cows.

The twins raced Jacob to the door; Jacob winning.

"It is good of you to join us," Noah said. "I do believe the cows have missed your voice." He nodded at the three boys at the barn door. "They try to sing, but it is not the same, Daniel. God has blessed you a wonderful voice." Noah took a deep breath. "Your singing teacher assured me of that fact many times when we talked."

127

Daniel frowned. He couldn't remember Miss Bronson and his father talking that many times.

Noah smiled. "Yes, Daniel, she and I spoke... maybe I should say discussed, even sometimes heatedly, about your singing." He took a deep breath. "It is not the Amish way."

Daniel waited. He knew something was about to happen.

Noah placed a strong hand on Daniel's shoulder.

"Elder Troyer has requested to no longer be *Vorsänger* (song leader); his voice is not what it was. He has asked if another could take his place."

Daniel stiffened. *Vorsänger?*

"Do not fear the Lord's calling," Noah said. "I have spoken with the other Elders of the church. It is they who recommended you."

Daniel stopped walking. The barn door a mere two feet away.

"Is there a problem, Daniel?" Noah asked.

"No," Daniel replied. "I am thinking. Do you feel I am the right person?"

Noah continued to the barn door. "The Elders do." He opened the door. "The cows are waiting."

Daniel stepped through the barn door opening. "I will accept the calling," he said as he passed his father. *Strange, Papa never said he approved of me being the Vorsänger*, Daniel thought.

"I thought you would," Noah said. "The Elders questioned if you could teach music in school." He paused. "Like your chorus instructor taught you. Reading notes."

Daniel glanced at his father. "Singing? We sing now."

"Yes, I know," Noah said. "We want you to teach them to read the notes. To sing parts."

Daniel scowled. "Parts? Is that Amish?"

Noah shrugged and smiled. "Could be. Why not?"

"I will need to get things around. I might be able to teach it after the start of the new year."

Noah nodded, grabbed a bucket, and headed for the back of the barn where the farthest cow waited.

CHAPTER TWENTY-ONE ~ End of and Beginning Year

Thursday, December 15, 1966 8:30 a.m.

Daniel took the package from the mailbox. He had been waiting for it, and now, it was finally here.

The music, he thought. *I can now teach the students how to sing parts. I will take this home and study it.*

Daniel placed the package in his satchel and nodded to Elizabeth Troyer to bring in the students.

After the opening, Daniel stood in the middle of the classroom, turned his back to the students and drew five straight lines on the blackboard. He drew circles on each line and between the lines. He wrote:

Do, Re, Me, Fa, So, La, Ti, Do.

Beside each word he wrote a letter, starting at the bottom line and working up each line with E, G, B, D, F. He then again started at the bottom, placing a letter on each open space, F, A, C, E. He turned back to the students.

"Today, we are going to add a new class to our learning. We are going to learn to sing."

"We know how to sing," John Mueller said. "We just finished singing."

"That is true," Daniel said. "We sang, but we sang in unison. Today we will start learning to read the notes."

Silence ensued. All students stared and watched Daniel.

"Is this a good choice?" Elizabeth Wyse asked. "I mean, to teach the children this? Have the church Elders been made aware?"

"This is according to the instructions of the church Elders," Daniel said.

He picked up his stick and touched it to the first circle, the one at the bottom. "This is the note E." He sang: Do.

"Now, join me. All of you; sing this note and hold it."

Daniel walked around the classroom, listening, telling some to raise their voice, others to lower the voice. Soon he heard the resonating sound of all the voices in unison.

"Very good. Now listen as I sing."

Daniel sang the scale of notes.

"Now, join me." He sang 'do' and the students joined him. He moved up the scale to 're' then 'me' then the rest of the notes. The students attempted to match his voice.

"We will do this each morning until the new year," Daniel said. "Now, I must be off to the mill. I will return."

He turned to Elizabeth Wyse. "They are your students. Do you have any questions? Elizabeth Troyer? Questions?"

The women shook their heads and Daniel headed out for the mill; Jason sat waiting in the yellow Mustang.

# # #

Thursday, December 15, 1966 7:20 p.m.

Daniel entered their house, stomping his feet to remove the last remnants of snow from his boots. Clara, the cow, and Bronk, the horse had been given their evening feed and bedded.

"Jacob brought this over from Mama." She lifted a book into the air. "It took some time, but Mama was able to find Great Grandpa Elias' copy of *The Ausbund*."

He grabbed the book, moved to the kitchen table, and lit the lantern. Martha followed, carrying Ezra on her hip. He placed the book on the table and carefully opened it.

"See?" Daniel held the book on the table for Martha to see. "It is quite old, published in 1834. It has notes." He turned the pages gently, moving to hymn 131, *O Gott Vater*. "It will take some time, but I can write the notes for the students to learn to sing." He smiled at Martha. "I hope to have it done for the new year."

130

Martha leaned in and kissed him on the cheek. "I am sure you will accomplish what you need in time." She turned and went back into the main room where the stove kept that room a little warmer.

# # #

Monday, December 19, 1966 7:10 p.m.

"Hurry," Martha called. "Your Mama said Mr. Jones would be to their house by seven-thirty."

"I'm coming," Daniel said. "I just needed to finish checking a few more tests so I can return them tomorrow." He sighed and then reached out to let Elizabeth grab his hand. "Let us go," he said and led the way out the door.

New fallen snow dusted the already snow-covered scene as they sloughed their way down the drive and across the road to Daniel's parents.

Daniel knew what this meeting was about. He could see Ruth and Joshua Mueller's buggy, as well as Luke and Miriam Yoder's buggy already in the road. Coming down the road were two more buggies and Daniel was sure they were Rachel and Jacob Metz and Hannah and John Heffel.

Tonight, if all went well, Richard and Judy Jones would finalize selling the farm to them.

Daniel tried to realize the size of farm they would have. Five hundred acres was an immense amount of ground.

We can raise cattle to sell, Daniel thought.

"Did I tell you? Your mother is making ice cream, strawberry flavored. She got fresh strawberries at the store, peeled the seeds off, and will mash the rest into the fresh snow ice cream."

"Peeled?" Daniel asked.

Martha nodded in the light snow blowing in the breeze. "She wants to start new plants with the seeds for the farm. If all goes well, we can pick strawberries this coming spring and summer."

"One does not pick strawberries their first year," Daniel said.

Martha pulled down her scarf covering her mouth and smiled. "Silly. She wants to start them soon in the greenhouse, then let them chill like it is winter." She sighed. "Then we plant them in the spring and they will think it is their second year."

#

"Tomorrow, I will go with Mr. Jones to the lawyer and finalize his selling of the farm to us." Noah sighed. "He accepted our offer of forty thousand now, and six years of ten thousand plus interest to finish paying off the debt." He quietly rocked his chair. "We were very fortunate to have re-negotiated our contract with Meadow Markets." He smiled. "The extra income helped in the deal."

He stopped rocking and leaned forward into the room.

"By next year this time, we all should once more have money in our funds. I spoke with the Elders and if there is a hardship, the community will aid us."

#

Monday, January 2, 1967 8:30 a.m.

Daniel opened his satchel and removed the sheets of music.

I hope the students can read this, he thought. He shrugged. *The older ones should have no problem. The younger?* Again, he shrugged.

"Call the students in, Elizabeth Troyer," Daniel said.

With the final words of The Lord's Prayer, Daniel stepped back to his desk and picked up the sheets of music.

"I have this music. It has been asked I teach you students how to read the notes." He broke the music into two groups. "I want the girls to get the sheets of music with "G" on them. The boys will receive the "B" sheets." He handed the "G" group to Elizabeth Troyer and the "B" group to Elizabeth Wyse.

Daniel turned to the students. "You are all familiar with this hymn. He pointed his instructor stick at the notes the students had been learning to sing the prior year.

"The first note is 'do' - let me hear it."

All the students matched his tone.

132

"The next one for the girls is the same. Boys, you will drop down two notes." He sang the note.

The boys matched him. The harmonics filled him with joy. He worked the students through the first ten notes, the first opening phrase.

"From the beginning, again, please," he said.

The girls sang the melody, the boys sang the counterpoint harmonic. Daniel closed his eyes. The music was intense. Even the students noted the difference of their singing versus what they sang on Sunday mornings.

"Repeat this one more time," Daniel said. "Slowly, like on Sunday."

Daniel gazed up at the clock. He was sure Jason was waiting for him outside.

"Mrs. Wyse, please take over. I will be back shortly."

He hastened between the desks for the back of the school room and the door.

Jason sat in his yellow Mustang, waiting.

"I thought you would honk," Daniel said, getting into the car.

"Nah," Jason said. "I heard the singing. It was nice." He put the car in gear and headed for the mill.

# # #

Thursday, January 5, 1967 9:00 a.m.

The school room door opened and a lone figure stood in the shadows. Daniel frowned as the children stumbled in their singing, finally coming to a halt.

"What is this heresy?" the man shouted. "What are you teaching the children?" The figure closed the door and moved into the light of the room.

Daniel stared at an angry Esau Augsburger.

"We are learning to sing," Daniel said.

"I heard my children singing yesterday," Esau said, moving to the center of the class room. "O Gott Vater, in harmony. We sing the hymn in unison." He lifted an arm into the air, a finger pointing at the ceiling. "We do not stand out."

133

Daniel cast a glance about the class room. The students were silent, waiting. Josiah Augsburger had his head bent down, afraid to look up.

"We are singing in unison, Mr. Augsburger. The girls are singing the melody; the boys are singing two notes different."

"Ah-ha!" Esau shouted. "They are not, I repeat, not singing in unison."

"But they are," Daniel replied. "It was the request of the Elders I teach them to read notes and learn to sing them."

"This is not what the Amish have taught," Esau said.

"Mr. Augsburger," Daniel called. "May I show you something? Please?"

"What?" Esau said.

"This," Daniel said and brought his great grandfather's hymnal out of his satchel. "This was my great-grandfather's. Look. It has notes. This is what I am teaching the children."

Esau glanced at the book. "It is nothing but lines with funny characters."

"Those are called musical notes, Mr. Augsburger. This is what I am teaching the children."

"Josiah. Rebecca. Philip. David. Bethany and Anna. Out to the buggy. I will take this up with the Bishop and Elders. I will not have my children learning this heresy."

"Before you leave, Mr. Augsburger, taking your children away from their learning, may I remind you of Psalm 100?

"Make a joyful noise to the Lord, all the earth! Serve the Lord with gladness! Come into His presence with singing! Know that the Lord, He is God!

"We are finished with the singing lessons for today. Allow your children to remain and do their daily lessons. If you discuss this with the Bishop and Elders, come Sunday morning, you may hear a difference in the singing. If I have erred, I have you to thank for putting me on the proper path."

Esau struggled with himself. "The children will stay," he said. "I will visit your father... the Bishop, and get this straightened away."

He turned and headed for the door. "This is heresy," he mumbled as the door closed behind him.

"I see my ride is waiting. I will return. Mrs. Wyse, you are in charge in my absence."

# # #

Thursday, January 5, 1967 5:30 p.m.

Daniel entered the house. The smell of fried chicken filled the air. Martha was in the kitchen cooking.

"Your father waits for you in the main room," she said.

Daniel frowned and headed into the main room where his father sat playing with Sarah and Ezra.

"You wish to see me?" Daniel asked.

"I was visited by Esau Augsburger," Noah said.

"As was I," Daniel added.

Noah nodded and smiled. "We talked. We will see… nay, listen this Sunday to what you have taught the children this week. The Elders and I will discuss what action to take. Mr. Augsburger has agreed to those terms. He feels it is heresy."

"Will I be shunned?" Daniel asked.

Noah got up and walked to Daniel, placing a strong hand on Daniel's shoulder. "No, my son, I do not see that happening. I feel Esau Augsburger is too set in his ways and cannot see the future."

"The future?" Daniel repeated.

"The Amish are not set in their ways with no chance of change. We accept change slowly, but we change. You have water inside your house." He smiled. "I now have water inside my house, too." He winked. "Your mother enjoys the luxury. It is called change."

Noah headed for the door. "Smells delicious, Martha."

He turned back to Daniel. "By the way, listening to the twins sing with Jacob. I think you are doing the right thing." He grinned. "They sang *O Gott Vater* last night to the cows. Jacob sang what we sing in church; the twins sang what you taught them." He nodded. "It meets with my approval."

Noah opened the door and left.

135

#

Sunday, January 8, 1967 4:30 p.m.

"Come, walk with me," Noah said.

Daniel followed, unsure of what his father wished to discuss. He had listened to members of the community speak about the children's voices during church. Most enjoyed the sound.

"I have spoken with Esau Augsburger," Noah said. "The children will be allowed to learn this new singing you are teaching. The Elders feel you are doing the right thing."

Daniel sighed relief. *I will not be shunned,* he thought.

#

Saturday, January 14, 1967 3 p.m.

Daniel strolled into the barn to check on Clara. She was due any day. He was greeted with her baying loudly. Clara lay on the straw covered floor of her stall. She was in labor.

Daniel stepped up on the railing of the stall to see if all was well. This was not her first birthing. She knew what to do and, as Daniel could see, she had it under control. Daniel waited.

Hooves! A nose! Daniel noted. *She is delivering.*

He watched, nodding approval.

Clara again contracted and suddenly the calf's front legs and head were totally visible.

She contracted a couple more times and then the calf was laying on the straw of the stall.

"Very good," Daniel said as Clara attempted to stand, but once more collapsed back down.

Daniel frowned. *Has the birth damaged Clara?* he thought.

Once more Clara bellowed long and strong.

Daniel was about to intervene when he saw it; another set of hooves and nose was showing.

"Twins?" Daniel whispered.

Ten minutes later, a second calf lay beside its sister.

A perfect match, Daniel thought as he watched Clara begin to clean her calves.

He waited, watching to see when the calves would stand. Moments later, the older calf struggled to its feet and began its search for the utter. The second calf followed suit and both were nursing in no time.

"Twins," Daniel whispered again. "I will need to get milk from my parents. Clara has two mouths to feed."

He gave Clara extra feed and hustled back to the house to let Martha know the news.

CHAPTER TWENTY-TWO ~ The Development

Wednesday, March 15, 1967 4 a.m.

Daniel heard the footsteps on the porch before the knocking on the door. He hustled to answer it for fear the pounding would wake the children. He opened the door to see his brother-in-law, Jacob Metz.

"What is the problem?" Daniel asked.

"It is your sister, Rachel. She is in labor and I need another to help. I did not wish to wake Mama. Will Martha come?"

"Of course, I will," Martha said, surprising both men who stared at her with wide eyes.

"You knocking not only awoke Daniel, but also me." She cocked an ear to the other bedroom. "The children are still asleep."

"I will harness Bronk," Daniel said.

"No need," Jacob said. "I have a buggy here, ready." He pointed to the driveway.

"Give me a minute," Martha said, and turned to Daniel. "The children are still asleep. If you have issues, take them to your mother and she can help you." She placed a loving hand on his cheek. "But you are a grown man and should be able to handle two small children. I will be back as soon as possible."

She grabbed her coat, slipped on her shoes, and headed out into the March snows. The wind whipped her coat about her, but her bonnet held true.

Daniel stood at the doorway watching them leave.

# # #

Daniel got the children around and went to the barn. He placed the children in the buckboard. *It will be cold*, he thought. He placed a heavy blanket around them. Harnessing Bronk, he jumped up and headed across the road to his parent's house.

"Mama," he called, entering the kitchen. "Martha has gone with Jacob to help Rachel with her delivery."

Rebecca turned from the stove. "Rachel is delivering?" She took three steps to the staircase. "Mary. Come take care of breakfast for the family. I need go to Rachel's. It is her time."

Mary hastened down the steps. "I am here, Mama. I will fix breakfast."

"Can you watch Sarah and Ezra for me? I need to teach and work at the mill."

Mary nodded. "It is no problem; they are young."

"Daniel," Rebecca said. "Harness Beauty for me."

"Already done," Noah said, coming into the kitchen. "I was returning when I saw Daniel enter. I heard him tell you about Rachel; I knew you would leave. Beauty is in the driveway with the small buggy attached." He leaned in and gave her a peck on the cheek. "Be off."

Martha stepped into the kitchen. "Rachel had a boy; his name is Simon Phillip."

"I will be back shortly," Rebecca said, and hustled out the door.

Martha frowned.

"I am sure you did a proper job, Martha," Noah said. "It is my wife's way. She must check to make sure all is correct."

Martha smiled and nodded. "Let me help, Mary," Martha said and went to the stove.

# # #

Tuesday, April 4, 1967 10:45 a.m.

Again, Ben Hopkins popped into Daniel's office.

"You're still here," Ben said and took a seat. "I was hoping you'd be here. I feared you'd be headed back to the school."

"I have been waiting for you to return to take me," Daniel said. "Now that you are here. We should leave."

"Fine," Ben said. "But we will talk in the car. My delivery to DeMotte this morning gave me some interesting tidbits of information."

Daniel began to stand, then paused. "Oh?"

Ben motioned for Daniel to have a seat. "Take a breather, young man," he said. "Let me share the details."

Daniel sat, but frowned. "Is it very important?"

"Depends on who you are," Ben replied. "Remember those development guys from last year wanting to create Amish Acres?"

Daniel nodded.

"I'm pretty sure I told you that ol' man Barrington told them to check with his cousin who lived north of Madison."

Again, Daniel nodded.

"They started development of Lake Hakihet."

"Lake what?" Daniel asked.

"Lake Hakihet. I had to ask what that meant. There are some Indian mounds near the development, so they decided to go with an Indian name. The Lenni Lenape tribe lived in this area." Ben shrugged. "Hakihet. It is Lenape for farmer. So, it is Lake Farmer or better, Farmer Lake since it will be created from farmland."

"No Amish Acres?" Daniel asked.

Ben grinned. "Nope. From what I heard, the lake will be something like three hundred and fifty-some acres and there will be another almost three hundred acres of different sized home lots and open parkland."

Daniel eased back into his chair. "Impressive."

"I'd say," Ben said. "They were able to get permission to dam the Saint Joe River to create this new lake."

Daniel shook his head. "How do you get all this news?"

"I talk. They talk. I listen. They talk." Ben shrugged. "And, from to time, my eyes tell me more than what others are revealing."

"Is that true?" Daniel asked.

"Like how is Martha? I heard she is pregnant, again."

Daniel frowned. "How do you know this, Ben? Martha told me last month she thought she was pregnant."

Ben laughed. "I told you. People talk, I listen."

Daniel continued to frown. "Who is gossiping about my family?"

"Don't fret it, Danny," Ben said. "I was talking with Jacob. I think Martha told your mother and she was telling your father when Jacob heard."

Daniel cringed at 'Danny,' but sighed. *I will need to talk to Jacob*, he thought, and shrugged. "I will tell you. This way, you will not learn of it through the gossip grapevine. We are expecting our next child in October."

Ben leaned in conspiratorially. "Don't come down on Jacob too hard. I think he is trying to be one of the guys." He smiled. "Jason mentioned they were trying for a baby."

Daniel's eyes widened. "Jason and Patty? A baby?"

Ben shrugged. "That's what I heard."

Daniel began to laugh.

"What's so funny?" Ben asked.

"Imagine. Jason, a father. He is the man with the yellow Mustang." Daniel leaned back in his chair in a full laugh. "Not what I would call a family car."

Ben placed a hand to his face, trying to cover his snicker. "Patty does drive that 1956 red and white Oldsmobile convertible. It could be used as a family car."

Daniel shrugged. "I still like my buggy." *I will also need to talk to Jason*, Daniel thought.

Monday, April 10, 1967 5:20 p.m.

Daniel ambled into the house. It had been a long first day of the week. He placed his hat on the rack and headed for his rocking chair.

He shook his head. "The students at school seemed to not want to learn," he started. "Elizabeth Wyse had to take her youngest son home because he was sick. Elizabeth Troyer attempted to pick up the slack, but she was young." He sighed. "When I got back to the mill, Benjamin Heffel was working on a new project; again, doing what he wanted. I spoke with Mr. Sullivan and had Benjamin talk with him. After that discussion, Bob Sullivan stopped at my office. Mr. Sullivan told me he had reprimanded Benjamin Heffel. He had explained to Benjamin that he cannot just decide what he wants to make." He paused. "He told Benjamin that he needs to get things approved and scheduled. He also told him if he did it again, he would be fired. Mr. Sullivan does not like doing that, but we cannot have staff doing what they want, when they want." Daniel took a deep breath and rocked, staring out the window. "I do not want to see Benjamin lose his job, but he cannot decide what he wants to do. Then Mr. Sullivan told Benjamin if he wanted to what he wants, perhaps he should consider quitting and starting his own business." Daniel shrugged. "He might quit. He is Amish, and they are known to be somewhat independent."

He gazed at Martha who had been silent, his thoughts immediately changed. She was weeping, upset.

"Why are crying?" he asked.

Sarah clutched Martha's dress; her face hidden in its folds. Martha held Ezra close and rocked her body back and forth on the settee. Ezra whimpered.

Martha sobbed, tears flowing down her cheeks.

Daniel stood from his rocker and eased close, falling to the floor before her.

"What happened?" he whispered.

"The baby," Martha sobbed. "I lost the baby." She tried to wipe the tears from her eyes. "I was over to your parent's house, and… and…"

Martha broke down, again. Tears flowing. Little Sarah whimpered and held tightly to Martha's dress.

Daniel frowned, trying to make sense of the scene.

"I miscarried," Martha said. "It was early this morning. Your mother was sure, but we went to Dr. Braeburn." She took a deep breath. "He confirmed it. I lost the baby."

Daniel reached and held her one hand. "It was the Lord's decision," he said. "We will have more."

"Will we?" Martha asked. "I almost lost Sarah. We were very lucky with Ezra. Now, this one has been lost. Will we have a large family I so desire?"

"Remember, Martha," Daniel said. "The Lord gives and takes. We will have a large family… if the Lord so grants. Even Dr. Braeburn has said a miscarriage is not a sign of never having more."

Martha sniffed. "True. But... but... I so wanted this child."

"As did I," Daniel said. "We will wait and see if the Lord grants us future children."

He squeezed her hand, leaned up, and kissed her on the forehead. "I love you, my blue-haired Marti."

Martha smiled. "You have not called me Marti in a long time."

"I remember a time I called you that and you told me your name was Martha. I had been chastised."

"Right so, my husband," Martha replied.

Daniel reached for Sarah who pulled away, sinking back and behind Martha.

"Daddy loves you, Sarah," Daniel said.

She opened her arms and jumped into Daniel's waiting hands.

"My little girl," Daniel said and whirled her into the air. "You like to fly."

Martha wiped the tears from her eyes and tried to smile.

There will be more, she thought.

\# \# \#

Saturday, October 28, 1967 7:20 p.m.

Daniel noticed the car lights turn into the driveway.

I wonder who that can be? he thought.

Suddenly there was a knock on the front door.

Martha gave Daniel a quizzical look.

"I will get it," Daniel said and walked to the front door. "Good evening."

"Hi, Danny-boy," Jason said rapidly. "I'm a father. A boy."

"Come in," Daniel said cringing, and stepped back to let Jason in.

"Good evening, Martha," Jason said. "Did you hear? I'm a father. A boy. Jason Daniel Muirs. Eight pounds, nine ounces, twenty and one-half inches long."

Jason stood there grinning.

"Sit," Martha said. "How is Patty?"

Jason grabbed a seat on the settee. "She is doing fine." He continued to grin. "I am pretty sure she won't want to do that again.

It was a rough delivery." He paused. "I have a son. A son!" He reached into his coat pocket and pulled out a cigar. "Here." He handed it to Daniel.

"I know," Jason said. "Give it to somebody you know who does smoke." He shrugged. "I mean, there are a lot of guys at work."

Daniel took the cigar and placed it on the table by his chair.

"You said your son's name is Jason Daniel?" Martha asked.

Jason nodded. "Jason after me, and Daniel after my best friend." He gazed at Daniel. "You."

"Will it not be difficult with both of you having the same name?" Daniel asked.

"Nope." Jason eased back in the settee. "We'll call him by his initials - J.D." He shrugged. "I'm Jason. He's J.D."

Daniel nodded understanding.

"When does Patty come home?" Martha asked.

"Well," Jason said. "J.D. is doing fine, but like I said, Patty had it rough. They said maybe on Monday."

Martha nodded. "The family will be there, so we will wait until the end of the week to visit and see your new son."

"You can come on Monday when she gets home," Jason said barely controlling himself.

Martha shook her head. "You say it was rough. Remember, I have delivered two children and they were relatively easy. Patty will endure her family, but friends? They had best wait until later." Martha held up her index finger to stop any further conversation from Jason. "We will wait until next weekend to visit."

Jason shrugged. "Fine. Okay."

"Would you like something to eat? Drink? I have some leftover meatloaf."

Jason's face paled. "I haven't eaten all day. Until this very moment, I haven't even been hungry."

"The meatloaf is delicious," Daniel said.

"You sit there and talk with Daniel," Martha said. "I will go to the kitchen and fix you a plate... meatloaf, mashed potatoes, green beans, and corn bread."

Jason gazed at Martha. "Thank you. My mouth is drooling."

CHAPTER TWENTY-THREE ~ Vacation Plans

Monday, June 10, 1968 7:30 p.m.

Emma Noble sat in the rocker, watching her daughter.

"You want to do what?" she asked Martha.

"I want to visit my uncle and aunt in Bird-in-Hand."

Emma cocked her head and stared at Martha's very pregnant body.

"Uh-huh," she mumbled. "I'm here because you are due almost anytime, and you are talking about taking a trip. A trip by car that will take at least seven hours by car." She paused and cocked an eye at Martha. "Can you sit for that length of time?"

"I did not mean today or tomorrow," Martha said. "Next month Daniel will have two weeks of vacation. We have spoken often of visiting Uncle Longenfelter. Daniel enjoyed the time he spent with them."

"Do you think you will be wanting to travel with a baby next month?" Emma eased back into the rocker.

"Not next month, but perhaps in August." Martha stood and stretched, rubbing her belly.

"You said Daniel had two weeks next month." She frowned.

"Daniel will have two weeks on the first of July. He can take those days anytime he wishes."

Emma leaned forward in the rocker. "So, you wish to visit Jacob and Naomi Longenfelter in August. Is that correct?"

Martha nodded. "Yes, mother… that is, if you and father will drive us there."

Emma grimaced. "I think it would take the whole two weeks just to get there by buggy." She laughed. "I am sure your father will agree." She sighed. "Pick a date."

"I am sure Daniel will need to get approval but I think we could leave on Monday, August 19."

"I will call your father and tell him," Emma said. "I'd go have coffee with Judy Jones but they've moved south." She gazed at Martha. "Does the old house still have a working telephone?"

Martha nodded. "Yes. Papa Yoder decided to keep it for the neighboring Amish to use, if needed." She shrugged. "Only out-going calls since nobody is there to answer it."

Emma stood from the rocker. "I'll be back." She left, getting in her car and driving away.

Daniel stepped out of the barn in time to see Emma turn onto the country road.

I wonder where she is going? he thought, and continued on his way to the house with the bucket of milk.

Inside, he was greeted by Martha.

"Where did your mother go?" Daniel asked.

"She is going to the Jones house so she can use the phone to call my father." She placed her arms around his neck. "She wants to make sure father will drive us to Pennsylvania to see my uncle and aunt." She paused. "You do remember them?"

Daniel's memory flashed back to his trip to New York City and the visit to her relatives. He smiled, then frowned as he remembered the death of his Australian friend, Adam Brown.

Martha felt Daniel's body suddenly stiffen. "What is it?"

"I was remembering my trip to New York and the memory of Adam's death caught me off-guard."

Martha pulled Daniel closer. "It was tragic." She released him and stepped back. "Do you remember visiting my relatives?"

Daniel nodded. "I remember them." He frowned. "When will your father drive us to them?"

"After the baby," Martha said. "I said around August 19."

"I will notify Mr. Sullivan. I see no problem."

# # #

Thursday, June 13, 1968 6:15 a.m.

146

Daniel headed out to the barn to milk Clara and to feed the animals before heading to work. He sang to Clara, offering a rousing rendition of Ten Little Indians. He laughed. He grabbed the bucket of milk and headed for the houses, glancing over at the chicken coop. The rooster crowed and he decided to feed the chickens and collect the eggs for Martha.

Opening the kitchen door, he heard Martha moan. He frowned.

"Daniel?" Martha whimpered. "I am in labor. Wake my mother, she can assist.." She bent over in pain.

He placed the eggs and milk on the table and rushed to the bedroom where Emma Noble was staying.

"Martha is in labor," Daniel said as he knocked on the door.

A sleepy voice replied. "I will be right there."

Daniel rushed back to the kitchen. "I will also get Mama," Daniel said and headed back out the door.

Within minutes, Daniel returned with Rebecca and Mary.

"My Mama is here," Daniel said.

"Hush, Daniel," Rebecca said. "No need to wake the children. I am sure Mrs. Noble has things under control. Now, go join your father and have breakfast."

Rebecca turned to Martha. "Now, my dear, let us get this baby born. Ready?"

Martha bent over as a labor pain hit. "Yes," she whispered and ambled to the bedroom with Emma and Rebeccas assisting her.

# # #

Thursday, June 13 7:40 a.m.

Ben Hopkins pulled into Daniel's driveway and noticed Daniel running toward him from his parent's home. He backed up.

"Is there a problem?" Ben asked.

"Martha is delivering," Daniel said. "I will come into work later."

"Tell you what," Ben said. "I have to make a delivery to DeMotte this morning. I can come by on my return to see if you are ready to come to work."

147

"Thank you," Daniel said then continued on toward his home, up the steps and into the house.

"Say hello to your father," Rebecca said, holding up the small baby. "My name is Elizabeth Anne Yoder."

Daniel reached and took the small child into his arms.

"I have another daughter," he whispered. "She is beautiful and looks like her mother."

Rebecca nodded. "Little Elizabeth is pretty, indeed."

"And Martha?" Daniel asked.

"Resting in the bed," Emma said. "My daughter is fine." She grabbed her keys. "I will go can Dan and tell him he is a grandfather, again."

CHAPTER TWENTY-FOUR ~ Vacation

Monday, August 19, 1968 9:20 a.m.

Dan Noble pulled the station wagon into the driveway. On the porch, he saw Martha sitting in a rocker while Sarah and Ezra romped around her.

"My grandchildren are active," Dan said.

"Yes, they are," Emma agreed. "I hope they work off all the excess energy before we begin the trip."

Daniel strolled across the road from his parent's home.

"Everything arranged?" Martha asked.

Daniel nodded. "Between my father, and my siblings, the animals will be taken care of. We are ready to go."

Dan grabbed the three small suitcases from the porch. "Light luggage," he said, lifting them into the air.

"There is one big one inside," Daniel said. "I will get it."

Dan put the suitcases by the vehicle.

"All the luggage goes on top and I'll tie it down." He smiled as he unloaded their suitcases from the back of the car. "Then we're on our way."

Daniel lugged the big suitcase down the steps.

"Keep the black bag out so I can change Elizabeth, if needed."

Emma grinned. "Eight hours? I'm sure you'll change her at least once; more likely a dozen times."

#

Monday, August 19 6:35 p.m.

Dan pulled the car into Jacob Longenfelter's driveway. An older couple rushed from the doorway to greet them. On the porch stood five children.

"*gut'n owed*, (good evening) Emma," Jacob said, rushing to embrace his adoptive sister. "It has been long since I last saw you."

"gut'n owed, (good evening) Jacob." She hugged her adopted brother then turned to Naomi. "And my brother's wife." She embraced Naomi with a strong hug. "We had hoped to arrive earlier, but..." She turned to Daniel and Martha. "The young ones would begin to *rutsch* (squirm or shuffle). It is a long trip for small children."

"They what?" Dan asked.

"I may have become *Englische*," Emma said with a smile. "But I have not forgotten my Amish roots. After a time, the children would get ants in the pants."

"Daniel," Naomi said and reached out to hug him. "I would recognize my first son, with or without a beard. It is good to see you, again."

"And to see you." He gazed at the children still standing at the rail of the front porch. "First son?"

"We have a lot to discuss," Naomi said and pointed at the children. "We adopted three boys and two girls over the last few years." She motioned for the children to join them. "This is Simon, old eldest at sixteen. Next is John at fourteen; then Mary at thirteen with Ester at eleven, and the youngest, Ephraim, at ten." She turned to Daniel. "This is Daniel Yoder, his wife, Martha, our niece, their children, and her parents, your father's sister, your Aunt Emma and her husband, Uncle Dan."

The children greeted the newcomers.

Naomi turned to the others. "Come in. A meal awaits you." Looking at Martha, she smiled. "Allow me to hold the little *bobbeli* (baby)."

"Her name is Elizabeth," Martha said and offered the baby for Naomi to hold.

Naomi cradled Elizabeth in her arms. "It has been many years since I held one so small." She paused. "A niece or nephew." She sighed. "Never mine." Then she smiled. "Of course, John will not admit it, but he has been spending time with Esau Zook's eldest daughter, Hannah." Naomi winked. "Maybe, in time, a grandchild."

Jacob led the way into the house. Daniel noticed there had been changes since he had visited back in 1963. He hesitated. *That has been almost five years*, he thought, then shrugged. *Five children. Yes, there would be changes.*

# # #

Sunday, August 25, 1968 7:20 a.m.

"We are going to New York City today," Emma said as she munched on a slice of toast slathered with homemade strawberry jam. "Dan and I thought we'd see the sights since we're so close."

Martha frowned; she'd not heard her parents speak about going to the big city. She would have enjoyed visiting some of the old haunts of her time spent there. She also knew Daniel would enjoy revisiting with Mr. Cardinale.

"Why not go tomorrow," Martha offered. "Daniel and I would enjoy visiting, too."

"And what would we do as you enjoy church?" Emma asked.

"There is a nice cafe in Bird-in-Hand," Naomi offered. "It is the one where we met Martha when she brought Daniel to us the first time."

Martha nodded, remembering the quaint place. "You could enjoy a cup of coffee, a donut, relax, and then wander Bird-in-Hand, return to it for lunch, and continue your sight-seeing until late afternoon."

Emma shrugged. "I will discuss it with Dan. He has his heart set on New York, though."

# # #

Sunday, August 25 8:15 a.m.

"We are off to Bird-in-Hand," Dan said as he escorted Emma to the car. "We will return later this afternoon."

Naomi cuddled Elizabeth in her arms. "We are going to church at Bishop Stoltzfus' home."

151

Jacob helped Naomi into the buggy. Sarah jumped up and sat beside her. Martha followed. Daniel and Ezra sat in front with Jacob who had Jezebel harnessed to the buggy.

# # #

Sunday, August 25 8:40 a.m.

Jacob pulled the buggy into Bishop Elmer Stoltzfus' driveway. Other buggies were already lined up and their horses tethered, enjoying the fresh food and water.

"Welcome, Jacob Longenfelter," Bishop Stoltzfus said, walking to the buggy. "Who are our guests?"

"Do you remember that young man who visited several years back? Again, this is he; Daniel Yoder." Jacob slapped Daniel on the back.

Bishop Stoltzfus studied Daniel. "You have married," he finally said.

"Aye, I have," Daniel replied. "My wife, Martha, is over there talking to your daughter. With her are our three children. She is holding Elizabeth, our youngest; then there is Ezra, the boy, and Sarah, his older sister."

"You have a fine-looking family, Daniel Yoder," Bishop Stoltzfus said, noting a young couple walking toward them. "Do you remember my son, Mark? This is his wife, Judith." He turned to them and then pointed at Daniel. "This is Daniel Yoder who visited several years back."

"Welcome back, Mr. Yoder," Mark said.

"I was talking with your wife," Judith said. "Your baby daughter is very cute." She touched her stomach. "Perhaps soon," she added and glanced at Mark.

"Daniel," Bishop Stoltzfus said. "I should tell you my daughter was sure you would come back to Bird-in-Hand and court her."

Daniel gazed at Martha talking to Bethany, remembering how Mark said she was pushy and she was, indeed, pushy. He wondered if he should intervene, but knew his wife could handle a simple Amish girl, pushy or not.

"We should begin church," Bishop Stoltzfus said and led the way toward the barn where benches were set up.

When all had gathered, the *Vorsänger* (song leader) began to sing *O Gott Vater*. Daniel joined in, singing the secondary part he'd taught the students in school. He noticed the gazes and immediately switched to the melody. He noted Martha sitting on the opposite side beside Naomi. She winked and gave an almost unnoticeable nod. Daniel smiled.

# # #

"This meatloaf is very tasty," Daniel said as Bishop Stoltzfus approached. "All the food is delicious."

"Yes," Bishop Stoltzfus said as he sat beside Daniel. "The food is always good, but I am intrigued. Today, as we sang *O Gott Vater*, you sang a different tune." He shrugged. "The Lord has given you a beautiful voice."

"I am sorry and beg forgiveness," Daniel said. "I meant no offense. I did not mean to stand out."

"No. No." Bishop Stoltzfus said. "No offense." He grinned. "I am not calling *Meidung* (shunning) on you. I am curious where you learned that tune."

"I teach music at the school. The Elders requested I teach the children to read notes and sing parts. What I began to sing is what I call the boys' part. The girls sing the melody. I got the original music from my great-grandfather's copy of *The Ausbund*."

"That is interesting," Bishop Stoltzfus replied. "I did not know *The Ausbund* had notes."

"My great-grandfather's copy is dated 1834."

"I think I would like this in my church," Bishop Stoltzfus said. "Can you teach it to us?"

"I had to teach the children to read notes, then I gave them the song. Perhaps one from your congregation could visit me for a month or two to learn music."

Stoltzfus grinned. "I considered Bethany, but I do not think two months with her would be good for your family." He gazed about the area. "Ah, young Abram Zook." He motioned for the boy to come. "This is Daniel Yoder from Ohio. Will you sing for him?"

Abram frowned at the request. "Sing?"

"Can you do this?" Daniel sang the scale of do-re-mi. "Start with this note." Daniel sang the beginning do note.

Abram matched the note and followed Daniel up the scale.

"You have a nice voice," Daniel said, and turned to Bishop Stoltzfus. "If he wishes to learn; I can teach him."

"We are near harvest. If I can get parental approval, could he come after the new year? Not much to do in the winter, especially in January."

Daniel nodded and noticed the group beginning to play ball. He gazed at Bishop Stoltzfus. "I think I may join in the game," Daniel said.

"How long will you be staying with Jacob Longenfelter?"

"We leave next Saturday," Daniel replied.

"I will be in contact," the Bishop said and nodded toward the game. "They're picking teams. Best be on your way."

# # #

Monday, August 26, 1968 8 a.m.

Daniel stepped lively toward the car, towing Martha with him.

"The children," she said.

"They will be fine," Daniel replied. "Naomi will watch them like an eagle." He grinned. "We are going to New York City."

Martha nodded and got in the back seat of the car with her mother. Daniel hopped into the passenger front seat.

"What do you want to see first?" Dan Noble asked. "Statue of Liberty? Empire State Building? The Twin Towers? Broadway?"

"A Chinese laundry," Daniel said with a smile and gave the address from memory.

# # #

Mrs. Chang frowned then glared at the bearded man entering the laundry.

"You got tickie?" she asked. "No tickie. No laundry."

"I'm here to see you and Mr. Cardivale."

"Me?" Mrs. Chang was surprised. "Why me?"

"My name is Daniel, Mrs. Chang," Daniel said and smiled at her.

Once more she frowned, scrutinizing him. "Oh, velly funny. You grow beard. Daniel Yoder. Yes?"

Daniel nodded. "Do you remember my wife, Martha?"

Mrs. Chang shook her head up and down. "Come. We go see Antonio. He upstairs."

Daniel turned to leave.

"No. We go this way," Mrs. Chang said. "Follow me."

Daniel and Martha followed Mrs. Chang through the back room filled with presses and hanging clothes to an open area with the stairs against the wall.

"I remember the door, Mrs. Chang," Daniel said.

"We go upstairs," Mrs. Chang said and stepped off the stairs like an eight-year-old.

"Antonio!" Mrs. Chang yelled as she opened the door at the top of the stairs. "You got company."

Antonio Cardivale turned and frowned at the newcomers.

"Good morning, Mr. Cardivale," Daniel said.

"Good morning," Antonio replied. "Can I help you?"

Daniel grinned. "The beard confuses you?"

"Daniel Yoder?" Antonio whispered. "Is it truly you?" He turned to Martha. "And Martha?"

They nodded.

Antonio rushed to embrace them, kissing them on the cheeks.

"Come. Sing," Antonio said. "Students. This is Daniel Yoder. You've heard me speak of him. Listen to his voice."

Daniel felt the heat in his cheeks.

Once more Antonio faced Daniel and lifted his Italian arm into the air with a wave. "Sing."

Daniel inhaled deeply and began to sing *Where're You Walk*, hoping it would suffice. He didn't feel this was the place for *The Ant Song*.

"Bellissimo! Magnifico! (Beautiful. Magnificent.)" Antonio shouted, a tear forming in the left eye. "You come to my apartment. We eat supper."

Daniel shook his head. "We are only in town for a few hours. We are visiting Martha's aunt and uncle in Bird-in-Hand." He shrugged. "We cannot stay, but it is good to see you."

Martha leaned forward. "Please tell Mei Lien we said hello. My parents are waiting for us outside. We need to leave."

Antonio pointed to Daniel as he gazed at his students. "You sing like this. He big star on Broadway."

Daniel turned to head out the door and down the stairs.

Mr. Cardivale had no right to say that I was a big star on Broadway, Daniel thought. *Maybe if I had stayed.*

# # #

They walked into the darkened theater. On stage, several people milled about.

"Fine. Take it from the top," the voice in the darkness of the theater seats said.

"I would like to try out for the lead, Peter," Daniel said. His voice filling the theater.

"I'm sorry," Peter replied. "Tryouts were last week." There was a pause. "How do you know my name?"

"I sang for you before. It has been a few years."

In the dimness of the theater, Peter stood and started to walk toward Daniel and Martha.

"Perhaps you have an opening for a seamstress," Martha said.

Peter stood before them, staring at Daniel. "What are you? Some sort of weird Jewish person?" He inhaled deeply. "You sang for me? When?"

"That would be 1963 and the show was called *Specters of Ghostly Raw*." He paused. "I replaced Adam Brown. I am not Jewish; I am Amish."

Peter frowned and searched Daniel's eyes for recognition.

"Adam was killed. He was replaced by... oh, no, wait. Are you... ah... ah... Daniel Yoder?"

156

Daniel grinned and nodded.

"Well, this certainly threw me," Peter said and pulled on Daniel's beard. "Why the beard?"

"I am married," Daniel replied. "Do you remember Martha. She was the one who hid the costume."

Peter stepped back. "Martha? You're Amish, too?"

Martha shrugged. "We were both on *Rumschpringe*. I went back to Shipshewana and then met Daniel when I visited his hometown."

Peter turned to the silent group on stage. "Take five." He turned back to Daniel and Martha. "Are you here to tryout for a part in a play?"

Daniel shook his head. "Nay, Peter. We came to visit you. Did you ever do anything with Adam's play?"

"It was a big hit," Peter said. "It ran for three years."

"Sad that Mrs. Vandergoode killed him," Martha said.

"Yes," Daniel added. "I loved his song *Aborigine Stomp*."

"Well, Mrs. Vandergoode passed away in prison two years ago. I was her executor and she left me a tidy sum." He shrugged. "I've been able to explore and produce the plays I feel comfortable with." He paused. "Do you want to grab something to eat?"

"Not really," Martha said. "My parents are outside. They want to see where I lived and do the tourist thing."

Peter extended his hand to shake. "If you ever decide to hit Broadway, Daniel, see me. You are definitely a star."

Daniel shook his hand, turned and headed for the main door. *A star*, he thought. *Maybe Mr. Cardivale was right.*

CHAPTER TWENTY-FIVE ~ New Year, New Changes

Tuesday, January 14, 1969 7:20 p.m.

A knock on the front door startled Daniel who looked up from his school tests spread across the kitchen table.

"I will get it," Martha said, walking to the door.

An Amish gentleman stood there with his back to the door, looking around the area in the darkness. A young man was with him.

"Is this the Daniel Yoder residence?" he asked, turning around.

"Uncle Jacob! Come in," Martha said and held the door open for the two to enter. "Daniel, look who is here to visit."

Daniel frowned. His memory immediately snapped to Bird-in-Hand. *Young Abram Zook is here to learn to sing parts*. He stood and went to welcome them. As they walked to the main room, the back kitchen door snapped open. Jacob Yoder entered, stomping the snow from his feet.

"I saw the car," Jacob said between breaths. "I am guessing these are the people from Pennsylvania."

"Ah, Jacob. Come in," Daniel said. "Meet Abram Zook. I believe the two of you are close in age."

Jacob rushed into the main room.

"This is Martha's uncle, Jacob Longenfelter."

Jacob extended his hand. "gut'n owed, (good evening)" he said and turned to Abram. "We can go in the kitchen and talk," he whispered and led the young man away.

"Sit," Daniel said. "How long are you staying?"

"A few days," Jacob said. "The bus leaves the depot in DeMotte at eight-thirty each morning."

"You will stay with us," Martha said. "We have the room."

"*denki* (thank you)," Jacob Longenfelter said.

"Tomorrow, I will go to AJ's and call my mother to let her know you are here."

Jacob shook his head. "No need," he said. "I called her from DeMotte to let her know. They brought us here tonight."

"They? Here?" Martha repeated, and gazed at the front door. "Are they with you?"

"Your mother said she would return in a few minutes, enough to allow us to get comfortable."

Martha went to the front door just as the car pulled into the driveway. She opened the door and waved her parents to join them.

"We have plenty of space for everyone to stay," Martha said as her parents came into the house.

"Abram can stay with me," Jacob said from the kitchen.

"Just remember, young Jacob Yoder," Jacob Longenfelter said. "My nephew needs to be up for school tomorrow. No jabbering all night."

"School?" Jacob asked.

"My last year," Abram said. "I am in eighth grade."

"I graduated last year," Jacob said. "Now, I work at the mill as a janitor."

"Are the children asleep already?" Emma asked.

"I am awake," Elizabeth said from the doorway and ran to Emma. "Grandma Emmy." She held out her arms to embrace Emma.

"Me, too," Ezra said and followed his older sister into the room.

Emma held the two on her lap, one on each leg.

"The two of you are growing up so fast," Emma said and kissed them on the foreheads.

"I need to finish grading papers," Daniel said and stood to go to the kitchen. *This will allow my wife to talk with her parents and uncle*, he thought.

"First, I need to put these two back to bed," Martha said, grabbing Elizabeth and Ezra by the hands.

"Allow them to stay awake a bit longer," Emma said. "They're no bother for me."

"Come, Abram," Jacob Yoder said. "We will go to my house across the road." He stood and headed for the kitchen door.

"I may stay with them?" Abram asked Jacob Longenfelter.

The old man nodded. "Be up and ready for school in the morning." He gazed at Daniel. "That is the teacher."

Abram glanced at Daniel.

Jacob Yoder slapped Abram on the back. "Do not fret, Abram. He is my brother."

Abram nodded, then joined Jacob at the door. "See you tomorrow, Uncle Jacob."

"Perhaps not," Jacob Longenfelter replied. "I am going to Shipshewana with my sister to visit with my brother."

Martha's head snapped up. "May I go?"

Emma smiled and nodded. "Of course, I thought you'd want to go along... if it is okay with your husband."

"I will be at school and work," Daniel said from the kitchen. "It is fine with me." He frowned.

"Yes, I will take the children with me," Martha said.

"I think I will go to bed, if that is okay with everyone," Jacob Longenfelter said. "It has been a very long day."

"Is everyone going to bed so early?" Dan asked, gazing at Daniel then at those in the main room.

"I need to finish grading papers," Daniel said. "I will be awake for at least another hour."

"Daddy!" Martha exclaimed. "I am here. We can talk until Daniel wishes to go to bed. Remember, tomorrow, he has to milk the cow, feed the animals, then go to school and finally finish the day at the mill."

Dan nodded. *My son-in-law*, he thought. *Even if he is Amish, he works to provide for his family. He is a good man and my daughter has done well.*

# # #

Wednesday, January 15, 1969 7:30 p.m.

Daniel harnessed Bronk to the buckboard. Last night's snow was a thin layer of white, barely a quarter inch thick. He rode over to his parent's house to get his younger siblings and Abram Zook.

Entering the kitchen, Daniel was surprised to see all his siblings sitting at the kitchen table, ready to leave, including Abram Zook.

"What is this?" Daniel asked.

"We want to get to school early today," Ester said. "We want Abram to hear us sing."

Daniel nodded, knowing something was happening; he just didn't know what.

"Can we sing the Ant Song?" Ester asked.

Daniel made a face. "It is something I can consider."

"Please, Daniel... I mean, Mr. Yoder." Jonah said.

"Let us leave and I will consider it on the way," Daniel said and moved to the side so Anna, Joshua, Jonah, and Ester could head out. Abram grinned then shrugged before following the others out the door.

Daniel gazed at his mother, but she grimaced, shrugged, and shook her head. "I have no idea," she said.

Daniel closed the door and made his way to the buckboard.

"Bundle up," he said. "The wind is picking up."

# # #

Daniel called the last few students in from the outside.

"For those who do not know him, we have a temporary new student in the eighth grade. His name is Abram Zook and is from Bird-in-Hand, Pennsylvania. He is my wife's uncle's nephew and is here to learn how to sing parts. This morning, we will sing *O Gott Vater* so he will know how we sing it. First, we will open with prayer."

Everyone bowed their heads.

O Heavenly Father, guide us in the proper path of learning. We thank you for this beautiful day. We open our hearts and seek knowledge to know You and your way. We lift our voices in joyous song to you. Amen.

161

They immediately began to sing *O Gott Vater* with Daniel leading the boys. Abram watched and listened as he tried to follow the other boys, but gave up and sang the melody with the girls.

"Can we sing the Ant Song?" Rachel Heffel asked.

Daniel frowned. *That is twice today I have been asked to sing that song*, he thought.

"I see no reason why we cannot," Daniel said and began to sing.

The students joined in and Daniel stumbled, momentarily lost for words.

They are singing parts. Not two, but four, Daniel thought. The younger girls sang the melody with the younger boys singing a counterpart. What amazed Daniel, the older girls were singing soprano and the older boys whose voices were deeper were singing bass and baritone.

Daniel stopped singing, watching and listening to them. The students were smiling, and without hesitation, the eighth graders took charge and began to march around the room. The other classes followed suit, except Abram who didn't know the song or what was happening.

Elizabeth Wyse and Elizabeth Troyer stood to one side, watching and listening to the students. When the song ended, the students returned to their desks.

"How is this possible?" Daniel asked.

Mark Beiler stood. "We have been practicing this for over a year, Mr. Yoder."

Daniel frowned. "How? When?"

Mark grinned. "During recess." He shrugged. "Some of us older ones learned more during the weekly sings and then we helped the little ones." He paused. "We were waiting for the right time." He gazed at Abram. "With our new student who is here to learn to sing parts, we decided today was the right day." Once more he paused and stared at Daniel. "Were we wrong in what we did?"

"It was beautiful," Daniel said and shook his head. "There is nothing wrong in lifting your voice in song." He stood in the front of the class and nodded. "I am very happy." He paused. "We will now finish with the Lord's Prayer and I will be headed out to return later."

As Daniel headed for the door, Abram gave him a furtive look.

"I need to go to the mill and make sure my department knows what to do today. I will be back shortly. Stay and learn. Tonight, after we finish our evening meal, I will work with you on learning songs and their parts."

Abram nodded and turned his attention to Mrs. Wyse.

# # #

Daniel spent the next eight evenings except for Saturday and Sunday, teaching Abram how to sing the scale, create harmony and handle different vocal parts of the songs.

# # #

Saturday, January 25, 1969 7 a.m.

"It is time," Jacob Longenfelter said. "We must get to DeMotte so Abram and I can ride the eight-thirty bus back home."

"My friend, Ben Hopkins has just pulled in," Daniel said. "He will take you to DeMotte."

Martha gave Jacob a hug. "Please come back and bring Aunt Naomi with you."

Jacob frowned.

"And the children, of course," Martha added.

"It was good to see you," Jacob said. "And to see my adoptive brother, Paul and his family." He sighed. "Time seemed to fly, but I also spent time with my adoptive sister, Emma."

"May I ask why you say 'adoptive' when you speak of them?" Daniel asked.

"It is respect," Jacob said. "Their parents adopted me into the family and allowed me the honor of keeping my family name. I am the adopted; they are the adoptive." He shrugged. "Does that make sense to you?"

Daniel nodded.

Ben honked the car horn.

"You had best be on your way," Daniel said and turned to Abram. "I feel you know and understand how to sing parts."

"Yes, I do," Abram responded. "I will teach this to the youth back home. Bishop Stoltzfus will be pleased."

The two headed down the steps and through the light snow to the waiting car and Ben.

CHAPTER TWENTY-SIX ~ Baby Boom

Saturday, February 15, 1969 8:30 a.m.

"Here comes your mother," Martha said, gazing out the window at the snow-covered scene. "I wonder what she wants?"

Daniel shrugged. "Maybe she wants to play with the children."

Martha turned and stared at him. "I do not think that is why." She walked to the front door to open it.

Rebecca stomped the snow from her boots. She entered the room.

"I came to tell you..." She stared at Daniel. "Your sister, Ruth had her baby last night. A girl; they named her Judith." Rebecca eased herself into a rocker. "It is a good name."

"Why did you not come get me?" Martha asked. "I could have helped."

"It was early this morning," Rebecca said. "No reason to wake you and the children." She gently rocked. "This was probably one of Ruth's easiest births."

Daniel gazed at Martha. "Do I hitch up Bronk?"

Martha shook her head. "We will see them tomorrow at church." She turned her attention back to Rebecca.

They spoke in hushed whispers.

Daniel got up and left the room, realizing he was no longer needed. There were chores to do.

\# \# \#

Wednesday, February 26, 1969 8 p.m.

Daniel was checking student homework. Martha was nursing Elizabeth. Both were surprised by a sharp rap on the door and it opened. Rebecca entered.

"Are you available?" Rebecca asked. "Hannah is in labor."

Martha placed the young child in the cradle.

"Let me get my coat," Martha said and rushed to the kitchen. She turned to Daniel. "The older ones are asleep and Elizabeth should fall asleep shortly."

Martha followed Rebecca out the door.

# # #

Wednesday, February 26 8:20 p.m.

"You are just in time," John Heffel said as he opened the door. "Mama says I have a lovely little girl."

Rebecca and Martha entered the room.

"A girl?" Rebecca asked. "How is Hannah?"

"Your daughter is well," Sarah Heffel said as she came out of the bedroom into the main room. "This is our newest granddaughter. Say hello to Mary Rachel Heffel."

She held the baby up for Rebecca to see.

"She is beautiful," Martha whispered. "She has your eyes, John. Kind and gentle."

"Finally, a daughter," John said. He held his two sons close to him. "You have a little sister."

Tobias, the older brother, shrugged. Benjamin, now the middle child, frowned, unsure.

Rebecca reached out and took the baby into her arms.

"I will go see how Hannah is doing," Martha said and left the room.

# # #

Thursday, March 6, 1969 9:45 p.m.

Daniel heard the stomping of feet on the front porch. He frowned.

It is late, he thought. *Who is this?*

Daniel opened the door when he heard the soft knock. His brother, Luke, stood there, brushing away the early spring rain from his clothes.

"Is Martha available?" Luke asked. "Miriam is in labor."

"Go get your mother," Martha said as she entered from the kitchen, coat in hand. "I will meet you at the road."

"I did not want to wake her," Luke said.

Martha raised an eyebrow. "How mad do you think Mama will be if you do not get her?"

Luke hung his head. "I will get her and then come back here for you."

"No need," Martha said and pulled an umbrella from behind the door. "I will meet you at the road." She waved her hand at Luke. "Now, skedaddle."

Luke dashed from the porch and into the buggy, snapped the reins, turning the horse around and rushed across the road to his parent's darkened home.

# # #

Thursday, March 6 10:20 p.m.

Rebecca rushed into the bedroom. "How long between labor pains?" she asked.

"About five minutes," Miriam said between deep breaths.

Rebecca nodded. "Soon." She sat on the chair by the bed. "Squeeze my hand if it helps with the pain." She offered her hand to Miriam who took it and clamped a tight hand over it.

Martha leaned over Miriam and wiped the perspiration from her forehead. "Everything will be fine," Martha cooed.

"I want to push," Miriam said.

"Not yet," Rebecca softly said. "We must wait for labor to be about one minute apart."

Miriam's grasp tightened and Rebecca tried not to show any pain. She counted.

Miriam quickly huffed short breaths.

"Now," Rebecca said. "If you want to push, do so."

Miriam held her breath and pushed. She screamed.

"Again," Rebecca demanded.

Once more Miriam screamed and pushed.

The sound of a baby's first breath filled the room.

"You have a girl," Rebecca said.

Miriam gasped deeply. "Her name is Ester. Ester Lily Yoder."

Martha once more wiped the perspiration from Miriam's forehead then stood. She left the bedroom to notify Luke of the birth of his new daughter.

Monday, March 17, 1969 8:45 a.m.

Daniel opened the school door and stepped out into the chilly spring air. He frowned. Jason's yellow Mustang was not there. In its place was Ben Hopkins' vehicle. Ben leaned over and rolled down the window.

"Get in, Danny-boy," Ben yelled from inside the car.

Daniel made his way to the car and got in, hoping Ben didn't see him cringe.

"Jason didn't come to work this morning," Ben said. "Seems Patty decided it was time to deliver."

"Deliver?" Daniel repeated.

"From what I heard, Jason called in and said he was at the hospital, waiting for Patty to have their next baby."

Daniel shook his head. "I still cannot believe my friend, Jason, is a father."

Ben grinned. "You know. A little over three years ago, I couldn't believe that you were a father." He laughed. "But here you are with three and another one on the way."

Daniel could feel the heat in his cheeks and hoped Ben wouldn't notice.

Monday, March 17 10:05 a.m.

Jason knocked on the open office door and sauntered in. He placed two cigars in front of Daniel. "I hoped you'd still be here," he said.

Daniel looked up and gave Jason a questioning gaze. "Two?"

"Yup," Jason snapped. "Patty gave birth to twin girls. Identical girls." He sat down in the chair opposite Daniel. "I am father to three children now."

"Twin girls?" Daniel asked.

"Uh-huh," Jason said. "There is Jane Marie. Five pounds, six ounces, eighteen inches. And then there is Jean Marie. Four pounds, fifteen ounces, and seventeen and three-quarter inches." He paused and leaned back in the chair. "They have the most beautiful red hair, and the bluest of eyes that I hope they keep. Patty is sure their eyes will turn hazel."

"Is Patty okay?" Daniel asked.

Jason nodded. "This delivery was easier than when she had J.D."

"Martha will be pleased to hear this," Daniel said. "When does Patty get home?"

"The twins are doing well," Jason said. "I think maybe tomorrow." He leaned forward and placed his elbows on the desk. "You coming over?"

Daniel grinned. "I think not, Jason. Remember, we are friends, not family. Martha and I will be over this coming weekend." Daniel leaned back in his chair, twiddling a pencil in his fingers. He shook his head. "I cannot believe you have twin daughters."

Jason leaned back in his chair and laughed. "Unless I get Mr. Sullivan's job, I have my family. No more children."

"The Lord decides the size of the family," Daniel said then grinned. "Can you get all your family in your fancy yellow Mustang?"

"I think three children can sit in the back without too much problem. Now, as to the size of a family, that might be, Daniel," Jason said. "Still, there is a surgery that I can have done to be sure there are no more children."

Daniel's eyes widened.

Jason shrugged then shook his head. "I just can't afford any more children, Daniel." He stood. "I'd best be on my way." He snickered. "I do have a job I'd better be doing or…" He left the sentence unsaid and exited the office.

Daniel shook his head absently. *Martha will be surprised,* he thought.

#

Sunday, August 3, 1969 9:20 p.m.

Martha sat up in bed. "Daniel," she called. "It is time. Go get your mother."

Daniel hastily put on his pants and shirt and headed out of the house and across the road to his parent's home.

He knocked lightly on the door then entered, rushing up the stairs to his parent's room. He tapped on their door.

"Mama," Daniel whispered. "Mama? It is time. Martha needs you."

The door opened and he was face to face with his mother.

"Get out of the way, Daniel," she hissed then hastened down the stairs and out the kitchen door.

Daniel followed.

#

Rebecca appeared at the bedroom door, holding a small bundle.

"This is your son, Daniel," she said. "Martha says his name is to be Joshua Levi."

Daniel nodded. "I like that," he said and reached for the baby. "Another son." He pulled at the blanket partially covering the baby's face. "Joshua Levi Yoder." He lifted the baby into the air. "The Lord has blessed us." Once more he cradled the baby in the crook of his arm. "A son," he whispered.

CHAPTER TWENTY-SEVEN ~ Am-Lische

Tuesday, August 12, 1969 8:15 p.m.

"Papa?" Jacob stood at the doorway into the main room.

Noah looked up and stared at his young son. Jacob's expression told him what he needed to know.

"Come," Noah said and patted the chair next to him. "You wish to talk. Sit."

Jacob crossed the room, trying not to show how nervous he was.

"What is it you wish to talk about?" Noah asked.

"I wish to..." Jacob paused. "I wish to go on *Rumschpringe*."

Noah nodded. "I knew this moment would come." He gazed at his son. "Where will you go?" He hesitated. "New York? Like Daniel and Luke?"

Jacob shook his head. "Nay, Papa. I wish to go to DeMotte."

Noah frowned. "DeMotte?"

"Esau Stoltz lives in DeMotte. He works at the mill and I have been talking with him."

Noah remembered young Esau. *He left the community for Rumschpringe over a year ago*, Noah thought. *No, it has been almost two years and he has not returned.*

"So, you will live with this Esau Stoltz?" Noah asked.

Jacob shrugged. "I think so." He tried to smile. "I must talk with him about it."

"When will you leave?" Noah asked.

Again, Jacob shrugged. "Maybe tomorrow?"

Noah had the question on his lips, but held back, fearing the answer.

Jacob gazed at his father. "I am Amish, Papa. I am intrigued with the *Englische* world, but I do not think I want it for my life."

"Make your decision before joining the church, Jacob." Noah reached out and placed a firm hand on the boy's shoulder. "If you wish to be *Englische*, now is the time to decide; not later."

Jacob glanced at the floor between his feet then again looked at his father. "I am Amish."

Noah nodded. *Only time will decide*, he thought.

# # #

Wednesday, August 13, 1969 7:30 a.m.

Ben Hopkins honked the horn and Jacob glanced out the window. He sighed.

It is now, Jacob thought and grabbed the small suitcase by the stairs leading to the bedrooms upstairs. *I am on Rumschpringe.*

Daniel walked across the road. He noticed Jacob with the suitcase. *He has decided to go on Rumschpringe.* Daniel opened the front door and got in the passenger seat of Ben's car.

"Good morning, Ben," Daniel said then turned to Jacob in the backseat. "Are you Amish?"

Jacob glanced at Daniel, his hand tight on the suitcase's handle.

"*Rumschpringe?*" Ben asked as he pulled the car onto the road.

Jacob nodded. "Yes," he whispered. Once more he glanced at Daniel. "I am Amish, Daniel." He shrugged. "I just wish to test *Rumschpringe*."

"I know," Daniel replied. "Just remember..." Daniel hesitated then spoke in Amish. "The *Englische* is tempting as a lifestyle. I considered it when I was in New York."

Jacob blinked and stared at his older brother. "You did?"

Ben tried not to show any emotion as they spoke Amish.

Daniel changed back to English. "I was tempted," he said. "I thought of staying in New York."

"But you came back," Jacob said. "Why?"

"Let me guess," Ben said.

Daniel cocked an eye in Ben's direction.

"It was a girl," Ben said. "Right?"

172

Daniel nodded. "Yes. I fell in love with a young lady I met in New York. She feared I would leave the Amish and took me to her friends who were Amish. I was reminded of my roots. When we returned to New York City, she left and I did not know where she went." He shrugged. "I came home."

"That is Martha?" Jacob asked.

Daniel nodded.

"I am only going to DeMotte," Jacob said. "I have a friend who is on *Rumschpringe*."

"Esau Stoltz?" Ben asked.

Jacob nodded. "Yes. He works at the mill and is only two years older than me."

Ben nodded. "Interesting." He offered a weak smile and pulled into the mill's parking lot.

Jacob frowned. *Why is it interesting?* he thought as he grabbed the suitcase, got out of the car, and headed toward the factory. *Esau is Amish. I am Amish. We are on Rumschpringe*, he continued in thought. How *is this interesting?*

# # #

Wednesday, August 13 5:15 p.m.

Jacob stood by the 1958 Chevrolet Oldsmobile, waiting for Esau Stoltz to come. He saw Daniel come out of the factory and head for Ben's car. Daniel stopped and glanced over at Jacob.

"Enjoy *Rumschpringe*. See you tomorrow," Daniel yelled then continued on his way.

Jacob nodded and waved. *Rumschpringe*, he thought. *I am on my own until I return*. He sighed. *Today, I am a man.*

"You ready?" Esau asked as he approached, holding the keys to the car up in the air. "DeMotte, here we come."

Jacob put the suitcase in the backseat then got in the front passenger seat.

"*Rumschpringe*," Jacob said. "It starts now."

"I think you will enjoy being Am-Lische," Esau said.

Am-Lische? Jacob thought. *What is that?* "What is Am-Lische?" Jacob asked.

173

"Am-Lische?" Esau repeated. "It is a mix of Amish and Englische." He paused. "We are Amish who have adopted more of the Englische lifestyle than the *Ordnung* allows."

I am on Rumschpringe, Jacob thought. *I can be Englische if I so desire.*

"How long have you been on *Rumschpringe*?" Jacob asked.

"Almost two years," Esau replied and shrugged as they drove to DeMotte, speeding around the big "S" curve near Hayton. "I know we are allowed one year of *Rumschpringe*, but until I decide to return to the Amish way, I will stay on *Rumschpringe*." Again, he shrugged. "I like being Am-Lische."

Jacob turned and gazed at Esau. "Do your parents approve?" he asked.

"They hope that at some point I will return to the Amish and be baptized." He looked at Jacob and smiled. "They think I am Amish because I still look it rather than appearing *Englische*." He grinned. "That is part of being Am-Lische. It is similar to being Mennonite, but still retaining our Amish heritage."

Jacob nodded. *Perhaps being Am-Lische is good*, he thought.

CHAPTER TWENTY-EIGHT ~ News

Wednesday, September 3, 1969 5:30 p.m.

Martha watched Jason's yellow Mustang pull into the driveway and Daniel get out.

"He will be pleasantly surprised," Martha whispered, standing at the front door. She absently nodded at Jason as he waved.

Daniel entered the house. Three children rushed him as he closed the door. He knelt down and wrapped his arms around them. Martha held the youngest in her arms.

"My family," Daniel said, giving each child a kiss before standing to give little Joshua a kiss on the forehead.

Martha followed Daniel as he made his way into the main room and sit in his favorite rocker. She sat on the chair next to him.

"Did you know your sister, Rachel had her baby? A girl."

"Another girl?" Daniel asked.

"Ruth Marie Metz," Martha said. "Plus, I heard your brother, Jacob, will be visiting tonight. I think for the evening meal. We are invited."

Daniel sniffed the air, noting the lack of kitchen scents.

Martha reached over and grabbed Daniel's hand. "Plus, I heard your mother has news to share."

Daniel frowned. "News?"

"Let us go and I can help Mama with the meal," Martha said and stood. "Sarah, get your little brother and sister. We are going to see Grandma and Grandpa Yoder."

Little Sarah scampered around, grabbing her brother and sister by the hands. She led them to the front door. "We are ready, Mama."

Daniel stood, took Joshua from Martha and then helped her to her feet. He nodded toward Sarah. "We are ready."

Sarah opened the door and led her siblings across the porch and down the steps to the driveway.

An old car pulled along the driveway of Daniel's parent's home. Jacob jumped out and then the car continued on its way down the dusty road. Daniel noticed the driver was Esau Stoltz as it passed them. He gave a cordial nod, but Esau ignored him.

"I see your mother was right. Jacob is here," Martha said.

Daniel shook his head. "Strange. Jacob never mentioned about coming to visit."

"Perhaps it slipped his mind," Martha offered as Sarah ran up the steps to the kitchen door and opened it. "Go talk with him."

Daniel strolled into the main room where Jacob sat beside their father. On the bench by the window, Isaac Wyse, eldest son of Jeremiah and Elizabeth Wyse, sat, hands folded in his lap. Daniel frowned. *Why is he here?*

"gut'n owed (good evening), Papa. Jacob. Isaac."

Daniel sat on the bench by Isaac.

"Jacob was about to explain a new term to me," Noah Yoder said. "Again, now what is this Am-Lische?"

Jacob smiled. "It is Amish and *Englische*, mixed together. I am neither *Englische*, nor am I Amish. I am a mix of both. Being Amish, living in the *Englische* world, our group has adopted many of the *Englische* ways. We accept cars, some electricity and other *Englische* amenities."

"You have accepted?" Noah questioned. "How is that?"

"Like electricity," Jacob started. "We use it to light our rooms, have an electric stove since the apartment will not allow gas." He paused. "But we do not have a toaster or electric coffee maker. We keep some of our Amish ways."

Noah nodded. "What are you not telling me?"

Jacob froze, unsure. He stuttered. "I have told you…"

"You want to be a Mennonite," Noah finished. "Yes?"

"No!" Jacob exclaimed. "We retain our Amish ways."

Noah shook his head. "Nay, Jacob. You are accepting many *Englische* ways." He paused. "Do you have a television set?"

Again, Jacob stumbled. "We… I do not… yes, there is a TV in the apartment. It is not mine."

"So, you are *Englische* but play being Amish," Noah said.

"No, Papa," Jacob replied. "It is called being Am-Lische."

Noah shrugged. "You are not Amish in my eyes." He gazed toward the kitchen. "I think Mama has the meal ready."

Daniel looked at Isaac Wyse. "Are you staying for the meal?"

Isaac nodded, all the while keeping an eye on Noah.

Daniel frowned, unsure why Isaac Wyse was in the house, let alone staying for the evening meal.

"Let us go to the kitchen," Daniel said and led the way.

"Isaac," Rebecca said. "You sit beside Jacob." She nodded at the place. Mary sat opposite him at the table.

Everyone took a place at the long table. Noah made sure everyone was seated before he spoke.

"*Händt nunna*, (hands down)" he said and everyone bowed their heads with hands folded in their laps.

After a few minutes, Noah cleared his throat indicating the meal prayer was finished.

Food was passed and everyone filled their plates and ate in silence.

Daniel noticed the furtive glances between his sister, Mary and Isaac Wyse. He frowned but continued to eat.

"For those who are done," Rebecca said. "There is cherry pie for dessert." She motioned to Martha. "Pass the first pie from the sideboard."

Martha turned and grabbed the cherry pie and handed it to Rebecca.

"Mary made this pie," Rebecca said.

Daniel glanced at Mary who bowed her head so none could see her face. Isaac Wyse smiled.

Daniel realized what was happening. *I did not know Isaac Wyse was courting my sister*, he thought then shrugged. *I no longer attend the sing on Saturday nights; how would I know?*

Noah finished his slice of pie and was first to speak, turning to Isaac Wyse. "Did you find the pie good?"

"It was very good," Isaac said, lowering his head and glancing at Mary. "It was better than my mother's."

Daniel considered telling Elizabeth Wyse of her eldest son's words, but decided it better to not mention it.

"Papa?" Mary called. "I have chosen Isaac Wyse. We would like to marry next month."

"Yes, Bishop Yoder," Isaac said. "With your blessing."

Noah gazed at his daughter. "If this is what she wishes..." He nodded. "So be it. You are both baptized and members of the church. I will announce it this Sunday." He leaned back in his chair. "Have you a date?"

"Thursday, October 23rd," Isaac Wyse said.

A car horn honked from the driveway.

"Esau is here," Jacob said. "I must leave."

"Has he not the decency to come to the door and knock?" Noah asked, scowling at Jacob.

"He has a date tonight," Jacob replied. "He is in a rush."

"Is that the Am-Lische way?" Noah asked.

The horn honked again.

"Good-bye," Jacob said, stood from the table and headed for the kitchen door.

"You will come back?" Rebecca called.

Jacob stopped at the door, turned to those still at the table, and shrugged. He disappeared as the car honked a third time.

# # #

Thursday, September 4, 1969 7:55 a.m.

Daniel sat at his desk in the school, sorting the papers to hand out when class began.

Elizabeth Wyse opened the door. "You are early, Mr. Yoder," she said and closed the door before the wind blew everything into a disarray. "It certainly is a windy day."

"Yes, it is," Daniel said. "Did you speak with Isaac when he arrived home last night?"

Elizabeth grinned. "Yes. I hope it will be a beautiful fall day."

Daniel shook his head. "Who would have suspected we would become related through marriage?" He sighed, lifted the papers and shuffled them to straighten into a neat stack. "I did not know Mary was seeing anyone." He shrugged. "Of course, I no longer live at home."

"I considered saying something," Elizabeth said. "But I did not feel it my right." She sat on the chair near Daniel. "What if it did not work?"

"Your son is a perfect match for my sister," Daniel said. "Watching them last night, I was reminded of when I courted Martha."

Elizabeth grinned. "I am hoping they only have one wedding." She peeked at him from under her bonnet. "I am sorry. I spoke out of turn."

Daniel shrugged. "I love Martha and was willing to do whatever necessary to marry her."

"Shall I call the students in?" Elizabeth asked.

The door opened and Elizabeth Troyer stepped in.

Daniel stood and looked at Elizabeth Troyer. "Please call the students in." He turned to Elizabeth Wyse. "Can you pass these out to the student's desks?" He handed her the stack of papers. "I need to get to the mill as soon as possible today."

He gazed about the enlarged room. Fifty-one students this year, he thought and absently nodded his head.

The school was now almost twice the number of students when he began as a school teacher. A second stove had been added to heat the school's additional room in the winter. Curtains, when pulled from the walls, helped to delineate the classrooms and offer each class some privacy.

# # #

Thursday, September 4 9:05 a.m.

Daniel strode into his office and glanced at the stack of orders to be processed. He hung his hat on the hook then sat to review the orders. He skimmed the papers.

Three gnomes; he glanced at the inventory list and saw they had four in stock.

Two horses. Again, the inventory showed two in stock.

Four swings. Gazing at the inventory, Daniel noted two more swings would need to be made.

Five chairs. There were two in stock.

179

And… He frowned.

What is a ceremonial Indian elephant? he thought then noticed the attached Polaroid picture.

He gazed at the picture, unsure if he or his crew could create the request in a timely manner. Daniel stood and went to the office door and got the attention of his staff.

"Come into the office," he said.

Martin Smith and Benjamin Heffel strolled into the office and took seats opposite the desk.

"What's up, boss?" Martin asked.

"More orders," Daniel replied. "We have most of it in inventory…" He grinned. "If this sheet of paper is correct. But we will need to make a few items."

Benjamin shrugged. "We can do it."

"There is a new item," Daniel said and handed the picture to Benjamin. "Share it with Martin."

Both men looked at the picture of the ceremonial Indian elephant.

"Any specs?" Martin asked.

Daniel gazed at the request. "Between four and five feet in height," he said.

"The tricky part will be the trunk," Benjamin said. "We want to make sure it cannot be snapped off easily."

Daniel noted the comment on the request form.

Martin nodded in agreement. "The curled trunk and the tusks are going to be the difficult part." He shrugged. "The rest of the body is basically pretty blocky appearing."

"Do we want to attempt this?" Daniel asked.

Martin's eyes widened. "Of course!" he snapped. "We can make that one plus another for stock. I see it as a big selling item."

Daniel noted Jacob pushing the broom as he made his way into the department.

"Fine," Daniel said. "We now know what we need to do for the rest of the week." He snickered. "I mean, today and tomorrow."

Martin and Benjamin stood and left the office. Daniel followed them to the door and then called to Jacob. He motioned for him to come into the office.

"What do you want?" Jacob asked, a belligerence in his voice. "I have work to do."

"Sit," Daniel ordered. "I want to talk to you about this Am-Lische stupidity."

"It is not stupid," Jacob snapped. "It is my lifestyle."

Daniel shook his head. "You are Amish, but *Englische*, but still Amish." He sighed. "Does that not sound silly?"

"I am on *Rumschpringe*," Jacob said, leaning in toward Daniel's desk. "It is my choice."

"Yes, you are correct," Daniel replied. "If you decide to become *Englische*, so be it. But you must give up this silliness you call Am-Lische if you wish to become Amish and join the church."

Jacob shrugged. "It is my decision." He stood. "Now, I have a job to perform." He headed for the door. "I do not think Mr. Sullivan would approve of us discussing family issues during working hours." He pulled the door closed behind him as he left the office.

Daniel picked up the request forms and headed to see Mr. Sullivan. He wanted him to know the elephant would be done. After that, he would find Jason and go back to the school.

I hope Jacob sees the error of his ways, Daniel thought. As he walked the hallway to the main office, his mind raced with visions of his life before he was baptized and married. He absently nodded. *Yes, Jacob will return. He is Amish.*

CHAPTER TWENTY-NINE ~ Mary's Wedding

Wednesday, October 22, 1969 4:00 PM

Mary removed the blue dress from the sewing machine. She held it up to admire. *My wedding dress*, she thought. *Tomorrow I will be Mrs. Isaac Wise*.

"Go try it on," Rebecca said.

Mary raced up the steps to her bedroom, the blue dress flapping the breeze.

"Does it fit?" Rebecca asked up the stairwell.

"It fits perfect, Mama." Mary twirled to allow the skirt to open like a small upside-down tulip.

Mary sauntered down the staircase to show her mother the dress.

Rebecca pulled and tucked different areas on the dress to make sure it all adjusted properly.

"You will make a lovely bride," Rebecca said. "Now, take it off and I will wash and iron it for tomorrow."

Once more Mary hastened up the stairs to her room.

Rebecca sniffed the air. *The chicken*, she thought and rushed to the kitchen.

# # #

Wednesday, October 22 5:45 p.m.

Daniel stepped into the house and the scent of meatloaf assailed him. He also smelled chocolate chip cookies baking.

"Supper smells good, Martha," he said.

"That is for tomorrow," she replied. "Tonight, you get a hearty bean soup with cornbread."

Daniel nodded, realizing the extra scent was the soup cooking on the stove. He always enjoyed bean soup, especially the way Martha made it.

"Do you think Jacob will show for the wedding tomorrow?" Martha asked.

Daniel hesitated; he was unsure. "Jacob does not talk to me at the mill. I do not know if he will be here or not."

Martha shrugged. "It would be sad if Jacob did not show."

"We will find out tomorrow," Daniel said

# # #

Esau Stoltz pulled the car into the driveway, working around the buggies. Esau parked the car and Jacob jumped out of the passenger's seat.

"Jacob is here," Martha said, glancing out the kitchen window. "I am happy the whole family is here now."

Rebecca nodded and continued to work on the carrots.

Daniel stepped onto the back porch. He paused, debating whether to go down the steps or wait for Jacob to join him.

Jacob came up the steps. "gut'n mariye, (good morning) Daniel."

"gut'n mariye (good morning), Jacob." Daniel offered his hand to shake, intrigued with the Amish greeting.

Jacob ignored the hand and walked around Daniel into the house.

Daniel shrugged then walked down the steps to join his father with the other men.

"It is time for me to talk with Mary and Isaac," Noah said and turned to walk away.

Daniel stood there, unsure what to do. His brother, Luke, and his brothers-in-law were with Jeremiah Wyse.

"It is a beautiful day," Jeremiah said "The Lord has blessed this union with a perfect day for my eldest son to be married."

Luke leaned toward Daniel. "Was that Jacob I saw walk into the kitchen?" He nodded at the house. "And is that Esau, his friend?"

Daniel nodded. "I am not sure. But I think Jacob is not happy with me. We barely talk at the mill."

Luke put an arm around his younger brother. "I will have a talk with him."

Luke walked towards the back steps of the kitchen. Daniel went in search of others to talk with, leaving his brothers-in-law.

The kitchen screen door slammed against the wall as Jacob burst from the kitchen door.

Esau appeared at the door. "Where are you going?"

"I am leaving," Jacob yelled at his friend. He hesitated and glared at the group standing behind Esau. "I am tired of others telling me how to live my life. I am on *Rumschpringe*." He drew in a deep breath. "I will decide what I want."

Luke moved around Esau, pushing him to the side.

"Jacob," Luke started. "All I said was Am-Lische is not real. Either you are Amish, or you are *Englische*." Luke moved to the edge of the small porch and hesitated, deciding whether to take a step down. "As I see it, you are living *Englische* but dressing and pretending to be Amish."

Jacob frowned, his eyes narrowing in a glare. "I am Amish," he yelled. He stomped to the car and yanked the passenger door open. "Are you coming, Esau?" Jacob slid onto the seat.

Esau strode out of the house, across the small porch and down the steps. He quickly joined Jacob in the car.

"This is your sister's wedding," Esau whispered. "Do you want to do this now?" He motioned with his hand to the surrounding area. "They are all watching."

"I am not staying," Jacob said. "If you do not want to drive me, I will walk." He took a deep breath to regain his composure. "Mary will forgive me." He shrugged.

"Mary may forgive you, but be honest, Jacob. Will you forgive yourself?" He turned the key in the ignition. "Is this what you want?"

Jacob stared straight ahead. "Yes," he whispered. *I am Am-Lische, just like Esau,* he thought.

#

Saturday, November 15, 1969 3 p.m.

"Is that Ben Hopkins' car at your parent's house?" Martha asked as she nursed Joshua.

Daniel stood to look out the window. "It is." He scrutinized the young man getting out of the vehicle. "That is Jacob." Daniel frowned. "I wonder why he is visiting?"

"You can stand there and wonder," Martha said. "Or, you can go over and find out what is happening. Did Ben get out of the car?"

"No," Daniel replied. "He is pulling away." There was a pause. "Hm?"

Martha sighed. "So...?"

Daniel grabbed a jacket and headed out of the house. The crisp November air was refreshing to Daniel as he rushed across the road. He took the kitchen steps two at a time and was entering the house when he heard his father's voice.

"What is this about?" Noah asked.

Daniel crossed the kitchen, his mother putting an index finger to her lips. He stood at the doorway to the main room. Daniel cleared his throat.

Jacob looked up from where he sat in the chair on the opposite side of the room. He frowned.

"May Daniel join us?" Noah asked.

Jacob shrugged. "He is my brother."

Daniel strode across the room and sat in the chair next to his father, still unsure of what was happening.

"I am no longer Am-Lische, Papa," Jacob said. He shook his head. "Esau is a fool." He paused, hands folded together as he stared at his shoes. "I was a fool."

"How is that, my son?" Noah asked.

"Luke was right. I was living *Englische*, dressing Amish."

Noah nodded. "How did you come to realize this?"

Jacob sighed and sat upright in the chair. "Esau was fooling me. He had *Englische* clothes hidden in his room."

Noah frowned. "Hidden?"

"Esau left last night for a date after work. He said he was going to Fort Wayne and he winked at us in the living room as he left. He took with him a small bag." Jacob shrugged. "I did not question it. He said it was an overnight date." He paused. "After he had left, I thought I would borrow one of his shirts... mine were dirty." His stare

185

wandered to the suitcase sitting near the staircase in the kitchen. "All my clothes are dirty. But, when I checked his closet, not only did he have Amish clothes, but also *Englische* clothes. He came home this morning very drunk. He was wearing *Englische* clothes and his hair was slicked back to appear very *Englische*. He didn't go to Fort Wayne, he stayed in DeMotte." Jacob shrugged again. "I asked him if he was Amish. Esau could barely stand and focus. He slurred that he plays the Amish game for his family, but lives *Englische* and has done so for two years. He called it Am-Lische."

Daniel cleared his throat.

"I am sorry, Daniel," Jacob whispered. "You, Papa, and Luke were right." A tear welled in his eye. "I wish to be Amish." He shook his head ever so slightly. "I have no urge to continue with *Rumschpringe*."

"You have given up this Am-Lische lifestyle?" Noah asked.

"Yes, Papa. I am Amish," Jacob said. "I wish to join the church, to be baptized."

Noah nodded. "In due time, Jacob. Spring will be soon enough." He stood and held out his arms. "Welcome home, son."

Jacob stood and stumbled to his father, tears flowing down his cheeks. "d*enki (thank you)*," he whispered.

CHAPTER THIRTY ~ Time Passes

Tuesday, June 15, 1971 4:45 a.m.

Daniel sat on the edge of the bed. He listened to Martha sleep and he smiled, yet the dream was vivid. He gazed off into the corner of the room where a shadow danced as the moonlight cast a cool blue-white light into the room.

The dream. He sat in a room with several people and watched a young lady... an Amish lady sing as she sat on a ladder at the edge of the stage. *It was not really a ladder,* Daniel thought. *It was more of a make-shift golden staircase with white billowy stuff to look like clouds.*

Daniel smiled at the memory. He knew the young woman; she was a granddaughter.

He froze at the realization. *A granddaughter?* he thought. *Why would my granddaughter sit on a ladder and sing?*

Daniel tried to remember the words of the song, but they failed him. Yet, he knew he knew them. The dream troubled him.

Martha moaned and Daniel frowned. He'd heard that sound before; she was starting labor.

# # #

6:20 a.m.

Martha fought to sit up in the bed, finally winning. She turned and saw Daniel sitting on the edge of the bed.

"Awake?" she asked.

Daniel nodded in the dimness of the room as the rising sun made its appearance.

"I am in labor," Martha said.

"I know," Daniel replied. "I heard your moans earlier."

"Go get your mother," Martha said.

Daniel dressed and headed to his parent's home across the road. Within minutes, three figures rushed back across the road. His mother and sister, Anna, hustled before him as they headed to help Martha.

Daniel sat in his rocker, waiting. *Maybe I should go ask Mary,* Daniel thought. *She is living in the Jones' house on the farm.*

Martha screamed. Daniel jumped then bowed his head.

Heavenly Father. May I ask you take away some of the pain my wife is having. This child seems to be more difficult to birth than those before. I ask this in my Savior's name, Jesus. Amen.

Again, Martha screamed, but the intensity was less. Daniel continued.

Thank you, Heavenly Father. Amen.

Daniel heard the sound of a new baby. He waited. Rebecca appeared at the bedroom doorway.

"You have another son, Daniel." She held the baby out for Daniel. "Martha likes the name Joseph Mark."

Daniel nodded. "It is a strong name. I approve." He held his new son, pulling back the swaddling cloth to get a better look.

# # #

Monday, August 2, 1971 4 a.m.

Daniel awoke, his eyes wide, staring into the darkness of the room. The nearly new moon cast blue shadows. He sat on the edge of the bed.

Earlier he had prayed for an answer. He examined the dream that awoke him.

He had his answer. Daniel sighed heavily. Joseph moaned in the darkness and Martha stirred.

"Another dream?" she asked as she grabbed the baby.

"An answer," Daniel replied. "I have made a decision."

"You mean what you will tell Bob Sullivan?" she asked.

Daniel nodded in the shadowed darkness. "Aye."

# # #

Monday, August 2 8 a.m.

Daniel walked toward the main office of the mill.

"Where you off to?" Jason asked, noting Daniel wasn't headed toward his office.

"I need to talk with Mr. Sullivan," Daniel replied. "I..." He shrugged. "Yesterday, I spent several hours in prayer, hoping for an answer."

Jason nodded. "You have the answer?"

"Yes," Daniel said. "One I will share with Bob Sullivan."

Jason walked over and placed an arm over Daniel's shoulder. "Do you want to talk about it before you go see Mr. Sullivan?"

"The decision I have made is for the good of the family, the school, and the farm."

Jason frowned. "Powerful, dude."

"I must go now," Daniel said and headed for the main office of the mill.

"Good morning, Daniel," Cynthia said as Daniel walked into the office. "What can I do for you?"

"Good morning, Cynthia," Daniel replied. "Is Mr. Sullivan available? I need to talk with him."

Bob Sullivan rapped on the window between the offices and motioned for Daniel to come in.

Cynthia grinned. "He'll see you now."

Daniel nodded and stepped into Bob Sullivan's office.

"What seems to be the problem? Is there one?" Bob Sullivan asked. "Have a chair."

Daniel sat in the chair and placed his hands in his lap.

"I was going over the list of students I have this coming year for the school." He paused and took a deep breath. "There are sixty-two students."

189

Bob Sullivan leaned back in his chair, holding a pencil between his hands which he rolled between his index and thumbs. "Am I going to like this conversation?" he asked.

Daniel bent his head down and shook it. "I do not think so." He inhaled deeply and then gazed up at his boss. "I think I need to quit the mill, Mr. Sullivan." He grimaced with a shrug. "I have enjoyed working here, but the school keeps getting larger and larger." Daniel glanced off to the left at the picture of the mill with Bob Sullivan senior and a teen-aged Bob Sulivan junior. The picture was almost forty years old.

Bob Sullivan noticed Daniel's gaze. "I was a lot younger back then, just learning the business from my father."

Daniel nodded and inhaled deeply. "I need to become a full-time teacher. I am even going to ask for an enlargement of the school." He shrugged. "Hopefully, before school starts so there is more room. I have ten more students this year than I had last year."

Daniel leaned back in his chair; a sly grin crossing his lips.

"In fact, my eldest child, Sarah, begins school this coming September. She will be six on September the thirteenth."

Bob Sullivan dropped the pencil and shook his head. "Sarah is starting school?" He leaned forward and over his desk. "I can't believe it."

"So, Mr. Sullivan," Daniel continued. "I am quitting. I will continue for the next two weeks."

"Who will lead your department?" Bob Sullivan asked. "Can I at least keep you on as a consultant?"

Daniel frowned. *Consultant*, he thought.

"I guess with two weeks' notice," Bob Sullivan said. "I should be able to find somebody to lead your department."

"You need somebody who knows carving and woodworking," Daniel said. "I would recommend Benjamin Heffel, but I fear you and he would have issues. I think Martin Smith might be a good choice." Daniel hesitated to allow the thought to solidify in Bob Sullivan's mind. "Of course, you would still be short one employee in the department," Daniel continued. "May I suggest my brother, Jacob? If you remember, he helped us with the gnome issues."

Bob Sullivan again leaned back in his chair. The look of anxiety slipping from his face.

"Martin might be an excellent choice for the department lead," Bob Sullivan said. "And, yes, your brother, Jacob is a good worker and he did do great work when he was in your department." He picked up another pencil to fiddle with. "I don't know why I haven't moved him to your department before." Bob Sullivan grinned. "Of course, now I need to hire another janitor."

"If I may," Daniel said. "Benjamin has two nephews; siblings of my brother-in-law, John Heffel. Their names are Matthew and Noah. They might be available."

Bob Sullivan nodded. "I can ask." He gazed at Daniel. "Two weeks, eh? Are you interested in consulting?" He shrugged. "Not exactly sure what it will entail, but I'd like to keep you around, if possible."

Daniel smiled. "If you need help, I will try to be available."

Bob Sullivan stood and offered a hand to shake. "It has been a pleasure, Daniel Yoder, and I will miss you."

"Thank you," Daniel said, standing to shake hands.

"You know," Bob Sullivan said as Daniel walked to the door to leave. "Jason is going to miss you and those trips to the school to pick you up."

Daniel smiled. "I will, too. Jason and I have been friends for so many years. JD, his son, should start school in two years." Daniel snickered. "Jason and I met in second grade and have been friends all these years."

Bob Sullivan smiled. "I'm getting too old." He shook his head, paused, then placed a hand over his chest. He frowned as he rubbed the area over his heart. Once more he smiled. "I remember when you were just starting out as a janitor and I happened to notice your carving." He shrugged. "How life changed for us."

# # #

Monday, August 8 7:30 p.m.

"Papa?" Daniel called as he entered the main room where his father rocked while reading *The Budget*.

"Oh, Daniel," Noah said, placing the paper to the side. "Come in. You wish to talk?"

191

"Yes, Papa," Daniel said and sat in the chair beside his father. "I need more school space."

"More space?" Noah asked.

"Yes, Papa," Daniel replied. "I have sixty-two students this year." He paused. "That is ten more than last year." Daniel shrugged. "I know we built on a few years ago, but with more and more students; we need the space."

"I see no problem, Daniel," Noah said. "You are the teacher. You know best. I will mention it to the other Elders. When do you plan to start school?"

"I was thinking August 30, but I could wait until later."

"We extended the one side to make it a two-room school house. I see no reason for us not to extend the other side and make it a three room."

"Thank you, Papa," Daniel said. "Also, I will be a full-time school teacher from now on. I quit my job at the mill. This way I can help around the farm during the summer when we need more hands in the fields."

"Is that a wise choice?" Noah asked.

"I was thinking," Daniel replied. "What if we expanded the strawberry patch to include a pick-your-own area." He paused. "Also, what if we added a blueberry patch?"

Noah leaned back in his rocker and gently rocked back and forth while he thought. "Two very good ideas," he said. "I will discuss this with the others. "Blueberries," he mumbled.

Daniel grinned. "If we cut back on the cow pastures, maybe three or five acres, we could add an orchard."

"Apples? Peaches? Pears?" Noah asked.

Daniel shrugged. *Fresh made apple cider*, he thought. "Yes. And..." He paused. "Possibly, raspberries, too."

# # #

Saturday, August 28, 1971 8 a.m.

Daniel, Martha, and the kids pulled up to the school with Bronk pulling the buckboard. Some people had already arrived.

Martha and Sarah grabbed the baskets of food and headed for the cluster of women to the one side.

"gut'n mariye, (good morning)" Jeremiah Wyse said as Daniel strode up the group of men who stood analyzing the side of the school building. He shook his head. "Who would have thought my donation of land would bring such a large building to be?"

"We have taught many students," Daniel said. "May the Lord bless you for this."

Jeremiah nodded. "The Lord has indeed blessed me. My wife teaches here and my children have had a good Amish upbringing." He patted Daniel on the back. "You have done well, Daniel Yoder."

Daniel tried not to blush.

Ezra tugged on Daniel's pant leg. "Papa? Can I help?" He held up a hammer. "I know how to pound."

The group of men laughed and Daniel assured Ezra there would be work he could do.

Noah Yoder strode up with Jacob, Joshua, and Jonah following behind. In the distance, Daniel saw his mother, Anna, and Ester making their way to the other women. He could smell the food even at this distance.

"So, Daniel," Noah said. "Have you decided what you want put on this side of the school?"

Daniel gazed at his father, amazed to asked his input. He reached into his hat and pulled out a sheet of paper.

"I thought this would be useful," he said as he opened the folded paper. "One big room is nice, but I think it would be better to have two rooms."

Noah scrutinized the rough drawing, stroking his beard as he thought.

"You have four rooms in total, but only three teachers." Noah gazed at Daniel. "Is that correct?"

"We have over sixty students," Daniel said. "I think we need another teacher, too." He paused. "Having the older students help the younger ones does work, but it also takes away from their learning."

"Another teacher?" Noah asked. "Are not three teachers enough?"

"We can have four rooms, but only use three," Daniel said. "The extra room cold be used for storage and, if need be, in the future, another classroom.

"Ah," Noah said. "Thinking ahead. Wise." He folded the drawing. "So be it. Let us extend out this side and create two rooms."

Noah conferred with a few of the carpenters of the community and the best method was decided.

Men were quickly assigned duties and the side of the school was removed and a new structure started to appear.

Daniel stood back and looked at the skeleton of the new structure. *This is good*, he thought. *Another teacher would be good, but maybe I need wait until next year. Our community is growing.*

# # #

Monday, May 20, 1973 7:35 p.m.

Martha sat on the settee enjoying her pastime of reading the Bible aloud to the children before they went to bed.

"Oh!" she said. "Daniel, my water broke."

"Ezra," Daniel said. "Go get Grandma. Be careful crossing the road. "Now, hustle."

The young boy hurried out the door. Daniel helped Martha to the bedroom.

"I will clean this," Sarah said.

"denki (thank you)," Daniel said as they passed into the bedroom. "No more Bible reading tonight," he said. "Get ready for bed there is still school tomorrow."

Ezra burst into the room through the front door. "Grandma is coming. Anna and Ester, too."

Daniel nodded as he listened to Martha groan with labor pains.

The three women entered the house and immediately took note of the room and headed for the bedroom where Martha labored.

Daniel continued to listen to Martha's labors, the moans getting louder as the pains of labor increased. Daniel prayed.

194

Dear Heavenly Father. Please make this labor an easy one for Martha. I ask this in Jesus name. Amen.

Once more Martha groaned in labor, but Daniel felt it sounded much less than the earlier one.

Rebecca came to the door. "This will be a long labor, Daniel," she said. "She is slow to dilate." Rebecca shrugged. "Make sure the children are to bed and wait."

Daniel stood and headed up the stairs to the children's bedrooms to make sure they were all tucked in and possibly asleep.

Sarah crawled into bed as Daniel peeked in. "Joseph, Joshua, and Elizabeth are in bed. Ezra should be in bed by now. *gut'n nacht* (good night), Papa."

"*gut'n nacht* (good night), Sarah," Daniel replied. "Sweet dreams."

Daniel slowly trod down the stairs, finally stopping near the bottom and sitting on a step.

I am truly blessed, Daniel thought. *Six wonderful children and the seventh on the way.* He grinned. *Martha wanted a large family and we have one.*

Daniel listened to the sounds of the house. It was silent except for Martha's labor pains and an occasional whimper from above where the children slept. His mind wandered.

The fruit trees are blooming nicely this year. Papa may be able to allow others to pick this year. His mouth watered at the thought of fresh peach and apple pies. *Even the strawberries seem to have more flowers this year. It could be a bumper crop.*

Martha yelped and Daniel jumped from the staircase and headed to the main room.

Rebecca stood in the doorway to the bedroom. She shook her head. "This is going to be a rough birth," she said. "She is beginning to dilate but Martha wishes to deliver now." Again, she shook her head. "That is not good. I have had to tell her several times not to push."

Daniel fell to his knees and bowed his head.

Dear Heavenly Father. I beg forgiveness for bragging about my family. It is your wish, not mine. Please be with Martha during this delivery and take away the pain, if You will. I ask this in my Savior's name, Jesus, Your Son. Amen.

"Continue to pray, Daniel," Rebecca said and disappeared into the bedroom.

Daniel stood and leaned back in his rocker. *I must think of something else. Sixty-four students with eleven of them ready to graduate,* he thought. *Only a few more days of school.*

Without thinking, Daniel stood, placed his hands before him, cupped together. He moved his left foot at an angle from the right foot. He took three deep breaths, slowing exhaling. The words filled the room. Daniel sang *Where'er You Walk*; his diaphragm controlling the notes' intensity and duration.

Martha's labor pains intensified, but she was calm, relaxed, listening to Daniel sing in the other room.

"You are dilating," Rebecca said. "You should deliver soon."

Martha smiled then felt an urge to push. "I want to push," Martha whispered.

Rebecca nodded. "It is time."

Daniel continued to sing songs, working through all those he could remember from over the years; especially those he learned in New York when on *Rumschpringe.*

The sound of a newborn crying filled the room. In moments, Rebecca stood at the door holding a baby wrapped in blankets.

"You have a daughter. Martha says for you to name her."

Daniel held his newest daughter, gazing into her eyes. He frowned momentarily in thought.

"Welcome, Bethany Grace Yoder," he said.

Rebecca's brows knitted in thought then nodded. "That is a good name. I do not think we have any other Bethany in the family. I think Martha will agree." She hesitated then placed a hand to hip. "I do not believe Martha should not have any more children, Daniel. This birthing was difficult for her. This was a close call. We were able to stop the bleeding."

"Bleeding?" Daniel repeated and considered the words. "Do we need to go to the hospital?"

"Martha is fine," Rebecca said softly. "You and Martha will be happy with the family you have." Rebecca took Bethany and returned to the bedroom.

Daniel sat in the rocker, contemplating his mother's words. *No more children. Would Martha be content?*

CHAPTER THIRTY-ONE ~ Surprises

Thursday, April 18th, 1974 2:20 PM.

Jason pulled the yellow Mustang up to the schoolhouse, skidding tires as he stopped, causing gravel to fly in all directions. He rushed into the school building, startling the students and Daniel who was sitting at his desk.

"Daniel!" Jason yelled "I came to let you know Bob Sullivan just had a heart attack, and they have taken him to the hospital."

Daniel stood looking at Elizabeth Wyse, Elizabeth Troyer, and Miriam Graber.

Elizabeth Wyse approached Daniel and placed a hand on his shoulder. "You should go, Daniel. I will finish classes." She gazed at Elizabeth and Ezra. "I will take your children home and tell Martha."

Daniel straightened a few pages on the desk, then went with Jason to the car. Jason revved the engine, put the car in reverse, and spun the tires as he backed out of the school area. The tires squealed as Jason lurched the car forward.

Fifteen minutes later found them at the DeMotte Hospital. Jason led the way, and Daniel followed as they worked their way to the emergency area. They were informed Bob Sullivan had been taken to the third-floor cardiac unit. They took the elevator up to the third floor and immediately saw Ben Hopkins and Mrs. Sullivan talking as they entered the waiting area.

Mrs. Sullivan, with tears streaming down her face, stood and hugged Daniel when he approached.

"It is so good to see you, Daniel," Mrs. Sullivan said. "They say Bob will survive, but he will need to have a quadruple bypass to correct the situation."

"Will we be able to see Mr. Sullivan?" Daniel asked.

"This is very serious" Jason said, shaking his head. "Very serious. I think only immediate family is allowed in."

Mrs. Sullivan nodded her head as she sat back down and Ben Hopkins grabbed her hands to hold in comfort.

"I want Ben to run the business while Bob recuperates." She turned to Daniel "I know it would be an imposition, but would you come in to make sure that the carving department is under control? I know Martin has been running it, but I heard Bob make a comment about having to keep an eye on him."

Daniel nodded. "I can come in the mid-afternoon, but not in the morning."

Mrs. Sullivan nodded her head. "That will work." She smiled. "It could be several months, though. Is that okay?"

Daniel nodded.

A nurse appeared at the door of the waiting room. "Mrs. Sullivan? We are getting ready to take your husband in for surgery." She stepped to the side of the doorway. "Do you wish to see him before we begin?" The nurse gazed at the other three men. "Do you have any family who want to visit?"

Mrs. Sullivan walked stiffly toward the door. "We have no children," she said. "These are his close friends. Could they come in?" She shrugged. "They're like family to us."

"Only immediate family," the nurse said, slowly shaking her head. "I'm sorry."

# # #

Friday, April 19, 1974 3:15 p.m.

Jason pulled his yellow Mustang into the driveway of the mill and Daniel inhaled deeply.

"It's been a while since you were last here," Jason said, opening the door. "Some things have changed, but most have remained the same."

Daniel got out of the car and gave Jason a quizzical gaze.

"Tom Johnson, the lead in my department, is considering retiring next month." He hesitated. "Mr. Sullivan and I were talking and I might become the new lead if he does retire."

"Congratulations," Daniel said. "I mean, if you get the job."

Jason shrugged. "Guess it all depends on how Mr. Sullivan does with his recovery. I'm glad his surgery went well." He sighed. "Imagine. A quadruple bypass. You don't get one of those every day."

Daniel frowned but let it go. He knew Bob Sullivan had heart surgery and he knew quad meant four, but was uncertain of the exact procedure that was done. Daniel knew if he waited, someone would explain it. He walked toward the carving department. He gazed at the new sign over the department - Wood Initiatives.

"Daniel!" Martin called when he noticed the Amish man.

"Good afternoon, Martin," Daniel said, unsure of how things would resolve with him returning.

"Ben told me you were coming back to help straighten out this department." He shrugged with a smile. "I'm trying, but just not quite have gotten the hang of it." He shook his head. "Bob Sullivan has been really patient with me."

Daniel glanced about the area; three other men worked. He recognized Benjamin Heffel and Jacob, his brother. The other man Daniel was unfamiliar with.

"Come meet Frank Hughes," Martin said, gently pushing Daniel toward the new man. "We hired him about three months ago, right after the New Year."

"So, you are the Daniel Yoder I have heard so much about," Frank said. He stuck out his hand. "Glad to meet you."

Daniel shook hands and frowned at what Frank was working on. "What is this?"

"We started making this last year," Martin said. "Like the gnomes, a big seller. It is called a croquet set. There are six balls, six mallets, two stakes, and nine wickets. Like the gnomes, hot items since they're handmade."

Daniel nodded. "Let me go to the office and check things out, if I may."

"You bet," Martin replied. "I'll get back to work on my big project for a customer." He nodded to the left. "Eight foot tall."

Daniel gazed at the rough sculpted horse rearing on its back legs. "When is this due?"

"The customer wants it by the first of July," Martin said. He sighed. "I will have it done."

This job may be more than Martin can handle, Daniel thought. *I had best check the office and make sure everything is under control.*

"I am going to the office," Daniel said.

"If you have any questions," Martin said. "Just ask." He paused and offered a goofy grin. "It's a mess in there."

Daniel stepped into the office and was immediately assaulted by the disarray and confusion of paperwork on the desk.

I will be here late tonight, Daniel thought. *This will take a lot of work to straighten.*

Daniel sat at the desk and surveyed the mess. *Best just to make a stack of all the papers and figure out where each goes*, he thought.

Ben appeared at the doorway.

"Not the most organized manager," Ben whispered as he entered and sat at the chair on the opposite of the desk. "You have your work cut out for you."

Daniel nodded. "I might have to come in tomorrow." He sighed. "Papa is getting things around for the spring planting. He needs my help." Daniel gazed at the four-inch stack of paper he'd made. "Still, I promised Mrs. Sullivan I would help here."

"Tell you what," Ben said. "I need to come in tomorrow. How about I pick you up in the morning and we'll work until noon."

Daniel offered a weak smile. "That will work." He gazed at the top sheet of paper. It had Bob Sullivan's signature on it.

"Mr. Sullivan has been blessed," Daniel said. "He has a loving wife, a great business, and very dedicated workers." He smiled at Ben. "Without you, Ben, I do not believe this business would be still operating with him in the hospital. Truly, the Lord has blessed him."

"I'm going to let you in a big secret, Daniel." Ben leaned in over the desk. "You are the reason Bob Sullivan is profitable. He was just making due after his father passed. When he discovered your horse carving when you were going to high school and working here as a part-time janitor, it helped his business. You, Daniel, are the reason Bob Sullivan's mill has been profitable. Remember the furniture? The carved animals? The gnomes? Selling lumber and pallets is one thing, but what you created, all these beautiful carvings, that is where Bob made his money. He was really sorry to see you leave." Ben glanced out on the floor where Martin worked. "Yeah, he does great work and has some good ideas, but he doesn't have business savvy. You do, Daniel."

Daniel watched Martin work on the massive horse statue and considered Ben's words.

Did I make the right decision when I quit? Daniel thought. Once more he gazed at the stack of papers before him. He absently nodded. *I will help here until Bob Sullivan comes back and then I will make a decision.*

"I can see the wheels working," Ben said. "So, I'm guessing you are staying on?"

Daniel shrugged. "At least until Bob Sullivan returns."

"That is all I ask," Ben said. "Like Bob, I need your help." Again, he gazed out at Martin. "Good worker, bad manager."

Ben stood. "I will pick you up tomorrow morning, okay?"

Daniel nodded and watched Ben leave then once again, started work on the stack of papers, creating smaller stacks to be worked and filed.

# # #

Saturday, April 20 1:15 p.m.

Daniel jumped out of Ben's car that parked at the end of the driveway.

"Jason will pick you up on Monday," Ben said. "You accomplished a lot today. Thanks for working with me."

On the porch, Daniel saw his children waiting for him. "Papa!" they yelled in unison.

Martha came onto the porch carrying Bethany. She smiled.

Daniel strode up the driveway to the waiting family.

"Come in. Eat," Martha said.

There was an air about her that Daniel couldn't put his finger on.

Daniel sat at the table and waited for the children to sit. When everyone was situated, he said *"Händt nunna"* (hands down) and prayed. When done, he cleared his voice and food was passed around.

Martha continued to smile at Daniel during the meal which confused him, unsure of why the smile.

"Who wants cherry pie for dessert?" Martha asked.

Hands went up. Daniel nodded and Martha stood to get the pie from the counter.

"Do you want to go out on the front porch and eat your dessert?" Martha asked the children.

They stood in line to get their pie and rush outside into the fresh air.

Martha handed Daniel his pie and then sat down beside him with hers.

"You have something to say," Daniel said.

Martha nodded. "Yes, Daniel." She paused, placing her fork on the plate beside the pie. "I think I am pregnant, again."

Daniel's eyes widened. "Pregnant?" His memory immediately flashed his mother's warning when Bethany was born... *no more children*.

"Are you sure?" he asked.

"I will see Dr. Braeburn on Monday." She nodded. "Pretty sure. Early, but I think so."

"Mama said we should not have any more children," Daniel whispered and grabbed her hand. "Bethany was a rough delivery."

"I remember," Martha said. "Still, if I am pregnant, then it is the Lord's wish."

Daniel squeezed her hand. "It is in His hands."

# # #

Sunday, April 21 5:45 a.m.

Daniel strode to the barn with Ezra walking beside him. Joshua, still young, tagged Ezra and then ran forward.

"Beat you there, big brother," Joshua taunted.

Daniel remembered back when he would race Luke to the barn in the morning to milk the cows. He smiled as the memory of Jacob tagging him in the race to the barn when Luke had married.

Ezra took the challenge and faked racing, allowing Joshua to win and scramble to the hayloft to feed the cattle.

Family, Daniel thought. *The cycle continues.*

# # #

Monday, April 22 5:20 p.m.

"Daniel," Martha called as she hastened down the porch steps. "Your Mama wants us over for the evening meal."

Ben honked his horn as he drove off.

"I've already milked our cows, fed and bedded the animals. Now, hurry. You can help your father with his milking."

Martha joined Daniel in the driveway and as they crossed the road, they saw Noah, Jacob, Joshua and Jonah leave the house for the barn. When across the road, Sarah, Ezra, Elizabeth, and Joshua raced for the backdoor and disappeared in the house. Daniel's sibling twins raced ahead to the bar leaving Jacob and Noah behind with Jonah winning and going in the barn. Joshua sighed with defeat and headed for the horses to put them away for the day. Ester hurried out the kitchen door and stomped toward the chicken coop to collect the last of the eggs for the day and to make sure the chickens were safely collected into the coop to roost for the night. She waved her hands at the rooster to head him toward the coop. "Shoo! Get in there," Ester yelled at the rooster.

"I will help Mama with the meal," Martha said.

"Did you visit Dr. Braeburn today?" Daniel asked.

Martha nodded. "Yes. He says I am pregnant and probably due in early October."

Daniel silently counted the months. *She is in her second month,* he thought. *Another boy? Girl? Whichever, the Lord is blessing us.*

"I will go help Papa," Daniel said and gave Martha a quick peck on the cheek. He gazed at the big house. "I bet Anna is watching the children." He looked off to the chicken coop. "That is probably why Ester is stomping around. She wanted to play with the kids."

"Mama said there is news today," Martha said. "I wonder what it could be?"

"Maybe I will find out in the barn," Daniel said and hastened toward the barn's door.

He entered where Jonah scooped hay down on the cattle. His father, as always, was in the distance milking a cow. Jacob was at the first cow.

"Welcome, Daniel," Jacob said. "Did you come to help milk? Or to watch?" He grinned. "Or to sing?" He nodded. "That would be nice."

"I will help milk," Daniel said and grabbed a stool and bucket and counted about one-third of the cattle and began to milk.

"Sing a song," Noah said from the recesses of the barn. "The cows enjoy your singing."

"And sing," Daniel said and began to sing *Old MacDonald*.' He soon heard Jacob and Jonah join him. Then he heard his father singing. Daniel smiled and continued with more songs, sometimes singing alone, other times with his siblings and father joining him. He could hear Joshua singing from the other side of the barn as he worked with the horses.

"I heard Martha say there is news to be told," Daniel said.

"In time," Noah said. "All in due time."

Jacob laughed. "Yes, Daniel," he whispered. "All in due time."

# # #

Monday, April 22 7:35 p.m.

Daniel eased back from the table, feeling his stomach fully extended. Martha made a wicked meatloaf, but his mother's meatloaf was still his favorite and he had eaten too much.

Martha leaned over. "As usual, you gorged." She wrinkled her nose at him. "At times I think you are part pig."

Daniel grinned and nodded. "Today, I agree."

"Come, Daniel," Noah said. "Let us go to the main room."

The kitchen door opened. Miriam and Luke appeared with their six children.

"I saw Hannah and John coming down the road," Luke said.

"Ruth and Joshua, Rachel and Jacob, and Mary and Isaac should arrive shortly, too," Rebecca said.

Daniel frowned. "What news could there be for all the family to show?"

Luke slapped Daniel on the back. "It is good to see you," he said. "How goes things at work? I mean, school and at the mill?"

Daniel smiled and nodded. "Good to see you, too." He walked across the room to a chair and sat. "School is about over and I think all the students will pass." He shrugged. "Work at the mill is interesting. I did not think I would be working at the mill again."

"How is Mr. Sullivan doing?" Noah asked, sitting in his rocker.

"His surgery went well last week," Daniel said. "He is scheduled to come home this coming Friday." He leaned over in the chair and placed his arms on his upper legs. "Ben is running the mill during this time."

"And you are once more managing the carving department," John Heffel said as he entered the room. "gut'n owed, (good evening) everyone."

"Is your uncle upset?" Daniel asked, curious as to John's words.

"No," John replied. "He says the department needed you. Martin is a good worker, but a poor manager."

Daniel nodded. "I agree."

Isaac Wyse appeared at the door, followed by Joshua Mueller. The men sat in the room and discussed the future of the farm. Finally, Jacob Metz joined them. Moments later, the women appeared.

"The kitchen is clean," Rebecca said. "Now that the whole family is here, we can make the announcement."

Daniel frowned.

"Jacob. You first," Noah said.

"I am getting married. I have been courting Havilah Zook. We wish to marry this fall."

Noah nodded. "A date?"

"She wants to marry in September, Papa," Jacob said.

"I will make the announcement at the beginning of September," Noah said. He leaned back in his rocker. "I am blessed."

Anna stood. "I, too, wish to make an announcement."

Noah frowned, unsure of what his daughter wanted to say.

"Mr. Yoder," a strange voice from the kitchen called. "My name is Andrew Schmucker." The young man entered the room. "I have no *Schteckleimann* (go between), but I have come to ask for Anna, your daughter's hand in marriage."

"Andrew Schmucker has been courting me and we wish to marry. A fall wedding?" She shrugged. "In October?"

Noah glanced at his wife who stood by the doorway beside Andrew. *She knew*, he thought.

"Two weddings this year," Noah said. He squinted in thought. "Have you considered having one wedding?"

Jacob frowned. "One wedding? Which of us is not to marry?"

"Nay. Nay," Noah said. "Both of you marry in one wedding."

"Is that allowed?" Martha asked.

Noah shrugged. "I can ask the other Elders. If none object, are you willing to do that?"

"I will ask Havilah when I see her tonight," Jacob said then glanced at his sister. "Are you willing?"

Anna glanced at Andrew who ever so slightly nodded his head in agreement. He smiled.

"We have no issue with a double wedding if…" Anna hesitated. "If Havilah is willing."

Jacob nodded. "I am sure she will agree."

Martha stood. "I have an announcement, too." She glanced at Daniel. "Do you wish to tell?"

Daniel waved his hand. "You say it."

"I am pregnant," Martha blurted.

Rebecca's head snapped to gaze at Martha. "Pregnant?" she asked.

Martha sighed heavily. "Yes." She paused. "I know what you are thinking, Mama."

Rebecca shook her head. "It is none of my business."

Hannah stood. "I think the news tonight is wonderful." She embraced her younger sister. "You are getting married." Hannah then moved to Jacob. "And you, my dear brother. How did I not know this?"

Jacob grinned. "Simple, Hannah. You do not live at home anymore."

Noah stood. "Let us take time to thank the Lord. We pray."

He bowed his head and the others in the room joined, bowing their heads. After a few moments of silence, Noah cleared his throat.

"Lead us in a song, Daniel," Noah said.

Daniel lifted his voice, the words of *O Gott, Vader* filled the room and the rest of the family joined in. He followed that with *Das Loblied* and finally finished with a rousing rendition of *Ten Little Indians* which the children enjoyed.

CHAPTER THIRTY-TWO ~ Fall Activities

Tuesday, September 24, 1974 8:20 a.m.

Daniel helped to get the children around so they could cross the road to his parent's home for the double wedding of his brother and sister. Martha walked into the room, placed a hand to her full stomach and sat on the settee by the window.

"I am sorry, Daniel," Martha said. "This pregnancy is wearing me down. I find it difficult to do anything."

Daniel moved across the room and knelt before her, taking her hand in his. "My dear Marti," he said. "I love you and if this is too much, we can pass on the affair. I am sure Jacob and Anna will understand."

"Marti. A girl from New York City who married an Amish boy," Martha whispered. "And why would you think I would not want to attend your sibling's weddings." She leaned back on the settee and laughed. "A double wedding? We had a double wedding but it was at two separate times. This is at the same time. I would not miss this." She placed an arm behind her to help push. Daniel pulled on the opposite arm. Martha stood and took a few moments to compose herself. *Doctor Braeburn says I have less than a month to delivery,* she thought. "Let us cross the road." She placed a hand to her back and waddled across the room.

Martha waved the children out the door, down the steps and to their grandparent's house. The sun was shining and sky was a beautiful blue with white clouds drifting.

A light breeze blew across the road toward them. Daniel inhaled the scents of cooking foods. *Fried chicken*, he thought. *My favorite.*

Jacob stood talking with Benjamin Heffel, Jason Muirs, and Ben Hopkins. Daniel joined them.

"I heard rumor," Ben Hopkins said. "It could be that Bob Sullivan and his wife will attend." He shrugged. "I think, other than going to church last Sunday, this would be his next time out of the house since his surgery."

On cue, the white Lincoln Continental pulled into the driveway. Jason noticed it first.

"I'll be right back," Jason said. "I will allow them to get close, then I will park the car for them. Mr. Sullivan doesn't need to be doing a lot of walking... at least, not yet."

"Actually, Jason," Ben countered. "I think the boss man has been doing therapy and is quite capable of walking."

Jason stopped and turned to face the group of men. "Really?"

The car door opened and Bob Sullivan stepped out from the driver's side. Using a cane, we wobbled toward the group of men from the mill.

"Am I paying you to attend this wedding?" he asked as he approached. "Who is working the mill?"

Ben put an arm over Jacob's shoulder. "This young man invited the whole mill to his wedding. I only saw fit to close the mill for the day." He grinned. "Then I discovered some of the men didn't want to attend." His grin was wider. "I made sure they would work and are running the store."

Bob Sullivan gave a fake sigh of relief. "Whew! I thought I'd be out of business by the time I got back."

"When do you plan to return?" Daniel asked.

"Good question, young Yoder," Bob Sullivan replied. "My doctor says if therapy continues as well as it has been; I should be back in the office before Thanksgiving."

Daniel nodded.

Noah approached with Andrew following. "I need Jacob. We need to discuss a few things before the wedding."

Jacob and Noah headed for the house. Daniel remembered his talks with Martha and Bishop Schmucker before he was married... the second time as an Amish man.

Daniel excused himself from the group and strolled the yard, meeting other workers from the mill and members of the Amish community.

"See those chairs?" Jason said, startling Daniel. "That's where us *Englische* will sit to watch the wedding." He grinned. "Some of the guys from the mill have no idea what they're in for; I mean, how long this wedding will take."

Daniel nodded, remembering the *Englische* weddings where Jason was his best man and he was in Jason's wedding, and his Amish wedding where Jason was a guest. The *Englische* weddings were short, not even an hour. The Amish wedding lasted almost three hours.

People began to gather for the service. Daniel sat with the men and watched as Martha came in with his mother. Ezra, Joshua, Joseph, and Matthew rushed in and sat by him. Sarah carried Bethany and Elizabeth followed.

Noah and the Elders came into the center then Jacob and Havilah, and Anna and Andrew walked in and took their seats.

Daniel glanced at his wife on the opposite side. She fidgeted and he saw her grimace a couple of times. *Mama will notice her rutsching (squirming),* Daniel thought.

Rebecca noticed Martha's movements and leaned over to her.

"Come with me," she said and grabbed Martha's hand. She gazed at the children. "Stay here with Aunt Hannah," she said and then led Martha from the service and into the house.

"I am not in labor," Martha said as they climbed the steps of the kitchen porch.

"I agree, you might be in false labor," Rebecca said. "It is better to be safe than to be sorry."

The kitchen door opened and Dr. Braeburn stepped in. "May I be of assistance?" he asked.

"It is nothing," Martha said. "Mama is just being cautious."

Dr. Braeburn nodded. "Let me be the one to decide if it is nothing or not." He nodded toward the stairs. "I've been in this house more than once. Now, up those stairs and into a bedroom so I can examine you."

Martha struggled to the staircase, holding a hand to her stomach.

"Nothing?" Dr. Braeburn asked. "How much pain are you in?"

"It is not labor," Martha said and grabbed the handrail to assist her up the stairs.

"Take it slow and easy," Dr. Braeburn whispered. "It is not a race to the top."

At the third step, Martha paused to get her breath.

"Shall I help you, dear?" Dr. Braeburn asked.

"I will make it," Martha replied, and again continued up the steps.

She turned at the first doorway and made her way to the bed to sit.

# # #

Dr. Braeburn hastened down the steps. "She is fine. It was false labor as you thought, Mrs. Yoder." He walked over to the counter where Rebecca offered him a glass of water. He drank. "Martha will need to be on bed rest until delivery. Is there anyone who can be with her while Daniel is working?"

Rebecca nodded. "I will have Ester stay with them until it is time."

Dr. Braeburn nodded. "Now, I'd best get back to the wedding." He sniffed the air. "The food smells delicious."

"In time, Dr. Braeburn. In time," Rebecca said. She turned to the other three women working in the kitchen. "I will remain to help."

"No, you will not," the one replied. "You have two children getting married. Now, you get out there. We will finish up here in the kitchen and keep an eye on Martha." She nudged Rebecca toward the kitchen door. "Do not worry. We have it under control."

# # #

Wednesday, October 9, 1974 5:40 p.m.

Daniel waved from the front porch to Ben as he pulled from the driveway, then he strode into the house.

"Daniel!" Ester cried. "Martha is starting labor. I will go get Mama." She bolted from the bedroom and through the door to disappear.

He entered the bedroom. The children were standing around the bed watching their mother in labor.

"Sarah," Daniel said. "Take the children into the kitchen and feed them. I will join you shortly."

He knelt by the edge of the bed and held Martha's hand in his. He bowed his head.

Dear Lord. I beg of You. Give Martha the strength to carry this last child to birth. It is a blessing You have offered to us, and we accept it. Be with Martha during this delivery. In Jesus name, Amen.

Rebecca raced into the room. She gazed at Daniel on the floor holding Martha's hand and crying. She glanced at Martha on the bed and stopped.

"Is...?" she asked.

"Sleeping," Daniel whispered, and stood. "I need to go to the children in the kitchen." He wiped his eyes.

Rebecca nodded. "I and Ester will remain here." She hesitated. "Maybe you should get Dr. Braeburn... just in case." Again, she paused. "Either you, your father, or one of the twins should go to get him. Hook up Beauty."

Daniel left the room and checked on the children in the kitchen. Sarah had everything under control. The siblings were eating.

"I even said grace, Papa," Sarah said.

"Be not proud, Sarah," Daniel chastised. "I need to go talk to Grandpa Yoder. I will be back shortly."

Daniel left the house to find his father across the road. He relayed his mother's words.

"I will send Joshua," Noah said. "Now, you had best get back to Martha and the children."

Daniel raced back to his house and heard Martha scream as he entered the kitchen. The children all glanced toward the main room which led to the bedroom. Their eyes were wide.

"Do not fear," Daniel soothed. "Mama is fine. Your new brother or sister is coming today."

They nodded their heads and once more continued their evening meal.

Daniel walked into the main room and sat in his rocker, slowly moving back and forth, listening to the slight creak of the floor.

Again, and again, Martha screamed in pain. Daniel held his breath. Martha screamed again and Daniel fell to his knees from the rocker.

Dear Heavenly Father. Please, I beg of You, ease the pain of my wife. Amen.

Martha screamed again, but not with the urgent distress of earlier.

Daniel nodded. "Thank you, Lord," Daniel whispered.

A knock on the door caught his attention and Ezra ran to answer it.

"It is Dr. Braeburn," he yelled toward the bedroom. "Come in," he said, opening the door.

The doctor entered and immediately went to Daniel. "Where is Martha?" he asked.

Daniel nodded toward the bedroom door just as she screamed again.

"I will see what I can do," Dr. Braeburn said and hastened to the bedroom door where he knocked, announced himself, and entered.

Daniel waited. The children finished their meal and came to sit on the floor before him. Sarah brought over the Bible. Daniel opened it and began to read. The children listened.

Martha's labor pains eased and her screams became moans.

Daniel continued to read the Bible. Inwardly, he smiled as he told the tales of Biblical Daniel.

"Is this how you got your name, Papa?" Ezra interrupted.

"It is very possible," Daniel replied and continued to read about Daniel's adventures.

"Can you interpret dreams?" Sarah asked in a whisper.

Daniel shrugged. "Some, I guess. Let me continue." He read then realized the time. "It is best you all get to bed. There is school tomorrow for some."

Sarah, Ezra, and Elizabeth grimaced.

"Do we have to go to school tomorrow?" Sarah asked and gazed at the bedroom door. She gazed hopefully at her father. "I can stay and help with the new baby."

"Aunt Ester will be here," Daniel said. "You..." He tapped her on the nose. "You need to be in school." He waved his hand. "All of you, up to bed. I will be there shortly."

Dr. Braeburn stepped from the bedroom, quietly closing the door behind.

"Daniel," he whispered and motioned for him to come close.

Daniel stood and walked to the bedroom door and Dr. Braeburn. He frowned, trying to remember the last time he heard Martha moan.

"Is everything okay?" Daniel asked.

"I have given Martha an injection to help ease the pain and let her rest." He shook his head. "This is a very, very difficult delivery, Daniel." He paused and heaved a heavy sigh. "I am hoping to save both Martha and the child." He shrugged.

"Save?" Daniel echoed.

Dr. Braeburn nodded. "Martha should never have gotten pregnant." He sighed. "I will do what I can." He reached behind him and turned the knob on the door. He slipped inside.

Daniel stumbled back to his rocker and slumped into it.

What will I do without Martha? he thought. *What will the children do without a mother?*

A tear welled in his eye, then traced a path down his cheek. More tears followed. Daniel cried.

Soft hands wrapped around his shoulders. "Do not fear, my son," Rebecca said. "Martha is a strong woman; she will win this battle."

Daniel reached up and touched his mother's hand.

"How will I live without her?" he asked. "She is..."

"You are strong, Daniel. Pray." Rebecca turned went back into the bedroom.

Once more Daniel fell to the floor, hands grasped together in prayer.

My Heavenly Father. I pray You grant me one more blessing. Allow my wife to live, and also my soon-to-be-born child. I offer their lives into Your hands. I seek your guidance. In Jesus name, Amen.

"Papa?" Sarah's plaintiff voice called from upstairs.

"Coming," Daniel replied and headed for the stairs.

He sat on the edge of Sarah's bed.

"Is Mama going to be okay?" she asked.

"Mama will be just fine," Daniel assured his eldest daughter and stroked her brow, pushing the long, dark hair back.

Sarah reached up and hugged Daniel. "I love you, Papa."

Daniel grabbed her arms and leaned her back onto the bed. "Now, you go to sleep, Sarah. Tomorrow is school."

"Yes, Papa," she replied, pulling the blanket up to her neck and closing her eyes. "Good night," she whispered.

Daniel stood and waited, glancing over at Elizabeth who was already sleeping soundly. He went to the boy's bedroom. Ezra was asleep; Joshua and Joseph tossed in the early stages of sleep; and Matthew lay there, eyes wide open.

"Why are you not asleep like your brothers?" Daniel asked.

"Mama is hurting," Matthew whispered. "Why?"

Daniel rubbed Matthew's chest in a soothing circle. "Mama is fine," Daniel said. "Shut your eyes and go to sleep. All is well."

Matthew closed his eyes and Daniel continued to rub the young boy's chest. He began to sing; the words of *Where're You Walk* coming softly.

Assured Matthew was asleep, Daniel edged out of the room and headed back down the stairs.

Ester sat in the chair by Daniel's rocker.

"Mama said for me to come out here and be with you," she said.

Daniel nodded. "*denki*, (thank you) Ester. *denki*." He sat in the rocker, but held it still. He waited.

The wail of a baby filled the room.

"You have another child," Ester said, jumping from the chair to charge to the bedroom.

The door opened and Dr. Braeburn moved forward with a small bundle. "You have another son, Daniel."

Daniel gazed down at the little body wrapped in the blanket. "Did Martha name him?" he asked.

Dr. Braeburn shook his head. "No, she is resting."

"Your name is John Aaron Yoder," Daniel said.

"Dr. Braeburn!" Ester's voice cut the air. "Come quickly."

Dr. Braeburn turned and went back into the bedroom, leaving Daniel holding the small child. Daniel's eyes widened with fear. He approached the cracked bedroom door.

"We can stop the bleeding," Dr. Braeburn said. "She's lost a lot of blood, but..."

Daniel turned away and went to the rocker. Sitting, holding John, he closed his eyes.

Please, Heavenly Father. Save my wife. Amen.

He held John close and rocked. He rocked, listening. Time passed.

"Daniel," Dr. Braeburn called. "You may come in and see your wife. Martha is calling for you."

"Is everything okay?" Daniel asked.

Dr. Braeburn nodded. "Martha is fine." He stepped aside to allow Daniel entrance into the bedroom.

Daniel moved to the bed and lay the baby beside Martha.

"This is John Aaron," Daniel said. "Do you like it?"

"A perfect name," Martha whispered.

Daniel leaned down and kissed Martha. "I love you. Our family is complete."

Martha nodded, grabbed Daniel's hand and squeezed it.

# # #

Monday, November 11, 1974 3:35 p.m.

Jason pulled up; Daniel was waiting.

"In a rush to get to work?" Jason asked.

The school doors opened and students came rushing out.

"Wowzer!" Jason said. "Just in time." He pulled the car away from the school.

"Have you heard when Mr. Sullivan will be returning to work?" Daniel asked as they sped toward the mill.

"Mr. Sullivan is back," Jason said. "He was at work this morning when I clocked in." He gazed at Daniel. "He is looking really good."

"Then I do not need to go to the mill," Daniel said.

"Actually, Mr. Sullivan wants to talk to you when you get to the mill," Jason replied.

Daniel frowned. "Am I in trouble?"

"I don't think so, Danny-boy," Jason replied, then paused. "I'm sorry. Daniel."

"It is okay, Jason. I allow you and Ben Hopkins to call me that," Daniel said. "Others? No."

"Thank you," Jason said. "Or, should I say *denki*? (thank you)"

"You remember some Amish?" Daniel asked.

"Just a few words," Jason replied as he pulled into the parking lot of the mill. "Remember, Mr. Sullivan wants to see you."

Daniel nodded and got out of the car to walk toward the main office.

"Good afternoon, Cynthia," Daniel said, coming into the office.

"Ah, Daniel," she said, looking up from her typewriter. "Go on in. Mr. Sullivan will see you."

Bob Sullivan stood and waved at Daniel through the glass.

"You wanted to see me, Mr. Sullivan?" Daniel asked.

"Have a seat. First, I want to thank you for coming back and getting the department back on track." Bob sat. "Second. Would you consider coming back to work? If nothing more than what you are doing currently; after school?"

Daniel leaned back in his chair. "I will need to talk this with my family," Daniel said. "I teach and farm now. If Papa can do without me in the afternoons..."

"I'm not going to tell you what to do, Daniel." Bob picked up a pencil and rolled it between his index fingers and thumbs. "You have been working for me all summer which I thank the Lord for the help. Your family has continued to take care of the farm. Am I not right?"

Daniel sighed. "Yes. Correct."

"Do you think they can continue?" Bob asked, gazing at Daniel with pleading eyes.

Daniel shrugged. "I guess so, but still, I need to ask my wife and family. Can I give you my answer tomorrow?"

"No problem," Bob Sullivan said. "Your department awaits you, my young Yoder."

Daniel stood and left the office for his office out in the mill.

His mind raced with the words and thoughts. *Mr. Sullivan is correct. I have worked all summer here. Does the family need me to help with the farm?"*

He stepped into his office and sat at the desk. *My older children are able to help.* He shrugged. *Martha is still nursing John, but she is able to handle the some of the self-pick area.* He sighed and picked up a pencil. *I can...* He stopped thinking and stared out the window at the men working on different projects. *Exactly what can I do?* he thought and glared at the stack of papers on his desk. *I spend two hours each day after school here. During the summer I work for eight or nine hours here.* He shrugged. *I barely have time to do the chores around my farm, let alone help on the family farm.*

Daniel leaned back in his chair, his fingers rolling the pencil between his thumbs and index fingers, mimicking Bob Sullivan. *May the Lord give me a sign,* he thought.

Martin knocked on the doors frame. "Is there a problem, boss?"

Daniel shrugged. "Mr. Sullivan has asked me to continue to work here as supervisor."

He watched Martin for any indicative reaction.

"That would be great!" Martin yelled. He slumped into the chair facing Daniel. "I am so out of my environment trying to be the boss." He bowed his head momentarily then gazed up at Daniel. "I was about to quit. Since you've come back, I have really enjoyed working here." He paused. "Please stay."

Daniel heaved a heavy sigh. *The sign has been given,* he thought. *I will continue to work here part time.*

CHAPTER THIRTY-THREE ~ Sarah and Bethany

Thursday, May 9, 1965 8:30 a.m.

"Papa?" Sarah called.

"What is it?" Daniel replied. "Not getting nervous, are you?"

Sarah twirled in her beautiful blue dress. "No, Papa. I have waited almost three years for Amos Wagler to ask permission to marry me."

Daniel grinned, remembering Amos Wagler's feeble attempt to be his own *Schteckleimann* (go between). He'd stopped at the mill near the close of the day to ask permission to marry Sarah.

Gazing at his daughter, Daniel remembered back to the day he and Martha were married; the Amish marriage.

"You and Amos will be happy," Daniel said. "You have courted almost three years. You know each other." He took Sarah's hand. "Come," he said. "The time is near and I know the Bishop will want to talk with you and Amos."

Daniel led Sarah down the stairs from her bedroom. He glanced about the room.

No more will I come to tuck her into bed, he thought. *No more nights of reading the Bible together.*

Daniel led her down the stairs and into the main room. His father stood there with Amos.

Noah nodded at Sarah. "Let us go into the bedroom here for a small talk."

Daniel took a deep breath, holding back a tear. He strolled into the kitchen where Martha and the other women hurried about getting the food ready. He walked outside and joined a group of men talking. His brother Luke was among them

Luke slapped Daniel on the back. "My Naomi married last year," Luke whispered. "Do not think of it as losing a daughter, but of gaining another son."

Daniel cast an eye at Luke, shrugged, and nodded approval. He gazed up at the sky; a gorgeous cerulean blue with a few white clouds and a mild spring breeze. He inhaled the scents.

Jason Muirs strolled up to the group. He shook hands with Daniel.

"Never in my life did I ever think of you having a daughter to be married." He grinned. "JD is getting serious, but I'm trying to convince him to wait until he finishes college."

"I am amazed how long Sarah waited," Daniel said. "Considering how young Martha and I were when we married." He smiled. "She really wanted Amos Wagler as a husband."

"I can't believe he waited that long to ask," Jason said. "Didn't he realize another young Amish man could have stepped forward?"

"I knew she was totally enamored with Amos," Daniel said. "There were two others who came forward, asking for her hand, and I told them to wait." He shrugged. "I think it was a wise call."

Jason nodded.

Noah stepped out of the house and onto the front porch. "It is time," he said and led Sarah and Amos to the major group sitting and waiting.

# # #

Monday, June 3, 1985 10:35 a.m.

"Mama?" Bethany called.

Martha looked up from gardening to see her daughter, who gave the plaintive call.

"Can I go and visit Grandma Noble?"

"Why do you want to go visit Grandma Noble?" Martha asked. "You just visited Uncle Paul and Grandma Noble only three weeks ago for a weekend."

"I thought it would be fun. I do not get to see her that often."

"When Grandma Noble comes the next time, I may consider letting you go visit with her for a few days"

Bethany smiled. "I think Grandma is coming today."

Just then a car pulled into the driveway. It was Grandma Noble.

Bethany, along with her other siblings, ran to meet her. Martha stood, watching her mother get out of the passenger side of the car and her father get out of the driver's side. *I wonder why they are here,* she thought.

"School is out," Emma said. "Who wants to come and stay to visit with Grandma?"

Hands went into the air.

"Oh, my goodness," said Emma. "I can't take all of you at the same time." She smiled. "I am going to pick a number between one and twenty. The one who picks the closest to my number will get to come and stay first."

Martha frowned. *I think this might be rigged,* she thought.

Numbers were offered and the winner was Bethany.

Martha nodded her head. *Definitely rigged,* Martha thought.

Emma put an arm around Bethany's shoulder and hugged her close.

"You get to stay one week with Grandma Noble." Emma looked at the other children with their down-trodden faces. "The next one to visit will be Ezra. Then Elizabeth. Then Matthew." She continued to list the children in the order they would come.

Martha strolled over and hugged her mother, leaning in to whisper in her ear. "This was rigged and you know it," she said. "Bethany already asked if she could come to visit, and I said when you came to visit the next time, I would consider it. Suddenly, you appeared. I don't think this is coincidence."

Emma let go and stood back with a false shocked look on her face. "Why, Martha, I would never stoop to such low shenanigans." She grinned. "Bethany called the other day and asked."

Martha nodded.

"Any idea why my daughter wants to stay with you?" Martha asked.

Emma shrugged. "I don't know, but she is twelve years old."

"I only worry that she may start to enjoy the *Englische* lifestyle too much. "

"I will let each child stay with me a day. Then I will send them off to Uncle Paul so they still live their Amish life." She grinned. "I'm not going to let them sit in the living room and watch television all day." She shrugged. "Besides, I've already spoken with Uncle Paul and it was his idea."

Martha nodded approval. "Will you stay and have lunch with us?" Martha asked, glancing about for her father.

Dan Noble was being led to the barn by Ezra.

"Where are you going, Ezra," Martha asked.

"I am showing Grandpa Noble the big farm from behind the barn," Ezra replied. "He has never seen it."

"Come back here and get a meatloaf sandwich," Martha called. "Then Grandpa Noble can drive you over to the u-pick strawberries and see that. You can help Grandpa Yoder weed."

"Grandpa Yoder is right here," Noah said, coming up behind Emma and Martha. "It is good to see you, Emma Noble."

Emma and Martha turned to face Noah.

"It's good to see you, too, Noah," Emma said.

Martha gazed at the older man. He was slightly pale under the tan, sweating, and seemed winded. She frowned.

"Are you okay, Papa Yoder?" Martha asked.

Noah stood a few feet away, rubbing his left arm. "Just getting old, Martha. Not as young as I used to be."

"Come in the house and have some lemonade," Martha insisted. "Rest a bit. My dad can drive you and Ezra back over to the farm when they have finished eating."

Noah waved a hand to put her off. "Nay. I will continue on my way." He nodded toward the house. "You feed your family."

Dan Noble approached. "Good to see you, Noah." He held out a hand to shake.

"Always good to see family," Noah said and shook hands. "I hear Martha has meatloaf sandwiches to eat." Again, he nodded to the house. "Best get fed."

Noah continued on his way toward the edge of the barn and to the fields behind it.

Martha and Emma got the children up the porch steps and into the house. Martha stood watching Noah as he placed a hand on the barn to support him. She frowned and shook her head. *Perhaps Daniel should spend more time helping his father farm than working at the mill.*

# # #

Monday, June 14, 1985 11:30 a.m.

Dan Noble pulled the car into the Yoder driveway. Martha was sitting on the front porch watching John pull weeds from the nearby flower bed.

"I am home," Bethany said as she jumped from the car. "It was a great week. I spent a lot of time with Uncle Paul."

Martha nodded. "Welcome home, Bethany."

Emma Noble stepped from the car and made her way to the front porch. John quit working in the flower bed and headed to talk with Grandpa Noble.

Emma watched Bethany run inside the house. She sat down beside Martha on the swing.

"You wondered why Bethany wanted to stay with me." She grinned. "I know the answer." The grin morphed into a Cheshire cat smile. "Your little girl is growing up."

Martha frowned. "Of course, she is," she replied.

Emma shook her head. "No. What I mean, the reason is a young boy by the name of Jeremiah Graber."

Martha frowned.

"Your Uncle Paul was the one to figure it out," Emma continued. "It was Wednesday evening and there was a prayer service for the youth at his house. Young Jeremiah Graber was in attendance and Bethany kept watching him the whole evening. After the service, the two of them slipped out onto the front porch and sat together on the swing."

"Bethany is only twelve..." Martha said.

"And discovering boys," Emma finished the sentence. "Think back, my dear daughter. How old were you when you had your first crush?"

Martha giggled. "You mean Bobby Miller? I was... I was probably nine or ten." Her eyes widened. "How did Bethany meet this boy?"

"I think it was the last time she visited and was with my brother for one of the youth prayer services."

Martha shrugged. "Long distant romances never last."

Emma absently nodded. "Uh-huh." She paused. "Like you and Daniel?"

"That was different," Martha retorted. "We met in New York during *Rumschpringe*."

Emma shrugged. "Doesn't really matter how the circumstances are. The fact is, Bethany is infatuated with a boy in Shipshewana."

Martha shook her head. "No. This... this cannot work."

"Be careful, Martha," Emma said. "I remember a certain young girl who was headstrong on being Amish. I'm sure her daughter is probably the same." She paused and they slowly swung back and forth on the porch. "Let it run its course." She shrugged. "I'm sure there will a young man to catch her eye in this community."

"My little girl is growing up," Martha whispered. *What will Daniel think?* Martha's mind was a whirlwind of thoughts. *Will he allow her to go back to Shipshewana?*

CHAPTER THIRTY-FOUR ~ Grandpa Yoder

Tuesday, November 5, 1985 2:45 p.m.

Noah threw the harness over his shoulders and urged the team of horses to plow the field. In the distance, his grandson, John, worked another team. The harvest season was done. Noah was adamant the fields needed to be plowed before winter set in. He wanted to make sure the manure was spread so it could steep into the ground during the winter. Good Friday, the perfect day to plant potatoes would be March 28 next year. Not nearly enough time to prep the fields.

Noah felt the pain course down his left arm and the chest feel like somebody was sitting on him. He stumbled, then fell. The team of horses continued another few feet before stopping. He lay in the freshly turned dirt.

Dear God. Please, not now.

He tried to roll over, but the pain didn't allow him to move.

"Grandpa!" John yelled and came running. He glanced about the fields, hoping to see somebody.

Tobias Heffel, his cousin, was in the nearby orchard and heard John yell and saw him on his knees with Noah. He came running toward them.

"Bring the wagon," John ordered. "We need to get him to the doctor."

Tobias ran back to the farm house and got the wagon, harnessing two horses to it while telling Mary and Isaac Wyse what was happening.

"I think Grandpa Yoder has had a heart attack," Tobias said and lashed at the horses to race back to John and Noah.

Isaac Wyse joined the two young men and the three of them lifted Noah onto the wagon.

"The quickest way to the doctor is that way," John said, pointing at his parent's house. "Sorry, Grandpa, but it will be a little bumpy."

Tobias lashed at the horses and headed for Daniel's farm. John knelt on the floor of the wagon and tried to comfort his grandfather.

Martha stood on the porch as the wagon passed.

"We are taking Grandpa to the doctor," John yelled. "I think he had a heart attack."

Martha followed down the driveway and raced to the house across the road. She burst into the kitchen and startled Rebecca.

"They are taking Papa to the doctor," Martha blurted. "Come." She hesitated. "Ester? Please check my children and have Bethany watch them."

Martha headed to the barn and harnessed Beauty to the buckboard. She stopped to allow Rebecca to join her and then they headed toward Dr. Braeburn's office.

# # #

Tuesday, November 5, 1985 3:40 p.m.

Dr. Braeburn stepped into the waiting room.

"I have him resting," he said. "He had a mild heart attack..." He saw the shocked looks on the faces. "But he will survive. Noah is a strong person but he has to realize he is getting older. He is no longer the twenty-something Amish man who can do it all."

Martha comforted Rebecca who cried silently into Martha's shoulder.

"You say my husband will live?" Rebecca asked.

"Yes," Dr. Braeburn replied. "But he has to slow down. For the next three months he is to rest. No intensive work."

"But, what of the fields?" Rebecca asked.

Dr. Braeburn pointed at the young men in the room. "They can do the work. Noah must rest. Period." He shrugged. "Or, he will be put to rest." He shook his head. "I don't think we want that."

Rebecca wiped tears from her eyes. "No. I want my husband."

"I considered sending Noah to DeMotte's hospital, but I think I will keep him here in my office and watch him tonight." He sighed. "All of you can go home." He gazed at Rebecca. "If you wish, you can go in and see him. He's probably asleep, but..."

Martha helped Rebecca to her feet and supported her as they walked into the back of the office. Noah stretched out on the bed, appearing comfortable and at ease.

Rebecca frowned. "Is he alive?"

"Yes," Dr. Braeburn replied. "I gave him a sedative to relax him and ease the tension on his heart. He's sleeping."

Noah moaned and turned ever so slightly.

Rebecca went to him and stroked his forehead. "Sleep well, my dear," she whispered. "I will return tomorrow."

Martha looked at the clock on the wall of the waiting room as they returned to it.

"I want to let Daniel know," she said. "He should be at the mill now."

# # #

Tuesday, November 5 4:00 p.m.

Martha strode into the main office. "I need to see Daniel," she said.

"Good afternoon, Martha," Cynthia said. "If you wish, I can go get him."

Martha continued toward the hallway. "No need. I know where his office is located."

"But..." Cynthia attempted to intervene.

Martha turned the corner and stepped into the mill, spotting Daniel's office. She trudged her way toward his office.

"Daniel," Martha said as she stepped into his office. "Your father is at Dr. Braeburn's office. He had a heart attack." She paused and took a deep breath. "You need to quit this job and work at the farm."

228

"Noah had a heart attack?" Bob Sullivan asked behind Martha as he stood in the doorway.

"Yes, Mr. Sullivan," Martha replied. "You, of all people, should understand. I think Daniel needs to consider working the farm now. His father… his father, per Dr. Braeburn's orders will be on bed rest for the next three months. He is to do no, absolutely no strenuous work."

"Is Papa okay?" Daniel asked.

"He is resting," Martha said. "I need to take your mother home and get things around for you and the children to eat. In fact, I think I am going to have your mother stay with us tonight."

"Do you really think Noah's heart attack means Daniel must quit working here at the mill?" Bob Sullivan leaned against the door jam.

"Business is one thing, Mr. Sullivan," Martha said. "Family is another."

"Martha," Daniel called. "Your *Englische* is showing, again. You take Mama home and let Mr. Sullivan and I discuss what to do."

Martha grimaced. "As you wish." She turned and stormed from the office.

Bob Sullivan sat in the chair opposite Daniel's desk. "And?"

Daniel leaned over his desk. *Time to be a man*, he thought. "My wife is right, Mr. Sullivan," Daniel started. "I have questioned many times my working here and not helping at the farm. Now, with my father incapacitated; my presence at the farm is more important." He shrugged. "I will be quitting at the end of the week."

"Who will be in charge? Who will manage this department?"

"I have been showing Martin how I do things. I think he will be better at the job this time than last." Daniel shrugged. "If not, I suggest you hire another person. My brother, Jacob, is a good worker, but he is not a manager. Benjamin Heffel still continues to be a free agent, wanting to work on his projects. Frank Hughes? Perhaps if Martin does not work, you may consider him."

Bob Sullivan stood and cocked a questioning eye at Daniel. "I can't talk you out of this?"

Daniel shook his head. "No. I am done."

CHAPTER THIRTY-FIVE ~ New Year; New Surprises

Monday, January 20, 1986 10:30 a.m.

Noah sat at the kitchen table with the different seed and garden catalogs spread before him.

"Rebecca," Noah called. "I see here in this catalog they have thornless raspberries and blackberries." He paused. "They are costly. Do you think we should consider them?"

Rebecca stood at the sink scrubbing carrots. "They might be a good choice, Noah," she said. "Especially if you wish to have them as part of the u-pick operation." She gazed at her arms, remembering all the small scratches from picking the berries each summer.

"I will place an order with Aaron Shaw for many of the seeds we want."

Noah flipped a page and stared at the various carrots. He sighed. Another page and he surveyed the myriad of sweetcorn available. Noah glanced out the window toward the distant greenhouse.

Do we need to enlarge it? he thought. His mind wandered to the large greenhouse at the big farm behind Mary's house, the old Richard Jones home. He nodded absently as he considered the other greenhouses of the family: Luke and Hannah. He shook his head. *No need to enlarge*, he thought.

Noah flipped a few more pages and slowly run his finger down the list of potatoes.

"Planting potatoes isn't that far off," Noah said. "I will make sure to tell Aaron which potatoes we want to plant."

Rebecca nodded, all the while wondering exactly how much Noah planned to do this year. *I hope he allows the family to do the farming*, she thought.

Noah picked up the pencil and began to calculate how much seed potato he would need for the year. His fingers locked as the jolt of pain ran down the left arm. He gasped.

Rebecca turned at the sound, watching him.

Noah feebly smiled and shook his head. "It is nothing," he said while trying not to rub his arm.

She lifted the carrot and pointed it at him. "You had best plan to include the family in this year's farming." She shook the carrot. "Daniel quit his job at the mill to be available to help when school is not in session." She glared at Noah. "Do you understand?"

"Hush, Rebecca," Noah whispered. "I know my limits."

Rebecca blinked then turned back to the sink. "Uh-huh."

Noah continued to work on his list of needs for the new year of farming.

I hope Aaron can get all this, Noah thought.

# # #

Thursday, May 16, 1986 9 a.m.

Noah stood in the potato field, analyzing the crooked rows the grandchildren had planted. He shook his head.

I can take the walking plow and one of the work horses and try to cut between the rows, he thought.

Luke came up behind him. "What are you thinking, Papa?"

Noah grinned. "I am thinking my grandchildren need to learn how a straight row is made."

Luke gazed at the rows. "Probably not as straight as you would have planted," Luke said. "Still, they did it, the plants are growing, and we should have a good harvest."

Noah shook his head. "It will be difficult plowing between them."

"I can do it," Luke said. "I'll hitch up Duke to the walking plow."

Noah nodded. *Luke will make a good farmer*, he thought. *He thinks like me.*

He continued to stand in the field, waiting for Luke to return. He gazed back at the barn; there was no sign of Luke. Noah started to stroll back to the barn to see why there was a delay. Turning the corner of the barn, he noticed Mary hanging the laundry. He stepped inside the barn. The horse, Duke, was still in his stall. Noah frowned.

"Where is Luke?" Noah asked of Mary.

"He had to leave," Mary replied. "Naomi was delivering his first grandchild."

Noah nodded and turned back to the inside of the barn. He hitched Duke to the walking plow. He led the horse out to the field. Mary frowned but continued to hang her freshly cleaned laundry.

Noah pressed the plow into the ground and followed Duke as the horse worked its way between the newly sprouted potato plants.

Noah eased up on the plow and Duke halted. Noah gazed at the field, a little over half plowed. He removed his hat and wiped the sweat from his brow and inhaled deeply. He felt the catch in his chest and immediately brought his hand up to it. The pain subsided, but Noah felt weak. He leaned against the handles of the plow, hoping they would support him as his legs weakened. He slumped, still holding onto the handles, he tried to remain upright.

The catch in his chest exploded and sheer pain wracked his upper body. Noah inhaled then collapsed onto the ground. He lay there.

# # #

Luke, still excited at becoming a grandfather; a grandson, no less, gazed out at the potato field. He saw Duke standing with the walking plow attached. He couldn't see his father. Luke ran to the horse. As he approached, he noticed the straw hat flopping in the breeze. He saw his father.

"Papa!" he yelled and raced even faster.

Luke fell to his knees and grabbed his father up from the ground, holding him close. There was no breathing. Luke hugged Noah as he rocked back and forth, crying.

"Why?" Luke cried out to the sky.

# # #

Sunday, May 18, 1986 9 a.m.

232

Deacon Jacob Metz stood before the congregation.

"With the death of Bishop Yoder, we need to pick a new bishop."

He held five copies of the *Ausbund* and placed them on the table. "I now call on those in the lot to come forward." He paused before calling the names aloud. "Ezekiel Troyer. Rueben Metz. Daniel Yoder. Amos Schmucker. And Isaac Holtz."

Daniel was surprised his name was in the list, but it was his duty.

Each man stepped forward and stood before the table holding the *Ausbunds* with a string wrapped around each one. One of the books contained a slip of paper on which the words of Acts 1:24 had been written:

And they prayed, and said, Thou, Lord, which knowest the hearts of all men, show whether of these five thou has chosen.

In order of age, each man stepped forward to choose a hymn book, then stepped back to sit on the bench, and wait.

Deacon Metz stepped before Ezekiel Troyer and untied the string. He searched the hymn book for slip of paper. He found none.

Next, he moved to Amos Schmucker, repeating the procedure. Again, finding nothing.

He stepped before Daniel and removed the string. Daniel held his breath. He was a teacher, he would accept Bishop if it befell him, but he preferred it to pass. Suddenly he no longer felt he was the Daniel of the lion's den, but Jesus in the Garden of Gethsemane praying for the burden to pass. Jacob Metz riffled the *Ausbund*, but no slip fell out. Daniel sighed relief.

Deacon Metz moved to Rueben Metz who was three days younger than Daniel. He untied the string and opened the *Ausbund* and found nothing.

The four men looked to Isaac Holtz who was the youngest of them; almost a year younger than Daniel. Isaac offered the *Ausbund* to Deacon Jacob Metz and waited, knowing the slip of paper was in his book.

Deacon Metz paged through the book and found nothing. He frowned. The four men straightened on the bench. One of them still held the slip of paper. Who?

Jacob worked his way back to the beginning and again searched Ezekiel Troyer's book. He was careful, moving the pages to see if the slip of paper was caught. The slip flitted down from the book as he held it by the front and back, allowing the pages to move back and forth in the air.

Ezekiel's eyes widened.

"We have our new bishop," Deacon Metz said.

# # #

Monday, May 19, 1986 9:30 a.m.

Buggies pulled into the Yoder farm. The twins, Joshua and Jonah tied off the horses and moved the buggies to the side. Noah had been the bishop, the full community and several *Englische* were in attendance for the funeral. The twins took turns parking the cars off to the side of the driveway.

Noah's children greeted those attending and spoke with them. Saturday and Sunday had been spent getting the farm ready for the funeral. The barn had been cleaned and benches were arranged for everyone to see the coffin in the center. Extra benches were just outside the double doors to allow more seating.

Bishop Troyer stood in the shadows of the house's side, going over his notes. Being an elder was one thing, being the bishop was another. Minister Amos Schmucker approached Daniel.

"I know this is a strange request, but your father told me he wanted you to sing a song a Miss Br... Bran..."

"Miss Bronson," Daniel corrected.

"Yes, Miss Bronson. He wanted you to sing that song she taught you. He said it was peaceful."

Daniel shrugged. "If that is his wish."

Minister Schmucker walked away, leaving Daniel to wonder when he would sing.

Noah's plain pine casket lay in the center of the barn and the people passed by to give their last respects. Rebecca sat closest to the casket, continuing a circle around the casket by the immediate children: Ruth, Luke, Rachel, Daniel, Hannah, Mary, Jacob, Anna, Joshua, Jonah, and Ester. Respective spouses and their children sat behind.

The service began with Minister Amos Schmucker beginning a short sermon. When finished, he turned to Daniel.

"It was requested Bishop Yoder's son sing a song." He nodded.

Daniel stood and as he had been taught, placed his feet slightly apart, hands together, and sang *Where're You Walk*.

Bishop Troyer moved forward to begin the long sermon that would last perhaps an hour.

"Beautiful, Daniel," Bishop Troyer said. "I know Noah enjoyed listening." He walked up to the coffin, looked in, and then closed the lid. "We say goodbye to Bishop Noah Yoder." He turned to the congregation and continued his sermon.

"In closing," Bishop Troyer said. "We will sing *O Gott Vader*."

When the song finished, the pallbearers picked up the casket and headed for the family cemetery. Rebecca followed with the children in age sequence behind her.

Daniel gazed back at the house in the distance. He saw people beginning to re-arrange the benches and add tables. The meal would be ready when they returned.

The group stopped and Noah was lowered into the ground. Bishop Troyer said a prayer.

Daniel fought to hold back the tears. He'd seen death before; this wasn't the first time. For his children, they were doing their best to control their emotions; to be strong for Grandma Yoder, as they had been told.

CHAPTER THIRTY-SIX ~ Summer of 90

Saturday, June 2, 1990 11:20 a.m.

The car pulled into the driveway and Bethany ran out to meet it.

"Grandma Noble," she cried and hugged the woman as she got out of the car.

"Have you asked your mother?" she whispered.

Bethany shook her head. "Nay. I waited until you come."

Emma Noble rolled her eyes. "Putting me in the middle, yet again. Right?"

Bethany shrugged.

Dan Noble stepped out of the car. "Is she ready to go?"

Emma shook her head. "No, Dan. I need to go talk with Martha."

Dan slammed a hand on the car door. "I thought this was all arranged."

"Be patient," Emma said and walked with Bethany up the steps and into the house.

"Mama?" Bethany called.

"In the kitchen," Martha replied, turned and saw her mother. "Mother!" she exclaimed. "I did not know you were coming."

Emma glared at Bethany. "You were supposed to know, but somehow things have gotten twisted."

"Twisted?" Martha echoed.

"Yes. Bethany wishes to spend the summer in Shipshewana. A few days with me, most of the time with your Uncle Paul."

Martha glanced at Bethany. "Is this true?"

"Yes, Mama," Bethany replied. "Grandma Noble says I can get a job at E & S Market."

"Oh, you can, can you?" Martha asked, turning to face her mother. "And how and when was this decided?"

"That's the tricky part," Emma said with a chuckle and leaned against the wall. "Uh, we spoke of this when Bethany last visited and she went to E & S to see if they would hire her." Emma shrugged. "They will."

Martha stared at Bethany. "When were you planning to ask your mother and father?"

Bethany bowed her head to hide her eyes. "Uh, now."

"Absolutely not," Martha said. "You should have asked Papa last night."

"I am almost eighteen," Bethany started.

"No, you are seventeen as of two months ago," Martha countered.

"I can go on *Rumschpringe* and I do not need your approval."

"Bethany!" Emma exclaimed.

"Grandma, I want to go to Shipshewana. That is where... where..."

Martha narrowed her eyes. "Jeremiah Graber?"

"Yes," Bethany whispered. "I am giving him this summer to decide if he wishes to marry me. If not, I come home."

Martha's eyes widened. "If not, you will come home? What if he wants to marry?"

"I will come home and we will be married here and..." She shrugged. "I guess I will move to Shipshewana."

"What of your job at the farm? The u-pick operation? Who will do it in your absence?"

"I have many cousins, Mama," Bethany said. "Any of them would welcome the job so they do not have to work in the fields."

"Bethany!" Martha chastised. "You are to work in the field when not busy."

Bethany shrugged. "I am always busy so I cannot spend time weeding. I cannot look for weeds and keep an eye on the customers and cash register."

"So, you are going on *Rumschpringe,* is that correct?"

"Yes, Mama," Bethany replied.

Emma clapped her hands and leaned forward. "Now that everything is settled." She motioned toward the front door. "Can we go?" She looked at Martha. "Your father is out in the car waiting."

"Daddy is here?" Martha said. "Have him come in. We can eat lunch and…" She gazed at Bethany. "Then the three of you can leave."

"Sounds good to me," Emma replied and stepped to the door to motion Dan into the house.

"What?" he asked, coming in the door.

"We will eat lunch," Martha said. "I will visit with my parents and then the three of you will head back to Shipshewana."

"A tall glass of lemonade sounds good," Dan said and sat on a bench at the kitchen table. "Sandwiches?"

"I can fry up some bologna, give you cold meatloaf, or, if you wish, make a hamburger."

Dan shrugged. "Me? Just a plain bologna sandwich, no frying necessary."

Emma nodded. "Yes, that sounds good."

Bethany shrugged. "Yes."

Martha turned to the counter and made four sandwiches. *Bethany is leaving for Shipshewana,* she thought. *Daniel will not be happy.*

Friday, June 8th, 1990 6:15 p.m.

A strange car pulled into the driveway. Daniel was coming out of the barn when he noticed the car. It had an Indiana license. A young boy stepped out of the passenger side of the car. He was Amish.

The young man noticed Daniel standing near the barn entrance. He waved.

"Mr. Daniel Yoder?" he asked.

Daniel nodded. "Aye."

"My name is Jeremiah Graber." He stuck out his hand to shake. "I wish to talk with you privately, if I may."

Daniel nodded to the young man. "Let us go inside and discuss this."

Daniel opened the front door of the house, allowing Jeremiah to enter first.

"To the left, Mr. Graber," Daniel said and turned to notice Martha in the kitchen.

"Would you like to join us?" Daniel asked of Martha "This is Jeremiah Graber from Shipshewana."

Martha dropped the knife into the sink that she was using to peel the beets. She rinsed her hands, and wiped them on her apron then entered the main room. She appraised Jeremiah as she entered the room and sat on the settee near the window.

"Mr. Graber has come to discuss something important.

Martha stiffened. She recognized the name and knew immediately why Jeremiah Graber had come.

Jeremiah sat in the chair next to Daniel's rocker. "I have come to ask for Bethany's hand in marriage."

Daniel nodded. "Since I don't know you, may I ask what you do for a living?" Martha asked.

"I am a carpenter by trade. I work at the wood mill in Shipshewana. I also have a small farm across the road from my parent's home. It is similar to how Bethany explained your home." He shrugged. "I have not built a house; I still live with my parents. I will allow my wife to decide how the house will be."

"May I call you Jeremiah, Mr. Graber?" Daniel asked.

"Please," Jeremiah said. "I would prefer that. Mr. Graber is so formal."

"I'm therefore going to assume," Daniel said. "That you and Bethany will reside in Shipshewana." He paused. "At your farm?"

"Yes, sir," Jeremiah replied then glanced at Martha to see her reaction.

He shrugged. "If Bethany wishes to live here, I am sure I can find land to buy and I know there is a wood mill."

Daniel grinned. "I am quite familiar with the wood mill in Centertown. I worked there for several years."

Jeremiah's eyes widened. "You are the Daniel Yoder who carved at the mill?"

Daniel nodded.

"Customers came to our mill to buy the gnomes, horses, and other things you carved." He swelled with pride. "May I shake your hand? You are a legend at the Shipshewana mill." He grinned. "Mr. Beiler has often considered coming to Centertown and attempt to lure you away."

Daniel smiled, but decided not to let the topic change to about him. "So, you want my permission to marry my daughter. Is that correct?"

Jeremiah nodded.

"Do you love her?" Daniel asked.

"Very much so, Mr. Yoder," Jeremiah replied.

"How many years have you been seeing our daughter?" Martha asked.

Jeremiah blushed. "Several years. Only the last few years have she and I shared the sings together." He sat straight up in the chair. "Bethany is a wonderful young girl who makes me better by just being around her."

"May I ask how old you are?" Martha asked.

"I will be eighteen in August, Mrs. Yoder," Jeremiah replied. "I went on *Rumschpringe* last year for two months." He shrugged. "I did not enjoy it. I am Amish. I am now baptized."

Daniel nodded. *Bethany is very much like her mother,* he thought. *This young man is much like me.* He paused in his thoughts. I wonder if he sings. Daniel grinned.

Jeremiah frowned, unsure why Daniel was grinning.

"Do you sing, Jeremiah?" Daniel asked.

The young man studied Daniel unsure of the question.

"I am the teacher for the community," Daniel said. "I have been teaching the children to sing harmony."

"Yes," Jeremiah said. "I sing. Bethany has told me how you went to high school and sang in competition in Columbus and also went to New York City."

"Would you like to stay for the evening meal?" Martha asked.

"I really should be headed back to Shipshewana." Jeremiah sighed. "It is a long trip and my driver has been sitting the car, waiting."

Daniel gazed at Martha who nodded.

"You have our blessing, Jeremiah Graber. If Bethany has chosen you, then a marriage is soon to be." He paused. "This fall? Here?"

Jeremiah nodded. "A wedding here? Definitely. I will see Bethany tomorrow for the sing. I will ask her then."

Daniel and Martha nodded, stood, and saw Jeremiah to the door.

# # #

Wednesday, August 29, 1990 8:25 p.m.

Daniel sat at the kitchen table, once more going over the seating charts he'd made for the new school year.

Only sixty-one students this year, he thought and smiled. *Elizabeth Troyer has matured and is a great teacher. Elisabeth Wyse is now Ruby Mueller; a strong hand when needed.* He leaned back in his chair and shook his head. *Never did I think one of my children would want to be a teacher.* The image of Sarah, his eldest child, filled his mind.

The front door opened, startling Daniel from his reverie.

"Papa? Mama?" Bethany called.

"What is the problem?" Daniel asked, moving from the kitchen table to the front room.

Daniel watched through the open front door at the car sitting in the driveway. It looked familiar.

"Why are you home?" Daniel asked. There was concern in his voice.

Martha sauntered into the room from the bedroom.

"Bethany?" Martha was surprised to see her.

"My wedding is in two months. I need to get ready."

Martha patted her chest. "I thought the wedding was off." She sighed relief, then nodded. "We can prepare."

"Grandma Noble is sitting in the car," Bethany said.

Martha lurched for the doorway and motioned for her mother to come into the house.

Emma Noble moved the car to the side of the driveway and then walked into the house.

"Why did you not come in with Bethany?"

Emma shrugged. "To be honest, I really don't know."

Daniel hugged Bethany and then returned to the kitchen, allowing the three women to talk in the main room.

# # #

Thursday, August 30   10:15 a.m.

"I do wish we could get the material where we bought your wedding dress," Emma said as she drove the big "S" curve outside of Hayton on their way to DeMotte.

Martha sighed. "Yes, the Charles Store closed several years ago." She gazed out the window. "We just have the two so-called super stores. The fabric is limited."

Hannah leaned forward from the backseat. "If we need, we can always go to Fort Wayne. I am sure they have some fabric stores there."

"Why Hannah," Martha said. "That is almost an hour's drive away. I think not."

Hannah shrugged and gazed at Bethany beside her. "Better than settling for whatever."

Bethany nodded. "I want my dress to be special. I was thinking light blue."

# # #

Thursday, August 30   1 p.m.

Emma stomped to the car, shaking the keyring in her hand. "I can't believe that with these two so-called super stores, they don't have the fabric needed for the wedding."

"We need to rethink things," Martha soothed.

"No! We're going to Fort Wayne." Emma unlocked the doors of the car. "Everyone get in." As she bent to get in the car, Emma noticed the fast-food chain. "But, first, we'll get something to eat. Everyone want a hamburger, fries, and a shake?"

Martha shrugged. "I guess it is okay."

"Sounds good," Hannah and Bethany responded in unison.

# # #

Thursday, August 30 6:30 p.m.

Daniel gazed out the window as the car pulled into the driveway. He walked to the door.

Martha got out of the car and hustled toward the porch and began up the steps.

"I did not know we would be gone so long, Daniel," Martha said. "I am sorry."

Daniel smiled and shrugged. "I did my chores and worked on the student seating chart. There was meatloaf so John and I had a sandwich."

"Do you want me to fix you something to eat?"

"Nay," Daniel replied, hugging Bethany as she stepped up to the door.

"I'm sorry, Daniel," Emma said. "We went to DeMotte and they didn't have any fabric suitable for Bethany's wedding." She heaved a sigh. "We went to Fort Wayne." She lifted the bags of fabric. "Your daughter will be beautiful on her wedding day." She grinned and elbowed Daniel in the ribs. "Jeremiah is one lucky man."

Daniel nodded, stepped aside, and the four women walked into the house.

"I had best get home," Hannah said. "I am sure John is wondering where I am."

"I'll drive you," Emma said and headed for the door.

"I will be back tomorrow and size everyone to make the dresses." Hannah followed Emma out the door.

CHAPTER THIRTY-SEVEN ~ Bethany Wedding

Wednesday, October 10, 1990 11:20 a.m.

Bethany slipped on the dark blue dress. *I thought I wanted light blue,* Bethany thought. *But this darker shade is prettier.* She brushed her hands down her sides and front to remove any wrinkles and tugs.

Elizabeth, her older sister, strolled into the bedroom.

"You are so pretty," Elizabeth said and did a small pirouette to show off her light blue dress. "As one of your *newehockers* (bridesmaid), do you approve?"

"You look very pretty, too," Bethany replied. She giggled. "As the *Englische* say, you do not want to show up the bride."

The two giggled.

"Are you coming down?" Hannah yelled up the stairwell. "Or, do I come up there?"

"We are coming, Aunt Hannah," Bethany replied and pushed Elizabeth toward the door.

The two girls raced down the staircase and into the main room where Hannah waited with a discerning eye. Martha and Rebecca sat on the settee and Emma sat in a chair near the front door.

"Perfect," Martha whispered.

Rebecca and Emma nodded in agreement.

Bethany spun in a circle. "Tomorrow will be a perfect day."

All the ladies in the room nodded in agreement.

Hannah was silent as she scrutinized her work. She reached over and plucked at the fabric of Bethany's dress.

She nodded. "Perfect."

# # #

Thursday, October 11, 1990 8:30 a.m.

Bishop Ezekiel Troyer walked up the steps to Daniel's house. With him he had Jeremiah Graber.

"I wish to speak with the betrothed before the wedding," he said.

Daniel nodded and opened the door to allow the two men into the house. He turned to watch his youngest two sons, Matthew and John, direct the horses and buggies as they arrived. He noticed the bright yellow, sporty BMW Z1 come down the dusty road. Daniel shook his head.

Jason and his hot yellow cars, he thought.

He saw Patty was with him as they pulled into the driveway. Daniel smiled as he watched John's eyes widen with the prospect of driving the vehicle. Jason pulled up beside John.

"Where do you want me to park this?" Jason asked.

"I can park it for you, Mr. Muirs," John offered.

Jason surveyed the area, nodded, and stepped from the car.

"You take care of this. You hear?" Jason asked.

John nodded as he jumped into the driver's seat. Matthew held the door open for Patty then jumped into the passenger seat.

"You park it," Matthew said. "I will bring it back to Mr. Muir."

John nodded.

Jason helped Patty up the stairs to Daniel.

"Martha is inside," Daniel said and opened the door for Patty.

Jason gazed up at the gray sky. "Well, Danny-boy, not a clear day," he mumbled. "I hope the boys put the top up on the car."

Daniel cringed ever so slightly at the Danny-boy, but let it go and nodded, watching in the distance as the convertible top of the BMW lifted into the air to enclose the car. "They are."

A gust of wind whipped around the porch.

"Not a good day at all," Daniel said and searched the sky. "Perhaps it will hold off until after the wedding."

Jason nodded. "Here comes the rest of your family."

Daniel watched as Ezra, Joshua, and Joseph approached. Three women and a cluster of children followed with baskets of food. Just then a scent from the house's kitchen assailed Daniel.

245

Fried chicken, he thought. *My favorite.*

Bishop Troyer appeared with Bethany and Jeremiah. "It is time."

Bethany was adamant she wanted an outdoor wedding, so all the benches were set up between the house and barn. The barn had been set up with tables and benches for later.

Once more, the wind blew. Daniel looked off into the distance where the dark clouds rolled and churned in the distance to the north.

DeMotte is going to have a bad storm, he thought as he and his sons took seats on benches. Jason had joined the other *Englische* to watch the ceremony. He regarded the sky, shaking his head. He leaned in and whispered to Patty. "Be ready when the storm hits; go for the barn."

Patty nodded and glanced at the distance to the barn.

Once more the wind gusted and the trees in the yard swayed in the wind, dropping branches and leaves.

Daniel again looked to the north where DeMotte was engulfed in black clouds. He watched a distant cloud swirl and twirl and create a funnel, screwing toward the ground. Rain started to fall.

The *Englische* made a dash for the barn. The Amish, sitting on the benches, flipped umbrellas up and like black mushrooms caps, opened up so those below kept dry.

Bishop Troyer held tightly onto his papers and book with one hand while trying to keep the umbrella secure in his other hand. The wind kept whipping it up, trying to invert the black umbrella.

He quickly ended his sermon and the congregation sung two songs. Another minister spoke, making it a short sermon, and another song was sung.

Daniel stood. With the storm's winds nearly knocking him down, he sang the song Bethany had requested. The words of *Where're You Walk* filled the area. Even Jason who stood at the barn's door heard Daniel's voice over the wind.

Bishop Troyer quickly finished the final steps, and Bethany Yoder and Jeremiah Graber were married; husband and wife.

People quickly moved in different directions, with most heading for the barn, and several women heading to the house and kitchen where food was being prepared for the meal.

Daniel surveyed the sky as Jason ambled up beside him.

"What you looking for?" Jason asked.

"Another funnel," Daniel said. "I saw one between here and DeMotte earlier." He pointed. "There."

A swirling funnel was curling down from a low cloud.

"Everyone!" Daniel yelled. "Into the barn and stand in the corner or near a large support for protection."

He rushed into the house. "There is a tornado headed our way. Quick! Down to the basement."

Daniel opened the basement door and allowed the women to scurry down the steps to protection.

Bethany came running into the house.

"This is my wedding day," she cried. "It is not supposed to be raining."

Jeremiah was behind her.

Daniel waved the two of them to basement and he followed them down as the sound of a locomotive filled the room.

Daniel felt the basement stairs tremble and heard the rushing winds tear through the house. He shook his head, fearing the loss of their home, and he feared for those in the barn.

Suddenly, it was quiet with only the pitter-patter of light rain. Daniel cautiously walked up the steps and opened the basement door. The house, or at least the kitchen, still stood. He gazed out the window, the barn still stood, but the field to the south, on the other side of the ravine was devastated. He estimated the path of destruction to be close to fifty feet wide and maybe two hundred feet long. He opened the front door of the house and looked down the driveway and the road. His parent's home was gone; only shredded walls showed where the house had stood. The barn his father had built still stood; as did the *Dawdi* house and chicken coop.

The hand of the Lord has passed through the land and we were spared, Daniel thought.

# # #

Friday, October 12, 1990 10 a.m.

Daniel and Martha, with Bethany and Jeremiah, rode into town in the buggy with Beauty taking her trotting time.

Trees were down and a few buildings had a little damage. The mill was not touched, nor the school. The roof to the front porch of AJ Grocery was ripped away.

Emma and Dan Noble caught up with them in the car.

"Get in the car," Emma said. "We'll go into DeMotte and see what damage was done there."

Jeremiah nodded to Daniel. "I will take Bethany back home. You go with them."

Daniel and Martha got in the backseat of the car and gazed out the window at the wind's destructive paths. One house was destroyed, the one next to it left alone. It made no sense.

Dan Noble drove into the center of town. The destruction around the courthouse was unrealistic. The clock on the south face of the tower was missing, impaled in the curled-up furniture sign on the southeast side of the main drag. The trees that shaded so much of the courthouse square were broken and shredded. Only one tree remained of perhaps ten trees. One tree had fallen, destroying the small police tower where one paid their parking tickets.

Martha shook her head. "It looks like some little kid put their hands together with a hole in the middle and smashed down over the courthouse. Everything is destroyed."

"The town will rebuild," Dan Noble said. "Insurance will cover most of it."

"We will see how much damage was done to the Amish community, and if not much, we can help rebuild Centertown. If they want our help, we can help rebuild DeMotte, too."

Dan Noble shook his head. "Build your community first, Daniel. Then, consider Centertown. DeMotte? Let them do their own thing. I don't think they'll want Amish help."

Daniel shrugged. *Maybe my father-in-law is right.*

\# \# \#

As the Noble car pulled into Daniel's driveway, he noticed his mother going through the destruction of her house, searching for things not ruined.

"I will go tell Mama she can stay with us as long as she wishes," Daniel whispered to Martha.

She nodded then caught up with her parents on the steps to the house.

"When do you plan to go home?" Martha asked.

Emma shrugged. "Bethany and Jeremiah must visit for the next few days, we could go home tonight and come back next week... or we could stay?"

Martha smiled. "Mom. Dad. You are welcome to stay here as long as you wish. All the kids, except for John, have moved out. We have plenty of room."

"That's easy," Dan quipped. "We'll stay."

Martha smiled. "That was easy."

CHAPTER THIRTY-EIGHT ~ Shipshewana

Sunday, October 21, 1990 6 p.m.

Bethany and Jeremiah sat in the backseat of the Noble car, holding hands in the darkness as the vehicle raced toward its goal of Shipshewana.

"Once we get near, you will need to give me the directions to your parent's home," Dan Noble said.

"Very easy, Mr. Noble. Stay on Route 20; turn north on N 675 W..." Jeremiah said. "Go a mile and a..."

"The Graber house," Dan blurted. "I know it."

Emma giggled. "You should. It is literally around the corner from where my parents lived."

"In that case, we should be there in about fifteen to twenty minutes." Dan smiled in the light of the on-coming car.

Dan slowed the car. "It may take a little longer." He pointed at the red blinking lights of the horse-drawn buggy before them.

It moved to the side and Dan moved around the buggy. Four young Amish, two young men and two young ladies waved as they passed.

Jeremiah grinned. "They coming home from a sing." He gazed at Bethany. "We will not be doing that anymore." He sighed. "They were fun."

Bethany patted Jeremiah's hand. "We are married."

"Tomorrow I will go take care of my animals at my farm. You can come along to see where you want to build our home. Then I will go to work at the mill."

"I already know what I want our house to look like."

Another car passed with its headlights illuminating the Noble car.

Bethany saw Jeremiah's frown.

"I see a five bedroom, two story with a porch that goes from the front of the house and down the side to the kitchen door."

"Only five bedrooms?" Jeremiah asked.

Bethany blushed in the darkness. "More can be added if needed."

"Never in my mind did I ever envision having eleven grandchildren." Dan shook his head in the low light of the car's dashboard lighting. "Eight from Martha, and three from Bethan." He frowned in the darkness. "I don't think Alexander has any children, or at least, none that he is claiming." He shook his head in the dim light of the dashboard. "And, at my age, never once did I think I would have seven great-grandchildren."

"I wish to have a large family, Grandpa Dan," Bethany whispered. "Maybe ten."

Jeremiah squeezed Bethany's hand. "That is a nice number."

Dan turned onto the county road and headed north. He quickly pulled into the Graber farm.

"This is home," Jeremiah said. "At least, for the next few weeks until we can get our home built."

# # #

Saturday, November 3, 1990 8 a.m.

Jeremiah watched as the men of the Amish community gathered at his farm. The women and younger children had taken buggies and continued on to his parent's farm across the road. The mill had delivered some lumber; the remainder had been made by the Amish pallet business, using trees from his property. Doors, windows, and roofing were stored inside the barn.

He gazed at the big hole where the foundation of the basement stood.

It will be a beautiful house, Jeremiah thought. *Bethany has considered many things when she drew the plans of the house.*

Elijah Hochstetler ambled up to Jeremiah. *"gut'n mariye,* (good morning) young Jeremiah Graber." He smiled. "I see you, too, have chosen a bride from Centertown."

Jeremiah nodded, remembering Elijah's wife, Ruby, was also from Centertown. He smiled, considering how the circle of life and the family was all tied together. *I married Daniel's daughter and Ruby was Daniel's assistant teacher,* he thought.

"Here comes my brother, Bishop Amos Hochstetler." He slapped Jeremiah on the shoulder. "You will have a house by the end of the day."

Bishop Hochstetler gathered the men together. "Let us pray."

The group of men bowed their heads and Bishop Hochstetler thanked the Lord for a clear day and blessed the hands building the structure and praying for safety.

A cold November wind whipped the coats of the men as they broke into groups to begin to work.

Jeremiah gazed up at the bleak sky of grays. *At least it is not snowing,* he thought. *Not yet.* He bowed his head.

Please dear Lord. I ask You give us this day for the building of my home. Stay the snow. But it be Your will, not mine. Amen.

# # #

The first floor was almost totally finished when the parade of buggies carrying the women, children, and food came into the driveway.

Bethany smiled at Jeremiah as she road with his mother and two sisters. She jumped from the slow-moving buggy and joined him on the skeletal porch frame.

"Come inside," Jeremiah said and led her into the house.

Bethany gazed at the main room. "I did not realize it would be this large," she said.

"You wanted sixteen by twenty-four," Jeremiah said with a sly grin. "If we have the number of children you wish; the room will be just the right size."

Bethany nodded, noting the roughed-in stairwell leading to the unfinished upstairs.

"One bedroom down, four upstairs. Right?" she asked.

Jeremiah nodded. "Correct." He led her through an opening. "This is the kitchen." He pointed at the wall. "The men are already starting to build the cabinets."

Bethany nodded, noting the doorway to the basement.

"Almost like my parent's home," she said. "Just a tad larger and with a wrap-around porch for the children to play on when the weather is wet, or the ground muddy."

He hugged her. "Always thinking."

"There will be more than enough laundry to do," Bethany said. "No reason to add with children getting muddy."

"Tonight, we will have a house. Tomorrow, after church, we will begin to build our home," Jeremiah whispered into Bethany's ear.

"I will ask Grandma and Grandpa Noble if they will take me home this week and bring back our belongings from the wedding." Bethany gazed at the window by the front door. "The settee my father made will look nice there." She pointed to the left of the main door.

Jeremiah hugged Bethany as they stood in the middle of the room. "I love you."

# # #

Thursday, August 8, 1991 6:15 p.m.

Daniel came in from working on the farms. He'd done his chores then went over to the big farm to see what could be done since so many things were coming to harvest.

Mary pointed him to the sweet corn that needed to be collected for the next day's sales.

"The evening meal is about ready," Martha said as she bustled about in the kitchen.

Daniel frowned. His mother usually helped and she was absent. He glanced in the main room. She sat in her rocker, looking out the window, knitting an afghan. He smiled then strolled into the kitchen to give Martha a hug and kiss.

Martha chastised him, she was busy.

"John should be home shortly," Martha said. "He is probably still milking the cows at your parent's barn."

"Maybe I should..."

"*gut'n owed*," John said coming into the house.

"Then, again, maybe I will not need to go help with the cows." Daniel laughed.

"The table is set," Martha said, glancing at the four settings. She nodded to Daniel. "Go get Mama for supper."

John eased into a setting at the table as Daniel walked into the main room where his mother quietly sat in her rocker.

"Mama?" Daniel said.

There was no response.

"Mama?" Daniel's voice stronger.

Still, she did not respond. He touched her; she didn't move.

Daniel fell to his knees. "Mama!" he cried.

"Whatever is the problem?" Martha asked, walking into the main room.

"Mama is gone," Daniel mumbled, his head resting on her arm. "Oh, Mama," he whimpered.

Martha placed her arms about Daniel to comfort.

"John!" Martha called. "Go tell your aunts and uncles."

Daniel tried not to cry, but tears welled and crept paths down his cheeks.

\# \# \#

Monday, July 5, 1999 8:20 p.m.

Bethany sat in the chair next to Jeremiah. She rubbed her bulging stomach.

A twinge. She winced.

"Labor?" Jeremiah asked.

She nodded. "Number ten is ready to arrive."

Bethany gazed about the room at her nine children.

Aaron was the oldest, followed by Mary, then Ruth. They all read and studied the Bible on the kitchen table. Daniel, Ezekiel, and Issac played Chinese checkers at the one end of the main room. Rachel played with her doll, singing a soft song while Peter played

254

with a carved horse his Grandpa Daniel had made. Adam slept in the cradle.

Once more Bethany winced in pain. "It is time," she said.

"Aaron," Jeremiah said. "Harness a horse to the buggy and go get Grandma Graber." He gazed at Bethany. "You are about to have a new sibling."

Aaron stood from the table. "Yes, Papa." He hustled from the house and to the barn.

Jeremiah helped Bethany to the main floor bedroom.

"Do you want me to come sing to you, Mama?" Rachel asked, standing, holding her dolly.

Jeremiah nodded. "She would like that."

Rachel followed her parents into the bedroom and sat on the floor by the bed and began to sing a song her Grandpa Daniel had taught her; Ten Little Indians.

Grandma Graber strolled into the room and waved Jeremiah away.

"Your sister and I will help Bethany," Grandma Graber said. "You can watch the children." She gazed down at Rachel sitting on the floor. "What a pretty voice."

"Grandpa Daniel taught me to sing," Rachel said.

Grandma Graber nodded and smiled.

Bethany moaned and twitched on the bed. "The pains are getting closer."

"Jeremiah told me you wanted ten children," Grandma Graber said. "The Lord has truly blessed you. Now, shall we have this child?" She smiled at Bethany. "Boy? Girl?"

"A girl would be nice, but a boy is always welcome," Bethany replied. "Either." She closed her eyes as another labor pain wracked her body. "And soon," she added.

Grandma Graber looked down at Rachel. "You can go back out to the main room and play," she said.

Rachel shrugged, grabbed her dolly tightly to her and marched out the door, all the while singing verse one of The Ant Song. It was the only verse she knew.

# # #

Tuesday, September 4, 2012 8 a.m.

"Rachel Graber?" the man's voice called out.

"Yes," Rachel replied.

"Come in," the gentleman said. "My name is Joshua Holmes. I'm the General Manager for Blue Gate."

Rachel nodded.

"I see you're applying for kitchen help. Is that correct?" He appraised her Amish clothing.

Again, Rachel nodded. "Yes, sir."

"You do realize that means 3D?"

Rachel frowned.

"Dirty Dish Duty. D-D-D or as we call it 3D." He grinned and shrugged. "It sounds better than saying doing dishes."

"I do dishes at home," she replied.

"I think you'll work out just fine," Joshua Holmes replied.

# # #

Rachel followed the kitchen manager to the back of the kitchen and the multiple sinks.

"This is your work station," the manager said and removed a rubber apron from the wall to hand to Rachel. "Over there is Katy Hack. She does a lot of the food prep for the chefs." He pointed to another woman. "That is Viola Stuble. If I'm not around, ask her if you have questions." He turned and walked away.

Rachel put the rubber apron on and started pushing and moving pots and pans to begin her job. She was amazed at the number of dirty items.

It is a restaurant, she thought and began to hum as she worked her way through the large pile of dirty items.

"That's a pretty song you are humming," Katy Hack mentioned.

"It is one my grandfather taught me. It is called *Where're You Walk.*"

"Are there words to the song?"

Rachel nodded and began to sing.

256

"With a voice like that," Viola Stuble started. "Why are you working in the kitchen?"

"The 3D job is fine," Rachel said. "I am not a singer."

"Your voice belies you, Rachel," Katy said. "You've missed your calling."

Rachel grinned, then laughed. "My calling is Amish. Would you prefer I not sing?"

"No, no!" Viola said. "Sing. By all means, please sing. It will make the time go faster."

Rachel once more began to sing, filling the kitchen with her voice.

"Someday a young boy..." Katy said. "Of course, he will be *Englische* and you will become infatuated with him." She giggled. "Why, you might even consider becoming *Englische*."

"I think not," Rachel replied. "I am Amish."

"Oh, I think different," Viola replied. "You can't hide that voice." She shrugged. "Whether you are *Englische* or Amish, that voice is with you."

THE END

This page left blank

About the Author

My name is Robert S. Nailor but most people call me Bob.

I'm retired from the federal government. I was a computer geek and still do some programming yet today. One would think I should have plenty of time to write, but I actually seem to have less now. So, to make sure that things work out correctly, I force myself to sit down and write. That doesn't always work. Today, writing is fun and I find it relaxing. I get to visit those fantastic and strange places within my mind and well, if I don't come back right away, there is no longer somebody behind me writing on a pink sheet of paper.

I live with my wife, Violet, in a ranch home snuggled into a small wooded acre in NW Ohio. I was born in Sioux City, Iowa but my parents moved to Ohio in 1953. I have four sons and currently have ten grandchildren - 7 granddaughters and 3 grandsons. Plus, I have 11 great-grandchildren – 5 great-granddaughters and 6 great-grandsons.

My interests are camping (have RV, will travel), gardening, music, cooking and reading. So where do I travel? I've been in 46 of the 50 states and strangely, Hawaii is one of the states I've visited (U.S. Navy) but not Alaska. I have also visited two of our territories - Puerto Rico and the Virgin Islands. Traveling allows me to add the ambiance to my stories and also to some of the characters. Gardening is a bit gamey since we live in the country and have the wildlife visiting us constantly — deer, rabbits, raccoon, birds, squirrels plus many others. So, vegetables don't always make it to harvest, but what does is more than tasty. There are flowers, sometimes too many, to keep me busy. Music? I love New Age music and my favorite group is Mannheim Steamroller... and not just because of their fabulous Christmas albums; I was hooked on them before that. I also have created some of my own electronic music which I've been told is pretty good. Should I mention cooking? I love to cook and do gourmet cooking. Having worked with Boy Scouts for several years, I have taught many boys the basics of cooking beyond hot dogs and beans. I have won quite a few contests. As to what I read; well, obviously a lot of science fiction, fantasy and some Christian. Horror, romance, adventure and other genres are also great reads when they catch my attention with an intriguing tag line or cover.

Bibliography

Novels:
Eternal Blood ~ Book 1 in the Barry Hargrove detective mysteries
The Babbling Sphinx ~ Book 2 in the Barry Hargrove detective mysteries
Dragon Feast ~ Book 3 in the Barry Hargrove detective mysteries
The Secret Voice ~ Book 1 in The Amish Singer series
The New York Voice ~ Book 2 in The Amish Singer series
The Amish Voice ~ Book 3 in The Amish Singer series
The Vietnam Voice ~ Book 4 in The Amish Singer series
Pangaea, Eden Lost ~ a Barclay Havens, relic hunter mis-adventure
Three Steps: The Journeys of Ayrold ~ an Irish fantasy for today
2012 Timeline Apocalypse ~ the Mayan calendar comes to an end
At Death's Door ~ a collection of "light" horror stories about death
The Emerald ~ Book 1 in The Shiyula Realm series

Coming Soon...
The Englische Voice ~ book 6; does love really mend all?
The Topaz ~ book 2 in The Shiyula Realm series
Mommy Missing ~ book 4 in the Barry Hargrove mystery series

Anthologies I Am In:
52 Weeks of Writing Tips ~ tips to improve one's writing ability
Telling Tales of Terror ~ essays on how to write horror and dark fiction
Mother Goose Is Dead ~ a collection of favorite fairy tales, fractured
Dead Set: A Zombie Anthology ~ a collection of unusual zombie tales
The Complete Guide to Writing Paranormal-Vol 1 ~ various essays
Nights of Blood 2 ~ different takes on the vampire story
Guide to Writing Science Fiction ~ essays on writing science fiction
Firestorm of Dragons ~ an eclectic collection of dragon stories
Fantasy Writer's Companion ~ essays on writing fantasy
13 Night of Blood ~ 13 amazing vampire tales
Spirits of Blue & Gray ~ a collection of Civil War ghost stories

PLUS more at www.bobnailor.com

BOOK SIX ~ The Englische Voice

(Work in Progress – Beta; Subject to changes)

CHAPTER ONE ~ It Begins

Monday, May 13, 2013 8 a.m.

Rachel hummed her various tunes as she worked.

"Say, girl," Katy Hack called as she chopped lettuce. "Instead of humming, why don't you sing one of your songs for us."

"Yes," Viola Stuble agreed. "I'm older than both of you put together, so what I want, well, that's what goes. Sing, Rachel. Sing."

Rachel stopped humming and once more broke into *Where're You Walk,* filling the kitchen with her voice.

Joshua Holmes, the general manager for the restaurant sat outside the kitchen's swinging doors, working on next week's specials with Chef Harold Abbott.

"Did somebody turn the radio to a station with opera?" Joshua asked.

Harold shook his head. "No, that is Rachel singing. She has a beautiful voice."

"Rachel. Rachel." Joshua mumbled as he tried to place the name. "Oh, the 3D girl." He grinned. "I don't know who came up with the 3D name, but I do like it better than Dirty-Dish-Duty. He leaned back in his chair. "She can sing?"

Harold shrugged. "You're hearing her. That's her."

"We start a new production at the theater in six weeks." Joshua paused. "I want her to try out for Ladder Angel. Her voice is angelic and a perfect fit for the spot in the play."

"She won't do it," Harold said, shaking his head. "She's Amish."

"We'll see," Joshua replied and once more studied the sheets of paper in front of him. "We'll keep the potato carrot bisque and add this lemon rice soup as a second option for the daily soups."

Harold nodded and continued to listen to Rachel sing. He enjoyed listening to her voice.

# # #

Monday, May 13 2:30 p.m.

Joshua Holmes sat at his desk when the soft rap on the door caught his attention.

"Come in," he said and watched Rachel enter. "Have a seat, young lady." He motioned to a chair.

"Have I done something wrong?" Rachel asked, hesitantly sitting.

"No. No," Joshua said. "On the contrary. It is what you haven't done."

Rachel frowned. "What I haven't done? I do dishes. Is there more?"

"You sing, Miss Graber," Joshua said. "I've heard your voice."

Rachel shrugged. "I am sorry. I will stop singing."

Joshua shook his head. "No. No. That isn't the issue." He leaned back in his chair. "Why didn't you tell me you could sing?"

Rachel shrugged. "Everyone can sing, Mr. Holmes." She smiled. "Not everyone wants to sing."

"An Amish philosopher," Joshua said with a grin. "Interesting." He leaned forward over his desk. "What I want you to do is try out for the new play at the Blue Gate Theater." He paused. "Specifically, the ladder angel."

"I am Amish," Rachel said, remembering the stories of her grandfather and his trip to New York City. "I am not an actor."

"There is no acting, Miss Graber," Joshua said. "You will sit on a ladder... okay, call it a staircase, and you will sing." He shrugged. "That's it."

"No, Mr. Holmes," Rachel said. "That is not it. I am Amish and we do not play act." She clasped her hands together in a firm grip. "I am sure there is a costume involved."

Joshua squirmed in his seat, trying to figure out the best answer.

"Amish do not wear costumes." She stood.

264

"Please. Please sit, Miss Graber." Joshua stood and once more motioned for her to take a seat. "Let's not be hasty." He rubbed his first two fingers over his lips as he thought. "No costume. I think we could accommodate that." His mind ran rampant in thought. "In other words, you would consider doing the song if you could wear your daily Amish clothes?" He paused. "Or, perhaps a piece of cloth draped over the front from shoulder to shoulder?"

Rachel froze. She had been caught in her own words.

"Tell you what, Miss Graber," Joshua said. "I want to come try out for the part, sing the song and see what you think. If you are still against the idea, so be it." He stretched his hands across the desk. "Please?" he begged.

Rachel nodded.

"Thank you," Joshua said. "Tomorrow, 9 a.m., at the Blue Gate Theater. Come inside and you'll find me up near the stage."

Rachel stood to leave.

"You will be there tomorrow?" He cocked an eye at her.

Rachel nodded and left.

CHAPTER TWO ~ Punishment

May 16, 2013 4:46 p.m.

Less than a year and I'm so out of here! Evan slammed the bedroom door, punched the power button on the stereo, and leaped through the air to flop onto his bed. He grabbed the full-ear-covering, external noise canceling headphones from the bedside table, and snapped them over his ears.

"Screw them all," he mumbled as the twangs of a country song blared in his ears. "He has no idea what I want." Evan didn't hear the insistent knocking on the door.

"Since you won't answer." Nathan opened the bedroom door and stepped inside. He reached over and powered down the stereo system.

Evan responded instantly, glaring at his father, climbing out of the bed, stomping to the stereo and shoving his father's hand away before pressing the power back on. "You have no right," he screamed. "That's mine. Leave it alone."

Nathan grabbed the headphones and snapped them off Evan's head. "In actuality, this whole system is mine. I bought it, you took it." He placed the headphones on the console. "Now, you're going to listen to what I have to say. I've put up with your crap, and listened to your rantings." He glared at Evan. "So, you sit and listen to me. I'm your father."

"Sure, dad." Evan slurred the words at the older man standing before him in the expensive suit. "Tell me how much you love me. Tell me how lucky I am to have all this." The young man stretched out his arms and waved at the bedroom walls. "Yeah, like you always do. Tell me all about how good I have it." Evan looked down at the watch on his wrist. "Oh, wait a minute. Don't you have a date with somebody, somewhere, in about three minutes. Isn't this where you give me a hug, pass me fifty bucks and head out the door to party with a client?"

"You're only seventeen, Evan. You don't know everything about the world." Nathan edged closer to the door while glancing at the watch on his wrist. "Yes, I do have an engagement. And yes, it is a meeting with a very important client. You see those skis, that surfboard, your clothes, and this stereo?" He pointed, jabbing his index finger at the different items spread throughout the room. His eyes finally came to rest on Evan's feet. "When I was a kid, I didn't get two-hundred-dollar sneakers or three-hundred-dollar watches."

"Yeah, well, dad--" Evan didn't hold back on the snide. "You love me, remember? This is how you show me how much you love me."

Nathan raised his hand but let it fall back to his side. "Without my clients, you wouldn't have any of this. To be successful and have all this, I need to work. I'm sorry you're alone. Your mother died six years ago, but there was nothing I could do about that. It was an accident."

Evan glared at his dad. "You're the one who took her off life support. That wasn't an accident. It was you who finally killed her in the end. Sure, the thug did some damage, but you, YOU alone took her off the machine that was keeping her alive." A tear welled up. "While she was on the machine, at least there was hope."

"We'll talk about this when I get back home tonight." Nathan grabbed the bedroom door handle. "I'll be back." He reached into his pocket, pulled out the money clip, snapped a couple of bills free of the clip and placed them on the book shelf by the door. "Call for pizza, Chinese, whatever," he mumbled. "I should be home before ten. Get your homework done. We'll talk then."

Evan watched the door close and listened to it click shut. "We'll talk then," he whispered in mockery of his father's words. In one swift, quick movement, Evan lifted his right arm up, catching the bend with his left hand to stop it at mid-chest, allowing his hand to snap up and the sole finger flip defiantly into the air: the bird. "Up yours, dad!" He reached over and snatched the bills and wadded them into his jeans pocket. "Sure, I'll get Chinese. Happy Dragon is only three blocks away and I can get me a beer without anyone asking my age."

He snapped the power on the stereo system while pulling the headphone plug out. Music blasted through the room. Evan joined the song, singing as his voice blended with the country singer. He picked up the guitar and strummed with the song.

Yeah, less than a year, he thought. *I am so outta here and will be touring with some band, any band.*

Nathan hated the way Evan blamed him for Barb's death. Yet, there were secrets Evan didn't know. He silently leaned against the hallway wall and listened to Evan vibrate the walls with the loud music behind the closed door. Nathan's mind blurred with the images and memories of his wife in the hospital. The police thought it started as a simple hold-up which escalated to her being beaten, hit in the head with a brick and finally, brutally and sexually molested. He saw Barb's pained face in the recovery room after the operations. There was no way she would live. Even if she did respond and came out of the coma, she would be more vegetable than human. The doctors gave her less than a ten per cent chance of survival. For five days he was by her side, ignoring everything, and everyone, before he finally pulled the plug on the respirator. Evan didn't know about the rape. Nathan took a deep breath and softly let it out before walking the long hallway to the front door of the apartment: the big apartment filled with too many memories.

#

Evan strolled the street. He had his hood pulled up over his ball cap and his hands shoved down into his jeans. He wasn't looking for trouble, but he carried an air of trouble about him. People avoided looking at him, or even getting close.

He gazed up at the stupid neon light of a red dragon changing from smiling to non-smiling and then back to smiling again. Happy Dragon glowed in golden neon. Evan yanked open the door and entered the restaurant.

"Ah, Evan, you come eat here tonight?" Lin Ho smiled and welcomed the young man to the restaurant. "You lucky tonight. My brother has new shipment. You work, yes?"

Evan watched the small Chinese man. "I eat." He hesitated. "How much work?"

"Big shipment. Very big. Need much help. You make plenty money."

"Sure, I'll help after I finish eating." He smiled at Lin. "Make it Gong Bao Chicken and a bottle of Tsingtao."

Lin Ho bowed. "Follow me to seat." Lin scurried toward the back, near the kitchen doors. "You eat then I take you to my brother." He bowed again and chattered Chinese to a waitress who quickly disappeared and returned with the bottle of Tsingtao beer.

Evan consumed his meal, paid, leaving a nice tip before following Lin Ho. This time Lin rushed him through the kitchen and out the back door to a waiting car.

"He take you to my brother, and he wait for you. My brother pay you good."

Evan was always leery of being shanghaied, but felt pretty comfortable with Lin Ho. The driver zipped through the streets and alleys, finally stopping at the wharf. "We here," the mysterious and up-to-this-moment, silent driver said.

Evan got out and quickly spotted the activity. Another short Chinese man approached.

"You name Evan?"

Evan nodded.

"You work hard, I pay good. Follow me." The man headed back toward the activity. "Carry this inside. Follow man ahead of you. Repeat until all moved."

Evan watched for a few seconds as the collection of about six men marched from the warehouse to the ship, where they grabbed a bag, heaved it onto their shoulder and marched back to the building. He shrugged. *Definitely a no brainer*, he thought. Evan stepped into the line and grabbed a bag, hoisted it onto his shoulder noticing it wasn't as heavy as he thought it would be, and followed the silent man ahead of him.

Three hours later Evan got back in the car and counted his money as the silent driver wove a path back to the restaurant. Evan got out and made sure the one hundred plus dollars he'd earned was safely stuck in his pocket, opened the car door and headed home.

Nathan glanced up when the door opened.

"Where have you been?" he yelled as Evan entered the apartment. "You look like... like... What have you been doing? Fighting?"

"No," Evan replied. "I went to get me something to eat." Evan headed down the hallway toward his room. "Chinese, if you need to know."

"Get back here, Evan. We aren't finished. I want answers."

Evan twirled on his heel and glared at his father. "Me, too. I want answers. Where were you? Who did you see? What were you doing?" He narrowed his stare at his father. "See? I can play your game."

Nathan's eyes widened in surprise at his son's latest belligerent actions.

"If you must know, dad." Nathan heard the slurred last word from Evan as the boy flung his hoodie through the open bedroom door. "I got me a Chinese meal of Gong Bao Chicken and then I worked out with some new friends. Finally, I came home. Now, does that make you happy?" The boy spun around and headed into his room, and as tradition had been established, slammed the door behind him.

Nathan knocked on the door before opening it and walked to Evan's bedside. He held an envelope in his hand. "Since you seem to be answering questions, answer this one. Why is Mrs. Anderson sending me a letter about your refusal to turn in homework? You don't feel it is necessary to hand in English term papers?"

Evan rolled over on his bed to face his father. "You tell me, dad. You obviously did term papers on book reports when you were in school. Be honest. Did it help you with your work tonight? Exactly how many of those book reports have been critical in locking down a deal?"

"Fine," Nathan said and walked to the large window. "I'm not going to fight you about book reports. If they fail you, so be it. You fail." He looked out on the night scape of the big city, watching the lights flicker far below. "You don't seem to have any focus. It's obvious you have no respect for me." He stared at his son's athletic build. "You're willing to spend time working out, but not get a job. I've been thinking. For summer break, which will be in three short weeks, you'll spend the time with your grandmother in Indiana."

"What?" Evan rolled off the bed and stood. "With who? Where?"

"Grandma Curtz in Shipshewana, Indiana. I'll call her tomorrow to set it all up. Maybe during the summer, she can knock some sense into your stubborn mind."

"Who is Grandma Curtz?"

"My mother. I'll be honest, I left on bad terms and haven't visited her since my father passed away." He turned from the window and looked at Evan. "You were very young."

"If you don't like her, why are you sending me there?"

"I didn't say I don't like her. She and I don't see eye to eye on everything, but she raised me and I don't think I turned out all that bad. Maybe she can kick your ass and get you down the straight and narrow path before it is too late." Nathan snapped the envelope in his hand. "You have one year left until graduation with a couple of weeks left this school year, and they're already talking about kicking you out of this school. Do I need to recount all the schools you've been to in the last five years?" He slumped into the chair by the window. "Evan, I really don't know what to do anymore. I've tried to give you everything you want. Maybe my mother can give you what I've been overlooking." He sighed. "She's a very smart woman."

"I didn't even know I had a living grandparent," Evan said. "Where is this Ship-whatever place?"

"In northeast Indiana. The town is about six hundred people, mostly Amish. It's a busy place, but nothing like here."

"Amish?"

"Let's put it this way, Evan. In Shipshewana, you're going to find life very different. The Amish are a very simple folk who are--" Nathan smiled. "Tell you what. You'll find out when you get there." He stood up and walked to the door. "As I said, I'll get a hold of my mother and see if you can live with her for the summer."

"You can't make me do that." Evan folded his arms defiantly in front of him.

"You're only seventeen, Evan. Until you are eighteen, you're a minor and as much as you hate it, you have to do what I tell you. This August, when you turn eighteen, you can move out. If you decide to do that, we'll call it an early Christmas present." Nathan opened the door and stepped out. "Good night, son." He closed the door.

Evan dropped onto the bed and slammed his hands onto the mattress in frustration. "When I turn eighteen, you wait and see. I'll move out, that's for sure." He grabbed the headphones and slipped them over his head, and pushed the remote power button. "Just you wait and see." Johnny Cash sang "Will the Circle be Unbroken?" but it didn't soothe as memories of his mother's accident and funeral surged forward.

END OF READ.